ALWAYS AT THE BOOKSHOP PRETTY BEACH

POLLY BABBINGTON

AUTHORPOLLYBABBINGTON

Want more from Polly's world?

For sneak peeks into new settings, early chapters, downloadable Pretty Beach and Darling Island freebies and bits and bobs from Polly's writing days sign up for Babbington Letters.

AuthorPollyBabbington.com

© Copyright 2025 Polly Babbington

All rights reserved.

This book is a work of fiction. Names, characters, businesses, places, events, and incidents are either the products of the author's imagination or used in a fictitious manner. Any resemblance to actual persons, living or dead, or actual events is purely coincidental.

1

Daisy Henley stood behind the counter of the bookshop in Pretty Beach, sorting through a delivery of paperbacks that had arrived the afternoon before. Once she'd stacked the books and written their corresponding information cards, she looked around, inhaled and smiled. Ding-a-ling, life was good. The whole shop smelt of books, coffee and the lavender candle she'd lit when she'd opened up an hour before. Outside, Pretty Beach was going about its business as it had done more or less every day of her life. The trademark Pretty Beach blue and white bunting fluttered along the laneway in a breeze coming in off the sea, the sun was shining and the ferry honked from far off in the distance. So very comforting and told Daisy Henley that she was right where she wanted to be: home. The sights and sounds Daisy had grown up with, knew, and adored so very well, wrapped her in their very own sort of small-town love. All was right in Daisy's world.

Smiling, she waved as Nel, the local bus driver, hurried past and she watched a man with a dog pause and peer in at her window display. The bookshop, her ongoing little business venture, which she juggled with all the other things in her life, was ticking along beautifully. That in itself was something not to be sniffed at. After the drama with the corporate giant, GayesBooks, sweeping into Pretty Beach, Daisy had felt more than concerned that her business would hit a roadblock and wither away to nothing at all. That hadn't happened and in fact, touch wood, the bookshop was going from strength to strength. As, indeed, was its owner. Always good in that thing they call life.

Many things had settled into a rhythm for Daisy. In particular, the bookshop had become a very nice, stable part of her existence, she hadn't known she'd needed. Now she really couldn't imagine being without it. Not only had it provided her with a role and a purpose, it had slowly but surely started to beat to its own drum; customers came and went, the payment dongle, thankfully, pinged regularly, and the shop had even started turning an actual profit rather than just scraping by and breaking even. Not that Daisy was rolling in revenue and good times, far from it, but the constant draining anxiety and utter stress about money was no longer one of her closest companions. Thank the good person above for that. For Daisy, the grinding, relentless, soul-destroying worry about paying rent and where the money was coming from to settle her bills was a thing of the past. The sweet relief of that alone was something she couldn't quite put into words.

She picked up a copy of a novel doing the rounds on social media and turned it over to read the blurb. Though she'd already read most of it and had skimmed three reviews online and knew exactly what it was about, she reiterated to be sure. The delivery had included several copies, which meant her customers would ask for it, and Daisy liked to be prepared for the inevitable conversations about whether books lived up to the hype their publishing houses liked to push. Unfortunately, she was learning that they absolutely did not. More often than not, it was publishing hyperbole run on a huge marketing budget and a whole lot of wings and prayers. Placing the book carefully on the display table in the centre of the shop, she added a small handwritten card that read 'New Release - Ask Daisy for her thoughts...' and wondered who actually would do just that.

As she pottered and tidied, fairy lights twinkled softly in the corners, even though it was broad daylight. Daisy had learnt by hook or by crook that cosy was her business bestie: soft lighting, comfy corners, lovely old rugs, flickering candles, amazing soft furnishings and little lamps and throws were not only the bookshop's trademarks, but they much more importantly made sales. In fact, it sometimes felt as if her customers and followers gushed over the little bits and bobs in the shop even more than they loved the books themselves. Daisy had been a quick learner and anything that made people want to linger and browse was good for her business and, ultimately at the end of the day, for her.

Doing a quick pan around with her phone camera on cinematic mode, she zoomed in on the library trolley she'd rescued from Facebook Marketplace and focused on a huge vintage jug full of flowers on its top. The trolley, loaded with reads to dip and delve into and the wingback chairs just alongside it, looked so inviting that Daisy sometimes felt as if she herself could easily sit there all day with not a care in the world.

The bell above the door gave a jingle as Xian from the bakery just along the laneway shuffled into the shop. In a bottle green fluffy jumper and pink sliders, she had an iPad held out in front of her, a backpack on her back and headphones dangling around her neck.

'Morning, Daise. How are we? Good, I hope.' Xian headed straight for the wingback chairs. 'It's been chaos in the bakery. I have come here for peace and quiet and so that no one can annoy me. Can you provide me with that? I finished that Agatha Christie you recommended.'

Daisy chuckled. 'I think I might be able to fulfil your needs. What did you think?'

'Clever as anything, but I worked out who did it halfway through. Mind you, I've been reading crime novels for many years, so I suppose I would. It's how I taught myself English and French, for that matter, and I'm currently on a roll with Italian. Anything you think that I might like this week? I like a good dead body book, as you well know. The grislier the better.'

Daisy pulled out a novel she'd found when sorting through some of her Uncle Dennis's things. 'I've just finished this. It's set in a Scottish village: there's a missing person, local secrets, that sort of thing. There may or may not be a dead body.'

Xian took a quick gulp from a silver hip flask, then took the book and read the back cover. 'Hmm, a Scottish village. I do like a good remote setting. It makes it harder for the characters to escape, doesn't it? A bit like Pretty Beach, ha.'

'Exactly what I thought when I read it. Right, take a pew. Your usual cup of tea?'

Xian had a plastic shopping bag over each arm; she held one up. 'Yes, please. A nice tea and my Special Drink will do me well this morning. These are for you. Locals Only, though, so be careful who you give them to. Keep them under the table. Honestly, I need a sit down and a calm down.'

'Ooh, thank you. Will do.'

After putting the buns away and making Xian's tea, Daisy laughed to herself as she stood behind the counter and watched Xian in the wingback chair corner. Every now and then, Xian tapped on her iPad and then poured amber liquid from her hip flask into her mug of tea. Daisy couldn't quite work out how Xian wasn't permanently pickled, considering that she was almost constantly topping herself up with the liquid from her flask. Or perhaps that was the secret to her online trading reputation. Whatever it was, it worked for Xian and gave anyone who came into her vicinity a chuckle.

With no one else in the shop, about half an hour later, Daisy made herself a cup of tea and a fresh one for Xian, took two of the Locals Only cinnamon buns out, went and sat in the chair opposite Xian and hoped that no one else would come in. Xian sat forward in her chair, plopped some of her drink from her flask into the fresh mug of tea and smiled.

'Thank you. I am becoming like a piece of furniture in here, aren't I? It's so cosy. I can sit here and zone out and get on with my trading in peace.'

'Yep, you are. I like having you.'

Xian looked around. 'What a great idea it was of Pete's for you to start this place. Are we letting him take the credit for it, yet?'

Daisy laughed. 'Nah, he never gets to know we acknowledge it was his idea. Can you imagine? We'll never hear the end of it.'

'Very true. So, what's been happening with you this week?'

'More of the same. I'm happy and settled, so what more do I need? I was just thinking before you came in that this place has a little rhythm of its own now. I like it. It's done me well being here.'

'For sure. What about the lovely Miles? What's going on with him? Everything good in that department?'

Daisy nodded and thought about Miles. Like the bookshop, her relationship with him had settled nicely. It was as if he'd been in her life all along. To be honest, it was so good that she didn't really think about it. Like the bookshop, the Miles and Daisy story beat to its own drum. 'Yes, I can't complain.'

'Nope, I would not be complaining if I were you. So, what's happened with Elizabeth? Has there been any further talk about her coming to live down here?'

Daisy shook her head at the mention of Miles's mum, Elizabeth. 'Off and on. I don't see how she can continue living up there, to be honest. She's too scared to go out now. One of her friends also got mugged a few weeks ago. They not only stole her phone but also her watch and her bag. Did you hear about that newsreader who got mugged coming out of a shop on Oxford Street? A gang surrounded her, knocked her to the ground, emptied her bag and took her phone and stuff. Apparently, the police didn't even want to know. It's getting really scary if you ask me.'

'Lawless London, they're calling it.'

'I'd be cautious about going out if I were Elizabeth.'

'I don't blame her.'

'Miles has been keeping an eye open for property down here. It's so tightly held, though. I mean, he's talking about the Old Town.'

Xian made a face. 'Pah! He should be so lucky.'

Daisy rolled her eyes. 'I know. I said that!'

Xian cackled. 'Someone has to die for one of those houses to come up.'

'We went for a walk the other day and when we were on Strawberry Hill near Lottie's place, he was a bit taken by it all. I mean, who wouldn't like it there? I said to him that those houses hardly ever change hands.'

'Yeah, he has no chance.'

'I know.'

'So, you two are good?'

Daisy nodded and joked. 'We are. We're really good. I am very lucky that we threw chocolate ice cream at him and he's now part of our lives.'

'I bet. So no plans for anything in the next few months?'

Daisy shook her head. 'Nope, nothing at all. I have no plans except keeping this little bookshop going and making sure Miles and the twins are happy. Honestly, everything I have is right here in Pretty Beach and these four walls. What more do I need?'

Xian agreed. 'I make you right.'

Daisy nodded. She was completely and utterly happy with her lot in life. Couldn't argue with that. Not at all.

2

Daisy laughed as she settled herself into a cushioned wicker chair at The Sugar Wharf, a café on the far side of Pretty Beach. Looking at a little blackboard menu propped against the salt and pepper shakers, she smiled as she contemplated what to have to eat. Sitting with Maggie and Annabelle and about to have lunch, they'd been chatting about everything under the sun. The conversation had gone this way and that and taken all sorts of tangents and after talking about Annabelle's holiday plans, they were discussing how Daisy was now in a very serious relationship with Miles. Despite Daisy having wobbles in the early days and thinking that Miles might vanish, that had not happened. In actual fact, precisely the opposite had occurred and their love affair of the century had gone from strength to strength. She nodded, smiled and continued the conversation. 'Yes, Mags, as usual, you were absolutely right. Miles is completely different from what I expected when I first met him that day at the ice cream stall.'

Maggie tried not to look *too* smug as she adjusted a pair of oversized sunglasses on the top of her head and nodded her head knowingly. 'We did try to tell you from the very beginning that he wasn't going anywhere, despite your constant predictions of imminent doom and disaster. When I think about those early conversations we had, you were very worried.'

'I know, I know, I was being completely ridiculous about the whole thing,' Daisy admitted, fanning herself with a menu as she looked at the water view. 'I suppose I was so used to expecting the worst that I couldn't quite believe something might actually work out for once in my romantic life. However, here we are. I sit here as testimony to that very fact. I am officially a grown-up in a grown-up relationship. Go me.'

Annabelle chortled. 'Welcome to the club. 'It's all downhill from here.'

'It's understandable given everything you'd been through with the twins and all those years of barely keeping your head above water. We won't mention the bungee jumping thing.' Maggie turned the menu around to catch the light better as she squinted at the handwritten specials.

Annabelle continued. 'Nobody could blame you for being cautious about letting someone new into your world. You had the girls to think about.'

Daisy looked out at the water through the open doors of The Sugar Wharf. Pretty Beach was enjoying a sunny day and showing off about it. She watched as a small fishing boat with a cloud of seagulls following in its wake chugged past their table. 'Gosh, this is nice. The view from here never gets old, does it? I love where we live. I really do.'

Annabelle followed her gaze. 'There aren't many people who can say that, I reckon and yes, I love where we live, too.'

'I'll never get bored of it.' Maggie raised her eyebrows as she continued scanning the menu options. 'I'm thinking the Locals Only. Homemade croissant with garlic whipped cream cheese, red onion pickle and fresh herbs. Does that or does that not sound amazing? Who wouldn't like the idea of that?'

Annabelle looked up from her menu. 'That sounds divine.'

Maggie frowned. 'What was the other Locals Only again?'

'Mermaid Bay crab cakes with aioli.'

Annabelle swore. 'Yeah. They are calling my name, especially after that conversation I had with Phoebe last week. Apparently, the boats are bringing in amazing catches every morning, hence the reason those are on there, I guess.'

Daisy glanced around at the other diners scattered across the wooden deck, most of them locals she recognised from around Pretty Beach. 'I think I'm going to be completely predictable and order the Locals Only. Pheebs has never let me down yet with her creations. To be fair, they only get better.' Daisy lowered her voice. 'She's a blow-in technically, too.'

Maggie reached for a large vintage jug filled with edible flowers, ice and water sitting in the centre of their table and filled three blue hobnail glasses to the brim. 'Yeah, this place creates absolute magic in the kitchen. You just can't argue with it.'

A waitress they all knew, Emma, with sun-streaked hair tied back in a bun, approached their table, notepad in hand and a genuinely warm smile on her face. 'Good afternoon, ladies. How are we? Bells, how are you? All doing well?'

Annabelle smiled. Good, thanks, Em. How's your sister?'

'Great. I just got a message from her. How the other half live, eh?'

'Living it up in Thailand. Alright for some.'

'Yup.'

Emma inclined her chin in the direction of the kitchen. 'Locals Only? Today we have the croissants or the crab cakes.'

Maggie narrowed her eyes. 'I'm trying to decide. What do you think?'

Emma lowered her voice. 'The most delicious crab came in on this morning's boats. Phoebe made the crab cakes with herbs from the garden behind the café here. I've had way too many already and they are absolutely perfect for this weather. She's a genius.'

'I think I'll have the crab,' Annabelle decided. 'It's exactly what I'm in the mood for. You can never go wrong with the Locals Only.'

'And I'll definitely have the croissant.' Daisy nodded.

'Excellent. I'll put it through for you to save you going up.' Emma tapped her phone. 'To drink? We've got some lovely elderflower cordial and there's a huge batch of fresh lemonade with mint, or are you having wine?'

Daisy nodded. 'Lemonade for me, please.'

'I think a glass of Sauvignon Blanc for me. It's such a treat to have a proper lunch together like this, rather than just grabbing a quick bite between other commitments,' Annabelle noted.

Maggie agreed. 'I've got a relatively light afternoon ahead of me, so I can definitely indulge in a glass of wine without worrying about falling asleep during meetings.'

Daisy nodded. 'Ahh, it's so nice to be having one of our proper lunches. It's been too long.'

Annabelle folded her hands on the table and looked directly at Daisy. 'How are Miles and the twins getting on?'

Daisy tapped the timber on the side of the table. 'Touch wood, all is well. I don't think there's anything dramatic or newsworthy to report at the moment. Let's hope it stays that way. Though I'll curse myself for saying that, won't I?'

Maggie chuckled and joked. 'The fact that everything is going well is rather remarkable, given your historical tendency to assume that any good thing in your life is bound to end in disaster sooner rather than later.'

Daisy joked and bantered. 'I simply have a realistic understanding of how unpredictable life can be. I am responsible for two small children and trying to run a business at the same time.'

'Life sure is unpredictable.' Annabelle nodded. 'However, at the moment we're all doing well. Long may it last and last.'

Maggie raised her glass in a mock-solemn toast. 'To sisterly lunches in gorgeous surroundings with excellent wine and even better company. Oh, and Locals Only crab cakes that make everything better.'

Annabelle clinked her glass against Maggie's. 'We're so lucky to have each other, aren't we? I love having you two. Honestly, I don't know how I'd cope if something happened to one of us.'

Daisy joked. 'Speak for yourself. You two drive me potty.'

'Yeah.'

Maggie smiled. 'Seriously, Daise. It's so nice to see you so much more relaxed these days.'

'Do I seem more relaxed?' Daisy was surprised by her sisters' perspective on her emotional state. For sure, inside, she felt a trillion times better, but she didn't realise it was that obvious. 'I suppose I do feel more settled than I have in ages, but I thought that was mainly because of the bookshop doing well and the girls being happy at school.'

'Nah. You seem genuinely content in a way you haven't been for years, if you ask me, not that you really want my opinion on things.' Maggie laughed.

'I guess I am. I mean, Margot and Evie have blossomed, too, so I think it's a combination of it all. Things have worked out well and they love Miles. So far, so good.'

Maggie raised her eyebrows. 'I knew they'd be okay with him. I mean, come on, Daise, what's not to like about Miles?'

'They've been great. So much better than I dared hope when I was lying awake at night worrying about how to handle the whole thing. Children are supposedly remarkably adaptable when the adults in their lives are happy and secure. I've read that so many times, but I thought it was a load of old hogwash. Clearly, it's not.'

Annabelle sipped her wine. 'What have they said about it

lately? Some of the things they come out with are gold, especially Margot. I mean, we could make our millions writing a book about the things she says.'

Daisy chuckled. 'She asked me if Miles was going to be staying for breakfast more often, and when I said that was quite likely, she just nodded very seriously and said that was good because he makes much better pancakes than I do. Apparently, my pancakes are too thick and not fluffy enough, according to her very sophisticated palate. Miles's pancakes, however, cut the mustard.'

Maggie hooted. 'Out of the mouths of babes.'

'And what about Evie's take on the situation?'

'Evie told me that she likes the way Miles listens properly, which made me chuckle. Obviously, I don't.'

Annabelle laughed. 'That's a man worth keeping around. Anyone who can sit still and pay genuine attention while one of the twins works her way through an entire book about magical unicorns or talking animals deserves serious consideration for saint status. I mean, Piers gives it a good go, but Miles sounds better.'

'How is his mum getting on? Imagine being mugged twice. Did you hear about that newsreader who got mugged on Oxford Street? It's getting out of control. I am genuinely concerned now when the fast train pulls in up there. Someone told me they now remove all their jewellery and take an old phone into London with them.'

'I know. It's frightening.'

Daisy nodded. 'She's much better. I don't know how much longer she can live alone, though. When we went up there last week, it was clear that she's hardly been out. Would you go out if that was happening around you, left, right and centre? Imagine if that were here.'

Maggie tutted and shook her head. 'I don't blame her, to be honest. I wouldn't step foot out the door if I'd been mugged in broad daylight, not once but twice. It's not rocket science that she must be traumatised from that. I reckon she could have PTSD.'

'Yes, Miles's brother said the same thing.'

'What's his brother been like? Any better in actually helping the situation, or just going through the motions?'

Daisy shook her head. 'Nope, worse if anything. Honestly, I am not sure how those two are brothers. They are like chalk and cheese.'

Annabelle chuckled. 'Some might say that about us.'

'True.'

'So, what is Miles going to do about it?'

'No idea. I do know he's getting fed up going up and down there on the train all the time to keep an eye on her. It's just getting a bit old now.'

'Do you think he'll move down here permanently?'

'I don't know for sure. He's said a few things about buying something in the Old Town.'

Annabelle raised her eyebrows. 'Good luck with finding a property there. It's one in, one out.'

'Ooh, things are getting really serious.' Maggie giggled. 'Daise will be getting married soon. Ding dong, the bells are going to chime.'

'Pah, yeah right. That won't be happening.' Daisy dismissed Maggie immediately.

Maggie frowned. 'Why do you say it like that?'

Daisy contemplated for a minute. 'I don't know, really. I just, yeah, not on the cards. I didn't think, well, no, I don't know.'

Annabelle wrinkled her nose and made a face. 'We could do with a Henley wedding. You wouldn't say yes if he asked?'

Daisy mused. 'He's not going to ask. Actually, now you've said it: I really do not know. I feel like, don't take this the wrong way, Bells, but marriage seems a bit old-fashioned to me with, you know, our situation. I mean, I'm hardly the sweet and innocent youngster in a white dress.'

Maggie rolled her eyes. 'What does that matter? Sometimes, Daise, I really do not get you. You're weird.'

'I am. I own it.'

Emma returned to the table carrying a large tray and the conversation paused. Daisy's croissant was a picture, with whipped garlic cream cheese oozing from the sides, garnished with a tumble of microgreens and accompanied by a small portion of red onion pickle in a tiny vintage Cornishware pot.

The Locals Only crab cakes were of the same ilk. Sitting atop a bed of baby rocket leaves, they looked fabulous. Beside them, a small vintage blue and white floral dish, and a dollop of aioli looked ready to be tucked into. Maggie's second Sauvignon Blanc arrived in a beautiful vintage glass to die for. Daisy's elderflower cordial, in a tall glass with sprigs of fresh mint and slices of cucumber, looked the part, too.

Daisy took a bite of the croissant. 'Oh my goodness! How does the food in here always taste so good? It's just a croissant. Pheebs always seems to nail it.'

'There are no flies on her. She always goes for simple and always local. Also, she's serious about this place being good. I guess her business success is based on getting these little things correct. The cakes in here are next level, too.'

'True.' Annabelle cut into one of the crab cakes with her fork. 'These are divine. You can nigh-on taste Pretty Beach in them.' She dipped a small vintage silver spoon into the aioli. 'Mmm. I need to come here for my lunch every day. I must ask Pheebs what's in this aioli. The woman is a machine.'

Maggie gestured to the harbour. 'It's no wonder people make special journeys to Pretty Beach just to eat at this place. Watching the boats come and go while we eat makes me feel like we're on holiday rather than just having lunch five minutes from home. Love it.'

'Nice. Sitting here with you both, eating this gorgeous food and talking about how settled and happy you are, Daise, it strikes me that we've all come quite a long way from where we were a few years ago.'

Maggie smiled. 'Sometimes I think I take it for granted how lucky we are to live somewhere like this, to have each other, our health, and to have Mum in our corner.'

Daisy looked out at the sparkling water. 'Yeah, I know. I keep waiting for someone to tell me I have to give it all back. The bookshop, this life in Pretty Beach, Miles, you two...'

'Nup. You've earned every bit of happiness you have, and there's absolutely no reason why it shouldn't continue for as long as you want it to.'

'Besides, if anyone tries to take away your bookshop or interfere with your lovely life here, they'd have to deal with the entire Henley women clan and the Pretty Beach community, and we're quite formidable when we're protecting one of our own. GayesBooks: case in point.'

'Heaven help anyone who crosses the Henley sisters when we're all working together.'

Daisy nodded. Inside, she hoped there wouldn't be anything around the corner to test the Henley clan in any way. What she didn't know was what was on the cards.

3

The following week, Daisy had done the school run and dropped Miles at Pretty Beach station to get the fast train to London. She'd parked her car in the lane behind the bookshop, grabbed her tote bag from the footwell and made her way in through the back garden behind the shop. After letting herself in, she'd filled the dishwasher, put a load of washing on and cleaned the kitchen in double quick time. After making a cup of tea, she was in the bookshop, though it was closed, tidying, sorting and restocking the children's section. On seeing the postman on the pavement outside, she slid the bolts on the inner cage security door and then pulled open the main door. The bell jingled and the postman, Steve, with a small parcel-like envelope in his left hand, beamed.

'Morning, Daise. Lovely day for it. This one is recorded, so if you could just sign here for me that would be grand.'

'Oh, right, I'm not expecting anything.' Daisy frowned as she popped her signature on the electronic pad.

'A surprise for you maybe.' Steve looked in the direction of the library ladders. 'Looking good in here. How are you getting on with everything?'

'Yep, great, thanks. It's going really well, actually.'

'Always good to hear. I'm not surprised. I see things come and go in my job, pounding the pavements, and from day one, I was like, yep, she's going to kill it.'

'You're not surprised?'

'Come on. A true blue like you opening a place on the laneway. How was that ever going to fail? For a start, you had the whole town behind you.'

'Ha.'

Steve jerked his thumb in the direction of the end of the laneway. 'And you have those two in the bakery on your side. That's half the battle. Am I right? They saved this town from the evils of GayesBooks like the professionals they are. Never underestimate a sparkly woman and her mum with her Special Drink.'

Daisy giggled. 'I know. You have to laugh at how that all panned out. Trust me, I thought this shop's days were numbered.'

'Yup. When we were in that meeting, I really did have severe worries for you on the one hand. On the other, I thought it would all pan out okay once Pretty Beach rallied and it did.'

Daisy shook her head. 'To be honest, I thought it meant it was over before it really started for me.'

'And now look at you.'

'Keeping my head above water and myself out of trouble,' Daisy joked.

'You and me both.' Steve lifted his huge parcel bag up. 'Right, I'd better push on with this little lot. I have a few over near the funicular this morning, so I'll be earning my keep.'

'Yep, see you, Steve. Thanks.'

As her phone rang and Daisy dealt with a customer, she put the envelope to the side and didn't pay much attention to it at all. About an hour later, when she finally got to it, she frowned at a logo in the top corner from the Independent Retail Alliance.

The envelope was thick, serious-looking and padded. Daisy went a bit cold and frowned because thick envelopes from organisations usually meant either very good news or very bad news and she certainly wanted none of the latter. Her little business was keeping its head above water and she wanted it to remain that way. After the kerfuffle and threat from the Gayes-Books drama, she was not sure she wanted any news whatsoever. All she wanted to do was bob along in a little world of her own in Pretty Beach and keep it that way. She didn't need to build an empire: she just wanted to pay her bills.

Opening the envelope with a frown, she had to read the first few lines twice before the words properly sank in.

We are delighted to inform you that The Bookshop Pretty Beach has been nominated for an Independent Retail Alliance of the Year Award.

Daisy sat down heavily on the stool behind the counter and read the letter again much more slowly. The award, by the looks of the invitation, was a big deal; the sort of recognition that was very surprising for a small coastal bookshop like hers. Reading through, she genuinely wondered if they'd made a mistake. According to the letter, she'd initially been nominated by several customers who had emailed the Alliance about the bookshop's role in the Pretty Beach community and its success in building a loyal customer base while maintaining its individual character. The letter went on to explain that the judging process would involve a site visit from representatives of the Alliance, followed by a formal assessment. The winner would be announced at a ceremony in Bath and all nominees were invited to attend a formal gala evening, whether they won or not.

Daisy read the letter a third time, trying to process what it meant. The nomination itself was an honour, but the possibility of actually winning felt very alien to her. Letting the invitation drop onto the counter, she looked around the shop and thought about all the work she'd put in. Her mind zoomed back to all the late nights before it had opened when the twins had stayed with her mum and she'd worked late into the night. She'd spent hours arranging and constantly rotating displays once the shop's doors had opened and had put thought into everything from the tea that went into the pots to the little hand-stamped labels on the brown paper book bags. Shaking her head at all the cleaning, sorting and filing she'd done on Uncle Dennis's huge book collection, she pondered it all. As she looked around, she wondered why it had done well; it didn't take long to work out why. She'd thought about and curated everything, every single little detail. Careful consideration had gone into choosing which books to stock, she'd trawled online sites for special books and she'd researched how to create an atmosphere in retail environments that made people want to stay. She'd stalked Pinterest for bookshops all over the world and had done the whole thing on a shoestring budget. On reflection, she realised that social media had played a massive part in her success, too.

Just as she was about to text Miles to tell him about the nomination, there was a tap on the front door. Daisy looked up to see Lotta with a book under her arm, a huge tote bag over her shoulder with a book stuffed in the top and a little pot of lavender from the florist tucked into the crook of her elbow. Daisy smiled, went to the door, slid the bolt back and opened it. Lotta had become both a friend and a bit of a confidante in all things books. She was someone who understood the book business and had been instrumental in helping Daisy build her social media presence. Daisy, truth be told, knew that much of her initial out-of-the-gate success had come from Lotta's influence in the niche bookworm world. It had been a cog in the wheel of her success and one she was very grateful for.

Lotta beamed. 'Morning, lovely. I wondered if you'd be in here getting ready for tomorrow. I loved that reel you did on the library ladders. How are you? All good? What gorgeous weather we've been having.'

Daisy's voice came out slightly strangled. 'Morning.'

Lotta frowned. 'Are you alright? You look like you've seen a ghost. What's up?'

Daisy held up the nomination news. 'I'm fine. Just a bit in shock. The bookshop's been nominated for an award. As in a real, decent, national award. I, err, I can't believe it. I've just opened the letter and I'm a little bit gobsmacked.'

Lotta put her bag down, propped the pot of lavender on the counter and read the letter. 'Oh my word, Daise! This is prestigious by the looks of it. I know bookshops that have been trying to get nominated for this for a long time. Wowzas. This place is just the gift that keeps on giving. Amazing!'

'Right, I don't know what to think.'

'Think that you're on a roll. It's huge. Massive. This could change everything for you. The publicity alone is worth it and if you actually win...' Lotta trailed off, shaking her head in amazement. 'How are you not jumping up and down in excitement?'

Daisy looked around the bookshop. 'I suppose I'm still trying to work out if it's real. I didn't really think anyone knew about us, if you see what I mean. Stuck down here doing our own thing and you know how often I leave Pretty Beach. I've not really heard of this organisation.'

'Which makes the whole thing even sweeter. It's real, very wonderful, and you absolutely deserve it.' Lotta picked up the letter again and scanned through the details. 'You haven't just opened a bookshop, you've created a destination. I, for one, love it in here. I think that much is *very* obvious.'

Daisy wondered how that was true, but the evidence was right there in front of her. Without blowing her own trumpet, the bookshop looked fabulous, customers loved it and more importantly, it was making her an income. When she'd first taken on the old building and turned it into a bookshop, she'd been motivated by nothing short of desperation rather than some high-falutin entrepreneurial vision. She'd needed somewhere to live and a way to make money, and the bookshop had seemed like the least terrible option available to her. But somewhere along the way, it had become something more than just a business and apparently other people had noticed that, too. 'They want to do a site visit. Representatives from the Alliance will come and assess the bookshop. How hilarious! I mean, really? It's just me making it up as I go along. I can't quite see what they are going to assess, but anyway.'

'They'll see exactly what your customers see.' Lotta was firm as she nodded. 'I love this place. It's a bookshop run by someone who genuinely cares about books and the people who read them. That's rarer than you might think in this business. Trust me, I've seen people come and go and some of the big boys try and recreate all of this and they fail time and time again. The simple thing is that you cannot recreate it. It has to be in your blood. Ask me how I know.'

Holly from the bakery waved as she went past, took one look at their faces, stopped and pushed the door. 'What's happened in here this morning? One of you looks like they've won the lottery and one looks like they're about to be sick.'

'Daisy's been nominated for a national retail award,' Lotta announced before Daisy could speak.

Holly's reaction was even more dramatic than Lotta's had been. She literally squealed, put her bag down and grabbed Daisy's hands. 'Are you serious? What award? Daise! Wait until I tell Mum. Wait until I tell everyone!' Holly was practically bouncing with excitement.

Daisy protested and played it down, though she was starting to feel the reality of it sinking in. Winner or not, to be nominated alone was quite an achievement. 'It's just a nomination. I probably won't win.'

'Doesn't matter if you win or not. Being nominated is a

massive achievement. This is also good for Pretty Beach. We'll have a nationally recognised, award-nominated bookshop in our midst. That's the sort of thing that gets written up on websites and talked about on podcasts and brings the sort of people we want to our little town.'

The thought of write-ups and suchlike made Daisy's stomach clench. She'd worked hard to build up the bookshop's reputation, but it had always been on a local scale. Just her bumbling around, making it up as she went along, making pretty reels on social media and doing her own thing. The idea of national attention felt unbelievable and all around odd. 'I need to tell Miles and Mum and Annabelle and Maggie. Oh God, what if the Alliance wants to do interviews and photos?'

Lotta chuckled. 'Oh, they'll want to do interviews.'

Daisy touched her hair and joked. 'Goodness, I'll need to do something about this bird's nest. I'll need a glow-up.'

Holly cackled. 'I'm your girl for glow-ups. I have people I can call. A little nip and tuck here and there.'

Daisy chuckled. 'I meant going to the hairdresser.'

'Right, well, if you need anything else, tell me.' Holly made for the door. 'I need to get to work. Well done. This is so good for you *and* Pretty Beach, Daise.'

'Thanks.'

'Yes, I need to shoot off, too.' Lotta picked up her bag, pot of lavender and books. 'Well done, again, Daise.'

'Yep, thanks. See you.'

Holly beamed and winked. 'Well done, Daise. This is going to keep the gossip wheel turning for a while.'

After continuing with the cleaning and sorting, the nomination letter was still sitting on the counter. Daisy picked it up to read it and as she read through, she shook her head and doubted herself. It did feel as if they'd either made a mistake or that they were a bit over the top. She'd hardly created Harrods; it was just a local shop that was doing fairly well. When she'd first opened the bookshop, she'd been focused mostly on dragging herself out of a horrible rotating situation of money stress and survival. Despite loving books and the book world, she'd focused on making enough money to keep going so that she could provide a stable home for the twins. The idea that she'd had an impact on the community had never really occurred to her and that other people recognised it was all sorts of strange. Thinking about the customers who'd become friends, the reading clubs that met in the shop, the mums groups who came in after the school run, she began to see what the nomination committee had recognised. The bookshop was a little bit of comfort and connection in a small seaside town. The feeling she'd inadvertently created by cobbling together things she loved had rippled outward and provided a base for cosy, community things. A little welcoming space full to the brim with books, pretty bits and bobs and all of it felt a bit like home away from home. Just what had been in the vision in her head in the first place.

As she folded the letter and tucked it into the drawer behind the counter, next to the notebook Miles had given her, she smiled and wondered how it would all go. Getting nominated was nice, more than nice, but she would play it all by ear. Paying her bills was a billion times more interesting to Daisy than awards. Fancy nominations were all very well and good, but earning a crust was more important and was giving her enough to be getting on with. She would simply go with the flow and wait and see.

4

Daisy had just got off the ferry and was on her way to do a turnaround clean at one of Suntanned Pete's holiday cottages. She smiled at a woman who was pulling a suitcase in one hand and holding a dog lead in the other with a poodle who had been clipped to make him look as if he had four dancing feet. It was cold in Pretty Beach from a brisk breeze coming in off the coast. Choppy sea crashed around the ferry and it felt like there might be rain in the air. Daisy put her collar up and felt the air nipping at her ankles where her jeans didn't meet her trainers as she walked away from the wharf and thought about the day ahead.

Cobbles underneath her feet felt uneven and a whole load of seagulls were pecking away at a grassed area as Daisy walked in the direction of one of Pete's holiday cottages. Hustling along, she thought about the indie bookshop award and all that it meant. It had been quite a surprise for sure, but also very welcome in a way. For Daisy, who'd felt a little bit lost since having the twins, it felt nice to be wanted, noticed, liked and acknowledged. Pondering the whole thing as she walked, she thought about how far she'd come since Suntanned Pete had mentioned opening a bookshop to her. At the time, she'd thought he was totally barking up the wrong tree and bonkers. It seemed, however, good old Suntanned Pete knew what was what. He'd spotted a gap, she'd gone full steam ahead and filled it.

Musing the whole situation, she shook her head. It was as if that morning sitting with Pete on the swing in her mum's garden was a million moons ago. Loads had happened in the time since; good things, bad things and everything in between. Didn't her tired body and full brain know about it? Yes, for sure, but she'd do it all again in a heartbeat. It had absolutely been a journey; there'd been times when she'd felt like throwing in the towel, some lovely days and lots and lots of ups and downs. There had been the threat that the whole bookshop idea would come toppling down with the proposal of the corporation GayesBooks taking over a nearby building and there had been days when she'd wondered if it was really all worth it. There had been times when she'd worked long twelve-hour days to hardly make a penny, where she'd questioned everything. Now, here she was nominated for an award with an accompanying invitation to a fancy gala event. She'd had worse invitations in her life.

As she reached the cottage and keyed in the security code at the side gate, she shook her head at herself and hooted at what was going on in her life. Here she was, walking up the path to clean a holiday cottage for Suntanned Pete, the same as she'd been doing for years, but now she was also the owner of a bookshop that had been nominated for a national award. The whole thing felt surreal and she wasn't quite sure how to process it all. She did know she quite liked feeling successful. It felt good to be staring success in the face. She'd watched the people she loved in her life dancing with it for long enough. Now it seemed it was her time to have a little jig.

The cottage she was about to clean was one of Pete's nicer

ones, tucked away down a little lane with a view of the sea from the upstairs windows. As she unlocked the front door and stepped inside, she was greeted by the usual post-holiday chaos. Towels dumped on the bathroom floor, sand tracked through the hallway, and the lingering smell of bacon and coffee from someone else's breakfast that morning. The guests had clearly enjoyed their stay, judging by the state they'd left the place in. Tutting and rolling her eyes at a wet towel in the middle of the hallway, Daisy put her cleaning bag down by the door and surveyed the damage. It wasn't the worst she'd seen, but it would take a good few hours to get everything back together. Pete had high standards and his occupancy rate and reviews reflected them.

A few minutes later, she was pulling on a highly glamorous pair of bright yellow rubber gloves and getting ready to get on with the job at hand. After tying her hair back with one of the twins' love heart covered velvet scrunchies she'd slipped on her wrist just as she'd left home, she got to work. Starting in the kitchen, she cleared breakfast plates from a table and loaded them into the dishwasher. Someone had spilt orange juice on the worktop and left it to go sticky, and there were crumbs scattered across every surface. As she wiped and scrubbed, Daisy let the monotony of the cleaning calm her mind. While she worked, her thoughts kept drifting back to the letter tucked away in the drawer at the bookshop. The Independent Retail Alliance Award had totally scoped her out and not only that, thought that her little attempt at running a bookshop was a good one. Who would have thought? She still couldn't quite believe it was real. When she'd first read the letter, her immediate thought had been that they'd confused the bookshop with someone else's properly managed professional operation. But Lotta and Holly had both been adamant that it was legitimate and that the bookshop deserved the recognition.

As she moved into the sitting room and started plumping

cushions and folding throws, Daisy found herself thinking about what the award ceremony would involve. According to the letter, it was a formal gala evening in Bath, black tie one hundred per cent not optional. The thought of getting dressed up and sitting in a room full of retail professionals did not really fill Daisy with joy. Some people thrived on dressing up and being seen, enjoyed it even. Daisy Henley, nope, not so much. Poking pins in her eyes appeared more attractive than gallivanting around in black tie. She'd rather live out her comfy little cosy life in Pretty Beach than attend galas any day of the week. She'd been to precisely one black tie event in her entire life, a charity dinner that Annabelle had dragged her to years before and she'd felt uncomfortable, bored to the back teeth and like a fish out of water the entire evening. She'd sat at a table under a sparkly chandelier, eating posh food on white plates and sworn never ever again. Since then, nothing and no one had been able to convince her to attend anything like it. She'd vowed not to ever repeat the scenario and had mostly stuck to her guns. It looked like the guns would be changing.

Musing and pondering, she wondered if she did, indeed, end up attending the gala, what on earth she would wear? Her wardrobe consisted mainly of floral shirts, dungarees, lovely comfy cardigans, jeans, jumpers, and the odd floral dress for special occasions. She didn't own anything remotely suitable for a formal gala, and the thought of having to buy something made her physically wince. The bookshop was doing well, but she wasn't exactly rolling in money. Every penny that came in either went back into the business or towards the twins, or dropped into her savings pot.

She'd have to ask Annabelle for advice, or maybe borrow something from Maggie's extensive collection of designer outfits. The notion of borrowing a dress was good for many reasons: she wouldn't have to bother with the brain power of finding something, it was better than spending money she didn't really have on a dress she'd probably never wear again and she'd be able to slip it on and go.

Moving upstairs to tackle the bedrooms, Daisy stripped the sheets and bundled them into a laundry bag and as she vacuumed under the beds and wiped down the bedside tables, she continued to mull over the implications of the nomination. The site visit from the alliance representatives filled her with quiet dread. She hated the formality of it and had no idea what criteria they'd be judging against, but supposed she'd just have to be herself and hope for the best. The thought of strangers coming to evaluate her little attempt at entrepreneurship was daunting at best, but there wasn't much she could do about it if she wanted to be considered. Fairy lights and vintage furniture would probably look amateur to people who were used to slick retail environments, but it was all she had and that was that. All she could do was give it a good go.

As she vacuumed all the way along the tops of the skirting boards with the brush attachment, she wondered whether they'd want to interview her about her business philosophy and her vision for the bookshop. Ha ha ha. Umm, truth was, she didn't really have a grand vision or *any* vision at all. She'd started the bookshop because she'd needed somewhere to live as a side hustle way to make money, and it had evolved organically from there. She'd made decisions based on what she'd had at her disposal and what felt right rather than following any particular business strategy. There was no philosophy either. What even was one of those? She wondered if her acumen would be enough for a panel of retail experts, decided that it probably wouldn't and pondered if, bottom line, the whole thing would be a bit of a waste of time. Who really knew?

In the main bathroom, she scrubbed the shower cubicle and replaced the towels, thinking about the potential media attention that might come with the nomination. Lotta had mentioned interviews and photo shoots, and the thought made

Daisy's palms sweat. She liked to let the bookshop speak for itself, heck, she cringed when she was ever in a reel on Instagram, so the idea of being asked to articulate what made her business felt daunting. She chuckled to herself at what she might say: that she'd stumbled into bookselling by accident, had no idea what she was doing and had been making it up as she went along ever since. That was about the nuts and bolts of it. That her main qualification was loving books, not ever having to leave Pretty Beach, and wanting to create a space where other people could love books, too. It hardly sounded like the sort of inspiring entrepreneurial story that award ceremonies usually celebrated.

As she moved back downstairs to tackle the final bits and bobs of cleaning, a little film-like reel played in Daisy's imagination. She laughed as she saw herself in a fancy dress with some of Annabelle's sparkly jewellery, attending the award ceremony itself. Her hair was up, her gown was floor-length and a little bag was hanging off her arm. The thought of having to get up and possibly give a speech made her feel physically sick. The idea of addressing a room full of industry professionals was, to be quite frank, Daisy's idea of out-and-out, skin-numbing hell. Whatever, she'd go with the flow.

Suddenly, she shook her head as a voice told her to back herself and beef herself up for once in her blooming life. She would not be nervous or try not to be. She would instead trust her gut and roll with the fact that what she'd created was worth celebrating, even if she couldn't explain exactly how she'd done it or, really, why. All she knew was that her lovely little shop had saved her life, provided the twins with a place to call home and had given Daisy back a role in Pretty Beach. All of that was worth more than any award any day of the week.

Finishing up in the kitchen, she wiped down the final surfaces and checked everything was spotless. As she packed away her cleaning supplies, she thought about how different her life had become since she'd taken on the bookshop. Not that long before, she'd been doing exactly this same job, cleaning Pete's holiday cottages and scraping by financially. Back then, she'd tried to be independent and pay her own way, but most of the time, she'd felt as if she was not only failing but as if she was hopeless, too. The bookshop had been nothing more than a desperate idea and a last-ditch attempt to create some stability for herself and the twins. Now here she was, still cleaning cottages but also running a business that had been recognised on a national level. It was utterly remarkable how quickly things could change when you took a chance on something, put your head down, your nose to the grindstone and gave something a good old-fashioned go.

As she went around checking everything was spick and span, she wondered what Miles's reaction would be. No doubt he'd be all over it and probably start talking about booking a hotel room and making a proper weekend of it, treating it as a celebration regardless of whether she won or not. Perhaps that would be a good idea. Maybe it was time to start making a big old ding dong about the good things in her life, because for sure, she now had a few of them.

After replenishing the welcome pack, Daisy locked up the cottage and walked back towards the ferry and thought about how surreal it was to be nominated for an award that she'd never even heard of before. She'd spent so long focused on surviving, on keeping her head above water financially and emotionally, that the idea of being recognised for anything at all, really, felt alien. The more she thought about it, the more she realised that perhaps that was exactly why the bookshop worked. Because it hadn't been created with awards and all that old rubbish and jargon in mind. Nope, it had evolved from a genuine love for books and a desire to create something for herself. She'd put her heart, soul, late nights, elbow grease, early mornings, brain power and grind into every single little thing.

Every decision, every fairy light, every mismatched chair and cup of coffee had mattered. Perhaps all of that showed.

The ferry was pulling into the wharf as she reached the end of the lane and as she quickened her pace to catch it, she nodded to herself that yes, siree Mr President, she had done well. As she climbed aboard and found a seat, she looked back in the direction of the cottage she'd just cleaned and thought about the strange parallel lives she was living. In one life, Daisy the cleaner, scrubbing bathrooms and changing bed sheets for visitors who came to stay in Pretty Beach. In another, Daisy, the award-nominated bookshop owner, being recognised for creating something special. How very bizarre, indeed.

When she pondered it, both versions of herself felt equally real and important. She quite enjoyed the cleaning work for Pete and always had done. It was cathartic on days when her brain was a fuzz, it paid the bills and kept her grounded and allowed her to trundle along with the bookshop doing her own thing. The bookshop was her dream manifested and proof that sometimes taking a leap of faith was the way to go.

As the ferry chugged across the water towards Pretty Beach, Daisy pulled out her phone and scrolled through the photos she'd taken of the award letter. What a turn-up for the books. Fabulous. Fantastic. She felt good, happy, safe and positive. Me, oh my, she hoped that things stayed the same. Little did she know that in the future, that might not quite be the case.

5

A few days later, Daisy was walking down the far end of the laneway from the bookshop. She splashed through a puddle and took a sip of a takeaway coffee as she made her way past a row of cottages facing the wharf, wondering if she would ever stop feeling surprised by how well the bookshop was doing. Not that she was complaining, absolutely for sure, not. She'd struck gold with the whole venture and the business was a million times better than having to worry about money. However, despite all the backing herself attempts, underneath, the award nomination had thrown her completely. The doubting part of her made her wonder if she was actually any good at what she was doing or if it had all just been a lucky accident. Really, she wasn't at all sure.

Strolling along beside Pretty Beach Fire Station, she made her way past a community hall and into the Pretty Beach council offices. The place was quiet, thankfully, and there weren't many people in the queue at all, apart from a small, skinny man in faded red chinos who was raising his voice at one of the staff behind the counter because he'd thought it fair to park his Volvo in a disabled spot because his dog had hurt his ear.

Daisy touched one of the large ticket machines near the entrance, tapped on the screen, scanned her driving licence and waited for a printed ticket to come out. It appeared with a bar code and number and informed her that she had an approximate seven-minute wait. Shaking her head, she sat down as the loud man continued to complain. Three staff were sitting, staring at their screens, clicking, and appeared as if they were making a lot of effort to not do much at all. Oh, to be a Pretty Beach council worker. Yes please.

Daisy was not a lover of bureaucracy, red tape, councils, governments, politicians or anything of the like. Mostly the places wound her up and made her feel confined and in her adult life, she'd tried to give them as wide a berth as possible. She attempted to be patient, calm and attempted to ignore the debacle going on at counter number one with the man with the dog who, by all accounts, had a slice out of his ear. Just as she'd got her phone out and was checking her emails, there were a few pings from a speaker and an electronic voice called out ticket numbers. No one got up, Daisy checked the screen above the heads of the staff and waited as the numbers clicked over and hers was called.

As she got to the counter, she smiled to see old-school, true blue Pretty Beach resident Julie sitting propped up on a blue pillow on top of a high stool with a smile on her face. Wearing a dark blue Pretty Beach Council blazer topped with a bright turquoise string of chunky beads, Julie smiled. 'Oh, hiya Daise! Long time, no see. How are you? And your sisters? Everyone doing well, are they? I saw your mum the other day when I was on my way to the allotments. She's looking well.'

'Can't complain. We're all good, thanks. Nothing to report. You?'

'That's good to hear. Yes, great, my end. What can I do for you?'

'I have a problem with my ferry concession pass. I can't get it to work on the app itself and my card is caput.'

Julie made a little huff sound and tapped away on her keyboard. 'Yep, you and the rest of Pretty Beach. The old way was much better. I don't know why they have to constantly change systems and upgrade things that are working perfectly well. Honestly, we get all these new-fangled ideas every five minutes from the powers that be. We only went on a training course for a new system two years ago. Now it's changed again. And they wonder why our beautiful country is on the brink of bankruptcy. I'm no politician or economist, but I've managed a household budget for long enough.' Julie rolled her eyes. 'You'd think they would have, you know, asked the people who work with this stuff every day what they think, but no, that would have been way, way, way too simple. Honestly, I have been doing these passes all week long. It's a pain in the you know what.'

Daisy nodded. 'Yes, everyone's been saying.'

Julie tutted. 'I don't know why we bother with the staff feedback link either. I've decided I'm not filling that in any more. I tell them things and do they take it on board? Do they heck. It drives me doolally, Daise.'

'Always the same.'

'How're you getting on with the bookshop? Let's talk about that. It's much more interesting than council stuff,' Julie asked as she tapped her keyboard.

'Fabulous, though I'm still pinching myself that it's actually working and people keep coming in. It's going well.'

'Ahh, that's so good. So good. You've got Suntanned Pete to thank for that.' Julie made a funny face.

'Don't let him know.' Daisy joked.

'Seriously, you're doing brilliantly. I was just saying to Laura, actually, that the bookshop is great for this town. There aren't many people like you who'll take a chance on something and make it work. It's no walk in the park what you've done. Look at me, for instance. Would I do that? Nope, not a chance! It might be a bit boring in this place, but I get to sit here all day in the warm, do my job, go home and put my feet up and I get paid rain or shine, week in, week out. Having your own business is nowhere near as easy. I know which option I would take. You should be right proud of yourself, Daise. I'd be proud as punch if I were you.'

Daisy was a little bit taken aback. 'Ah, thank you. I suppose I am. It's not been all unicorns and roses, but honestly, it's working really well for me. It fits in with the girls and everything and I love it.'

'Yes, for sure. I've been around here a long time and you are the best thing to happen to that old building, not that I am saying that Dennis, God bless his soul, wasn't good, you know. You, my girl, have done a blooming amazing job and don't you let yourself forget it.' Julie winked an electric blue-mascara-d eye.

'Thanks, Julie. Coming from you, that's so nice.'

Julie narrowed her eyes so that her eyeliner looked even more strange than it usually did. She pursed her fuchsia lips, leant forward and lowered her voice. 'I heard through the grapevine about the award nomination. Would you look at that? Congratulations, my lovely. That's a real feather in your cap, that is. It can't be bad for Pretty Beach, either. We love an award or two down this neck of the woods, don't we?'

'Oh, thank you. I'm still not quite sure it's real, to be honest.'

'Course it's real and well deserved too. That little shop of yours has brought something special to Pretty Beach. My sister pops in every week now, she says it's like stepping into someone's sitting room, only better. She reckons it's the sitting room we all wish we had, complete with cosy lamps, library ladders, pretty lights and tea on tap. What more could anyone ask for?'

Daisy laughed. 'That's so lovely to hear. I do my best.'

'Give yourself a pat on the back, Daise. Not everyone could have done what you've done with that place.' Julie continued to chat as she clicked through the computer system, simultaneously muttering about concession cards, digital permits and bureaucracy, then looking up again with a glint in her eye. 'Did Holly say your fellow was scouting for a house down here, or was I hearing things?'

'Blimey, we can't move for someone knowing our business.'

'Nope, you can't. You should know that. Did you know Mrs Patterson might be moving to Birmingham and her cottage could be coming up for sale in the Old Town?'

'Really? Oh, I hadn't heard that.'

'Well, you wouldn't have done yet. It's all very hush-hush at the moment.'

'Interesting. They don't go up for sale around there very often.'

Julie continued clicking through the computer system, her fuchsia nails tapping against the keyboard as she worked through Daisy's ferry pass details. 'It's round the back there, near the cricket field, you know? One of those tall Victorian places up near the church. Lovely up there.'

Daisy nodded. 'The Old Town's nice, yes. We grew up there, so maybe I'm a bit biased.'

'Exactly right. Not that I'd want to live up there myself, mind you. Too many hills and steps for my liking and all that old plumbing in those places. Give me my nice bungalow any day of the week.'

'Fair enough. Though those old houses do have character, though.'

'Yes, like your mum's place. I love it, I do, but character's all very good until you're dealing with damp and dodgy electrics every winter.' Julie squinted at her screen and clicked her mouse several times. 'My cousin, you know, Sharon, lives up that way and she's always moaning about something falling apart.' Julie continued to work through the system, muttering under her breath about technology and why things couldn't just stay simple. 'The house I'm talking about is the one with the fancy ironwork, just along there from the old vicarage. You know the one. You would have walked that way to school back in the day.'

Daisy squinted. 'I think so. Is that the one with the unusual bay windows?'

'That's it. Mrs Patterson's been there for donkey's years. Lovely old lady, keeps herself to herself mostly. My Charlie went to school with Lilly. Her grandson comes down from Birmingham to check on her every now and then. I can't remember why her Mandy initially moved to Birmingham. Probably for university or something, or was it nursing? Anyway…'

'Right.'

'Word is they want to get going on it, though you didn't hear that from me. Can't blame them really. That house is far too big for one person rattling around in it.' Julie hit a few more keys and looked pleased with herself. 'There we go. Your ferry pass should work now. The system had you down as a visitor rather than a resident, just as most of the other residents in Pretty Beach don't live here, according to this. Typical really.' Julie rolled her eyes.

'Thanks, it's been on my list of jobs to come in here and get it sorted for ages.'

'Don't mention it. It's been nice chatting. Say hello to Bells and Maggie for me.'

'Will do. Same, great to see you.'

'Take care.'

Daisy tucked her renewed ferry pass into her bag and thanked Julie again before heading back out onto the street. As she walked away from the council offices, she found herself turning left instead of heading straight back to the bookshop. The route to the Old Town was one she'd walked countless times over the years. The streets grew narrower as she climbed a hill, old stone walls flanked either side and glimpses of gorgeous gardens popped through wrought iron gates. The architecture was different to a lot of Pretty Beach, especially the cottages and fishermen's houses down by the harbour. The Old Town was a jumble of more solid Victorian villas that had been built to impress and last. Many of them had been in families for generations, their upkeep just as impressive as their stature.

As she walked and pondered, she wondered if a house would indeed come up and if Miles would be interested. If so, what, in fact, would that mean for her? Things were getting serious with talk of house purchases. Daisy wasn't sure what she thought about that. She could but wait and see.

6

Daisy had just got back from the school run and was getting out of her car on the lane behind the bookshop. A movement caught her eye and she looked up to see Miles walking towards her holding an enormous bouquet of flowers in his arms that was so large it practically obscured the whole of his face. The beautifully wrapped flowers, a gorgeous jumble of whites and creams, were clearly extortionately expensive and had been bought with intention. The sort of intention Daisy liked. They were far from Miles' first attempt at giving her flowers. In the early days, he'd turned up with ten bunches of "I'm sorry" flowers from the Spar. This, however, was an arrangement from a fancy florist rather than the corner shop and made anyone who might receive them swoon and then some. Oh, did Daisy Henley swoon? Indeed, she did. Who doesn't want a handsome man to douse one in flowers? Said no one ever.

'Good grief, what on earth is all this about? Who's the lucky person getting these?' Daisy laughed as Miles struggled to manoeuvre the bouquet as he got to her car and kissed her.

'Congratulations is what these are all about. You are a

nominee for a very prestigious award, so we are celebrating. It's my job to present you with flowers. I started as I mean to go on in this relationship, ha.'

Daisy shook her head, pretended to protest, but secretly adored it, him and the flowers. 'You didn't need to do that. I'm just happy to have been nominated.'

'I wanted to. The whole of Pretty Beach is talking about the nomination. I just popped into the bakery and Holly was practically bouncing off the walls with excitement.'

'News travels fast around here. Holly was passing the shop when I'd just received the invitation, so she was one of the first to know, as usual. I reckon she sniffs out gossip in this town.'

Miles chuckled. 'She was telling anyone who'd listen that Pretty Beach now has a nationally recognised bookshop. I mean, technically, she's right.'

Daisy pushed open the gate and they walked through the back to the kitchen. She took the flowers, which were indeed impressive up close and laid them carefully in the sink. White roses, lilies and things she couldn't identify, all arranged in a cleverly curated posy of absolute lushness, looked back at her. The bouquet was nearly as big as the kitchen but fitted in so very well with just about everything, mostly Daisy's happy, grateful current state of mind. 'They're gorgeous, but you didn't need to do all this. Really, you didn't. It's just a nomination. There's no way I'll win, anyway.'

'It's not every day your girlfriend gets nominated for a national retail award. This is huge, Daise. You shouldn't minimise it. I'm not going to let you do that.'

'I keep feeling as if they've made some sort of mistake and I'll get another letter saying something different.'

Miles shook his head and hugged her. 'Nope, they haven't made a mistake. You've built something special here and other people have noticed. That doesn't happen by accident. If you're not going to toot your own horn, I am.'

'We're English, we don't do horn tooting.' Daisy joked and breathed in the scent of the flowers mixed with the smell of Miles. 'I'm still getting my head around it all. Yesterday morning, I was cleaning one of Pete's cottages, thinking about how surreal it all is. I'm actually over the moon. How lucky am I?'

Miles shook his head. 'Nup, not having that either. Luck is not involved in any shape or form. You work incredibly hard, you've created a business that people love, and now you're being recognised for it. That seems perfectly logical to me.'

'When you put it like that. Anyway, how was London? Did you get everything sorted with your mum? How is she feeling?'

'All fine on the surface, but she's still not got her confidence back about going out. I don't know how it's all going to work out for the best. She keeps saying that she doesn't want to be a burden, which is driving me up the wall. I don't even know where that came from. How she thinks she's a burden is beyond me. I just want her to be okay. You know?'

'Oh dear. Hopefully, it will improve. I still have to make myself believe that someone mugs a senior citizen twice. If you saw that in a movie or something, you wouldn't believe it.'

Miles looked from the kitchen through into the bookshop. 'Anyway. Tell me everything about this nomination. What exactly does it involve? It wasn't very clear in the photo you sent me.'

Daisy went through into the bookshop, opened the drawer behind the counter, pulled out the letter and handed it to Miles. 'Have a read of that and tell me what you think.'

Miles scanned the letter, raised his eyebrows, slipped his phone out of his pocket and tapped. 'The Independent Retail Alliance is not some local chamber of commerce thing. Being nominated for this is a genuine achievement.'

'That's what Lotta and Holly said. It's all a bit funny, really. I still feel like an amateur playing at being a businesswoman, but there you go.' Daisy pumped her fists in the air and did a funny little jig. 'Go me.'

Miles gestured to the shop. 'Look at what you've built. This isn't amateur anything, this is professional retail done with heart and soul. It's how shops used to be in the old days, Daise.'

'I suppose it does look quite nice when you put it like that.'

'It looks more than nice and most places get it completely wrong, which is precisely why you're doing well. I mean, look what's on offer: sterile chain stores with no personality or chaotic independent places where you can't find anything. You've found the perfect balance between organisation and character.'

Daisy chuckled 'You sound very knowledgeable and serious. I just tried to create the sort of place I'd want to spend time in myself.'

'Exactly. And that's why it works so well.' Miles looked at the letter again. 'So what happens next? There's a site visit from the judging panel?'

'Yes. They want to come and assess the bookshop, talk to customers, and evaluate the business model. I've basically been making it up as I go along since I opened.'

'Everyone makes it up as they go along. The difference is that you've made good decisions based on instinct rather than following some textbook formula.'

'I just like pottering around reading in Pretty Beach. It's not rocket science.'

Miles winked. 'I'm always right. Let's make a proper weekend of it, we can stay somewhere nice, maybe see a show.'

'What in the world am I going to wear? I don't own anything suitable for a formal gala.'

'That's easily sorted. Maggie and Bells to the rescue.'

Daisy arranged the flowers properly in a vase. 'I thought the same.'

'This is a big deal, Daise, even if you don't want to admit it.'

'I'm starting to realise that.' Daisy touched one of the flower petals. 'Thank you for the flowers and for, you know, being proud of me.'

Daisy closed her eyes as Miles hugged her. Perhaps he was right about the nomination being well deserved. Perhaps it was time to stop second-guessing herself and start believing that good things could happen and would *continue* to happen. That her life had turned around. That there weren't bad things around the corner. The thing was: Daisy was well aware that, really, you never did know.

7

Daisy was having a thoroughly nice time on a lovely day in Pretty Beach. Walking hand in hand with Miles, they made their way through the town, past the wharf to the fishing area and headed in the direction of the funicular railway. They had special Locals Only passes to a ticketed event on the funicular railway and the twins were exponentially excited about going up and down in the carriages. It was part of the Pretty Beach heritage trail and much loved by locals and visitors alike. The railway and all that went with it, via riding up and down the cliff, had been part of Daisy's life forever, and brought back nostalgic memories of both being a little girl and her teenage years.

Daisy chatted away to Miles as they walked in the direction of the railway's little ticket office at the bottom. He stopped and stared with his chin lifted as they approached and squinted at a carriage coming down the side of the cliff. 'Wow, that is something else.'

Daisy nodded and saw the old railway with different eyes as Miles shook his head. 'I guess it is.'

The Pretty Beach Funicular Railway had been carrying

passengers up and down the cliff top for over a century, its lovely old timber carriages a really beloved fixture against the cliff face. The Victorian engineering marvel consisted of two carriages connected by a steel cable system, one ascending whilst the other descended, meeting halfway on a passing loop. As Daisy followed Miles' gaze, she agreed that it never failed to delight children and adults alike. The lower station sat tucked between fishermen's cottages and the lifeboat station, whilst the upper terminus opened onto cliff top walks with spectacular views across out to sea that had seen many a Henley family walk. The railway's original brass fittings and wooden bench seats had been lovingly maintained, and the gentle clunk and whir of the winding mechanism provided a soundtrack that was as much a part of Pretty Beach as the honk of the ferry in the distance. Daisy, like many locals, felt lucky to have it in her life.

As they got closer, Daisy smiled and watched as the twins got excited to go up on the railway. Strolling, they chatted about Miles's mum and how she was coping with being in the flat in London on her own. It had been an ongoing conversation and worry for months. The more Miles went to see her, the more he was none the wiser about how it was going to go.

'So do you think she is scared of going out all the time or just to that same area where she got mugged?' Daisy asked.

'I think *all* the time. She hasn't really been going anywhere and she's started to do Waitrose food orders on her phone, and even then, I don't think she likes being near the front door when her shopping arrives. I don't know how long she can go on like this.' Miles shook his head and held his hands up. 'What more can I do?'

'And how has your brother been?'

Miles tutted and shook his head. 'He says he doesn't like going to see her because it makes *him* upset. He says he can't stand the idea of her being vulnerable and that it's not good for his mental health. Which is annoying me, to be honest. How does he think I like it? Sure, I love seeing Mum like this! Yeah, it's super great for my mental health. But, anyway, it is what it is. He's always been weird about stuff like this. Sometimes I wonder if he ever grew up, you know? What do you think I should do?'

Daisy had heard various debatable things about Miles's brother, all of which made her feel very grateful for Annabelle and Maggie. She shook her head. 'I don't know. It's very hard to work out what to do in this situation. Have you thought anything else about buying a property here?'

'Yep. It could be the answer. I know one thing: I'm sick of going up and down, too. I need a base that's more permanent.'

Daisy wasn't sure what she thought about the idea, but she wanted Miles around more and his mum loved it when she visited. 'The answer would be a property with a granny flat. If, of course, she would be happy to live like that. Then you'd be able to keep an eye on her, but she wouldn't feel like a burden to you.'

'Yes, you know that would work. I've been looking and nothing comes up in the Old Town.'

Daisy remembered her conversation with Julie. 'Apparently, there's one coming up over that way in the near future, I forgot to mention it. I'm not sure what it's like or if it has an annexe. If it does come up, maybe it could be converted or something. Anyway, it's a thought.'

'How do you know?'

'When I was getting my ferry pass sorted out at the council, Julie, who dealt with my problem, told me. She knows everything about everyone.'

'Right.'

'What would you do about your mum's flat if she did come down here?'

'Don't know. I guess it could go up for sale or rent. Unbelievably, because of the crime levels, even though it's one of the most expensive areas up there, the property prices are falling. Who would have thought? Goodness knows what my brother will think about that, you know what he's like. I've told you how he has issues with money and his inheritance. It has to be said that he has issues with everything.'

'You think he would have an issue with her being down here?' Daisy questioned.

'Maybe, maybe not, it would make his world easier and he's always been one for that. I mean, he can hardly get across London to see her, so I don't see how it makes much of a difference. Whatever I do, I assume it will be a problem for him.'

Daisy shuddered as she thought about Miles's attitude towards his brother. There wasn't a problem between them as such, but they weren't particularly close. It was in stark contrast to what she had with Annabelle and Maggie. One of the reasons that she felt so lucky about her family situation was that her eyes had been opened by Miles to how other siblings behaved. She was now more than aware that her sisters were worth their weight in gold. 'Let's just hope he wants what's best for her at the end of the day, not himself.'

'Hope so. Trust me, though, if he's involved, it won't be straightforward. He has this knack of making things awkward for all involved and more complicated than they need to be.'

They reached the funicular station just as a carriage was making its way down the cliff face. The engineering made a mechanical clank that had been the same for as long as Daisy could remember. The twins immediately pressed their faces against the glass of the waiting area, watching the descent with wide eyes.

'Can we go on it twice?' Margot asked as she bounced on her toes.

'We'll see how we go,' Daisy replied automatically, though she was still thinking about what Miles had said about his mum's flat and the possibility of finding something in Pretty

Beach. The whole conversation felt like it was heading somewhere she wasn't entirely ready to go, though she couldn't quite put her finger on why that was. She was very happy with their situation currently and didn't really want anything to rock the boat. She was quite happy having him in her life whenever and wherever she liked and it suited her well.

'I've been thinking about it more and more, actually,' Miles continued, as if he could read Daisy's thoughts. 'About bringing Mum down here permanently, I mean. She was so much better when she stayed in that cottage. Remember how she got her colour back? She kept talking about the food and the scenery and how it had given her a new lease of life. Every time I go back to London to see her, she seems to have retreated a bit further into herself. I really don't think it's healthy for her. Down here did her the world of good.'

Daisy agreed. 'I thought that the last time I came up there with you. She looked jaded and worn out. I guess being perpetually on guard isn't great for her health.'

Evie was earwigging. She tugged at Daisy's sleeve. 'Mummy, is Miles's mummy, Elizabeth, coming to live in Pretty Beach in the flat with Miles?'

'We don't know yet, sweetheart.'

'She could come and live in our bookshop,' Margot added helpfully. 'Old ladies like books, don't they? And we could make her tea all the time and she loves cinnamon buns.'

Miles chuckled. 'I think she would love that very much. She's always reading something, usually romance novels or autobiographies.'

'Like Mummy reads.' Evie nodded.

The funicular carriage reached the bottom with a huge thud and a hiss of brakes, and the operator, a man in his sixties who Daisy had known since she was the twins' age, opened the doors with a flourish.

'All aboard for the scenic route. Oh, hey, Daise, lovely to see you.'

'Hi.'

'Mind the gap and hold on tight.'

The twins scrambled into the carriage, claiming seats at the front and immediately pressed their noses against the glass. Miles and Daisy settled onto a wooden bench opposite them. As she watched Miles pick up Evie's bag from the floor, Daisy smiled and reflected on how natural it felt to be doing family things as if they had been doing them forever.

'The thing is,' Miles continued as the carriage began its ascent with a gentle lurch, 'I don't think Mum's going to get better while she's still in that flat. She associates it with what happened, and every time she looks out the window, she can see the exact spot where she was attacked. I think there's some sort of trauma response going on there, not that I really know what that means. Do you get me?'

Daisy watched the twins as they exclaimed over the view that was opening up below them, as Pretty Beach spread out like a postcard. The harbour, pastel cottages and the sea stretched away to the horizon. 'It's not surprising. It must be so horrible for her. Getting mugged once you can possibly put behind you, but twice and in the same spot gets a no from me. Honestly, I don't think many people would come away from that without being scared out of their wits. I can't even imagine it happening in Pretty Beach. It's so unheard of, it doesn't sound real.'

'I know. A place here would be so much better for her. She would be able to go out without being fearful.'

'What about work?'

'The thing is, I can work from anywhere these days unless something comes up. Most of my meetings are on video calls anyway, and when I do need to be in London, it's quick on the train. It just makes sense to buy something down here.'

The carriage climbed up the cliff face, the mechanical clank of the cable system banging underneath them. Daisy had travelled on the funicular hundreds of times over the years, but she never got tired of the view. The twins clearly loved it too, as the old-fashioned pleasure of the journey captivated them.

Evie beamed. 'Look, Mummy. You can see our bookshop from here.'

Daisy leaned forward to look where Evie was pointing. She could just about make out the bookshop, looking tiny and perfect in the laneway.

Margot clapped her hands. 'I love our bookshop. So much.'

Miles lowered his voice as the twins chatted to each other. 'I've been thinking about other things too. About us, I mean and about what happens next.'

Daisy felt her stomach do a flip. She was more than happy with the status quo. 'What do you mean? What does happen next? I thought we were perfectly happy as we are.'

'Well, if Mum does move down here, and if I do buy a place in Pretty Beach, then I suppose the question is whether we carry on as we are, with me having my own place and you having yours, or whether we think about something more, well, permanent.'

The twins were still exclaiming over the view and pointing out landmarks to each other, completely oblivious to the conversation happening behind them. Daisy was grateful for their distraction because it gave her a moment to process what Miles had just said without having to respond immediately.

'I mean, we practically live together anyway,' Miles continued, interpreting her silence as encouragement to elaborate. 'I'm at yours most nights, or you're at the flat when the girls have sleepovers. They are used to me being around, and I think we work well together as a sort of family unit.'

'Do we?'

Miles looked surprised by Daisy's tone. 'I thought we did. The twins seem happy enough with the arrangement...'

'It's just that there's a difference between liking the way things are and making them, well, you know, actually living together. I've, err, been on my own for, well, for the whole time since they were born. Yeah, that would be quite different, wouldn't it?'

The funicular reached the halfway point, where it passed the descending carriage with a wave from both operators. The twins waved enthusiastically at the passengers going down.

'You've said that before.'

'What exactly are you suggesting?' Daisy suspected she already knew and wasn't entirely sure how she felt about it.

'I'm suggesting that we stop pretending and acknowledge that we're in a proper relationship. I'm suggesting that if I buy a house in Pretty Beach, we think about it being *our* house rather than just mine and that we do it together.'

Daisy watched the view change as they continued their ascent and Pretty Beach became smaller and more perfect with distance. 'And what about the girls?'

'What about them? They already think of me as part of the family. Evie introduced me to her teacher as her mum's boyfriend and Margot asked me last week if I was going to be living with you forever. I take that as an indication that they like me.'

'Did she really?'

'She did, and when I said I didn't know, she told me she hoped I would because I make a better roast and pancakes than you do.'

Despite her growing unease about the direction of the conversation, Daisy smiled. 'She's not wrong about my cooking.'

'So what do you think?' Miles asked, reaching for Daisy's hand.

Daisy looked at their joined hands and tried to work out

why the idea of making things official made her feel unsettled. Surely, it would make her feel the opposite? It wasn't that she wasn't massively in love with Miles, because she was. It wasn't that she didn't want him in her life, because she *very* much did. It wasn't even that she was worried about the effect on the twins, because they clearly adored him and seemed to thrive on the stability his presence provided. It was that the magnitude of moving in with him, to her mind, was off the scale. She'd only just become used to having a partner in her life, let alone moving in with one. She tried to stall for time. 'I don't know.'

'You don't know if you want to live with me, or you don't know if you're ready to make that decision?'

'Both, I suppose.' Daisy watched as a seagull wheeled past the carriage window, riding the air currents. 'It's just that everything has been working so well as it is. Why do we need to change it?'

'Because I don't want to keep living out of a suitcase.' There was a slight edge to Miles's voice. It suggested the topic was one he'd been thinking about for a while. 'I want to know that this is going somewhere rather than just drifting along indefinitely.'

'I get it.'

'It's not all about you, you know.'

Daisy was taken aback at the way in which Miles had delivered the sentence. 'Sorry! What does that mean?'

'Look, Daise. I get it. You have everyone's attention; your mum, your sisters, me, half this town and you've had it tough, but you don't always get to call all the shots all the time.'

'Ouch! Tell me what you really think, why don't you?'

'Sorry. I didn't mean it to sound like that.'

'What *did* you mean it to sound like, then? Are you saying that I'm selfish?'

'I guess I am. You asked: I'm calling it.'

'Right. Okay, thanks, I didn't see that coming. At least you're honest.'

The funicular was approaching the top of the cliff and Daisy could see the upper station with its Victorian ironwork and the beginning of the coastal path that led along the clifftops. 'I thought you were happy with the way things are. What if we move in together and it doesn't work? What if you decide that living with me and the twins full-time is too much? What if you miss your independence and just having your own space?'

'Then we would deal with it like adults.'

'You can't know that for certain that won't happen.'

'No, I can't. But I can't know for certain that I won't be hit by a bus tomorrow either. At some point, you have to take a leap of faith.'

The carriage reached the top with a bump, and the operator opened the doors with a flourish. The twins immediately scrambled out, chattering about the view and the seagulls and whether they could see France.

Margot called back. 'Mummy! Come on. You're being really slow.'

Daisy got out of the carriage, not sure what to think that she'd just been told that she was selfish. The clifftop stretched away in both directions, with the coastal path winding along the edge and benches positioned at regular intervals for people to sit and admire the view. She took it all in as Miles's words and his brusque tone reverberated through her mind.

'Can we walk to the lighthouse?' Evie asked, pointing along the path to where the white tower was just visible in the distance.

'That's quite a long walk.'

'Look at all the boats,' Margot called out.

The four of them walked to a safety barrier preventing people from getting too close to the drop. The view was more than spectacular, with Pretty Beach spread out below and the sea dotted with everything from small fishing boats to ginormous vessels heading for the Channel ports.

Miles put his arm around Daisy's waist. 'So what do you think?'

'About which bit?' Daisy asked, though she knew perfectly well what he meant.

'About us making this official and about building something together instead of just seeing what happens.'

Daisy tried to stall for time. 'Can we talk about it properly, later? When we don't have to worry about the girls overhearing or falling off a cliff?'

'No worries. But we *do* need to talk about it properly at some point.'

'I know.' Daisy nodded and she *did* know, but it all felt very in her face and daunting. Selfish? A little part of her, the single mum who'd struggled part was fuming with Miles. He was calling her selfish. Balls to that. For quite a while in her life, it had been nothing more than a matter of having to be all consumed with keeping her head above water. It was clear that he had no clue. Being selfish had been a case of having to. He didn't have the foggiest.

8

Daisy stood in the doorway of Annabelle's kitchen and did what she always did when she arrived at her sister's house: felt slightly underdressed and more than a little bit like she'd accidentally wandered onto the set of a BBC show about people who had their lives sorted. Everything was lovely and just so. The kitchen stretched out in all its Shaker cupboard and gleaming surface glory, and Annabelle was doing a very good job of looking the part, too. It was all very nice and managed to look both impossibly posh and genuinely lived-in at the same time. Annabelle was a hard act to follow and didn't Daisy know about it.

The centrepiece island, the size of a small car, topped with marble that had cost more than Daisy's annual income, caught the light from perfectly placed pendant lamps hanging overhead. The Aga sat in the corner doing its job; the sort of huge old thing that appeared in cookery programmes presented by women with double-barrelled surnames, all four ovens and warming plates that could handle Christmas dinner for twenty without breaking a sweat. Along one wall, a butler's sink the size of a small bath sat beneath a window that looked out onto a garden where even the weeds were probably heritage varieties. Daisy laughed to herself about it all as she thought about the contrast to her kitchen behind the bookshop, took her jacket off, hung it on a hook by the back door and sat down at the island. Annabelle took a wine glass from open shelving and started to open a bottle of wine.

'How's Piers getting on in that new project?' Daisy asked as she made herself comfortable.

'Yeah, loads of the usual headaches, but it pays well and enables me to fund my homewares addiction.'

Daisy laughed. 'You're funny. I thought it was your very high-powered job that funded your addictions.'

'His efforts top me up.' Annabelle said with a straight face and passed over the wine glass now filled with wine.

Daisy looked over at the oiled timber worktop opposite her and a collection of terracotta pots filled with herbs lining the windowsill. The pots had little bees embedded in them and she thought that, knowing Annabelle, they'd probably been sourced from some artisan pottery in the Cotswolds. 'And I get your castoffs.'

'It's a win-win for all involved.' Annabelle laughed.

'Works for me, Bells. Any time you want to pass any of this my way.' Daisy shifted on her stool. A grouping of copper pans hanging from a rack above the island dangled over her head and below her, a wine fridge hummed quietly behind glass doors that revealed rows of bottles arranged in precision.

Annabelle took a huge platter from under the island and started to tumble green leaves from a brown paper bag. 'Anyway, enough about my addictions. How are you?'

'Yep, good. Very good.'

'How were Pete's places this week?'

'Fine, nothing to report there. No dirty nappies in beds, which is always a bonus.'

'Miles?'

'Also, good. He's worried about his mum. Goodness knows what's going to happen there.'

Maggie arrived just as Annabelle was opening a bottle of balsamic vinegar. Daisy frowned to herself as she took in Maggie's appearance. Despite Maggie's usual dramatic entrance, Daisy immediately felt as if something wasn't quite right with Maggie, but Daisy couldn't quite work out what. She appeared somewhat muted by what looked like genuine tiredness and she slumped onto the stool next to Daisy. Letting her handbag slide off her shoulder and drop onto the stool beside her with a soft thud, Daisy frowned. Something was *very* off.

Maggie smiled as Annabelle passed over an oversized glass of wine. Maggie took it gratefully at the same time as she slipped off her Trench coat and folded it over the stool on top of her bag. 'God, do I need this?'

'Rough day?' Daisy tried to study Maggie without making it obvious. Maggie, under her makeup, looked tired and unless Daisy was seeing things, there was an almost grey tinge to her. Her usually glossy, shiny hair was in its regular, just back from the salon blow-dried state, but it appeared dull, if that was the right word. There was something near her left temple, a patch of skin that looked angry and inflamed, though Maggie had clearly tried to cover it with makeup. Alarm bells started ringing for Daisy, big time.

'Rough week,' Maggie corrected as she took a gulp of wine. 'Rough month, if we are being completely honest. Some of my clients seem to think I exist purely to solve problems they have created through their own spectacular lack of organisation. I don't know what's going on, but I'm really tired all the time, too.'

Annabelle leaned against the island. 'You look like you need a proper holiday rather than just alcohol. Your colour is off, Mags.'

Daisy watched as Maggie unconsciously raised her hand

towards the patch of irritated skin before catching herself and dropping it again. Maggie fluffed her hair and then smoothed it so it covered the sore area.

'Tell me about it. Anyway, enough about my tragic existence. We are here to celebrate our baby sister and her completely mad award nomination. So proud of you, Daise. So proud.'

Daisy tried not to squirm under the combined attention of both sisters and automatically played down the nomination. 'It is just a nomination. There is no guarantee that anything will actually come of it.'

'Do not start with that!' Annabelle shook her head and admonished. 'This is a massive achievement and you are going to acknowledge it properly instead of trying to minimise it into nothing. The Henleys achieve things and celebrate them. Mum has always told us that.'

Maggie nodded and pressed her fingers against her temple. 'Absolutely right. You've built something special and we are going to milk it to the hilt. The whole of Pretty Beach is going to know about this.'

Daisy laughed. 'That ship's sailed; Holly and Xian have told everyone. Pretty Beach is already well aware.'

'My little sister is an entrepreneur.' Maggie joked.

'Most of my decisions are based on guesswork rather than proper business knowledge, but no one needs to know that, do they? Fake it until you make it is the vibe I'm going for.' Daisy swirled the wine in her glass and watched the way it caught the light.

'Faking it is infinitely more valuable than textbook theory. Ask me how I know.' Maggie touched her temple again.

Annabelle slid a small dish of olives across the island. 'So proud of you, Daise, and my silent investment status by way of my donations of styling products.'

Maggie nodded and chortled. 'Mine too. Actually, yeah, when you have hit global domination of bookshops, I want my cut. When you're the Starbucks of the book world, don't forget who helped you clean that shop on week one.'

'You two deserve the nomination more than me. I'm not really looking forward to the site visit. So not my cup of tea.'

Daisy watched as Maggie touched the sore skin again. If she weren't Maggie's sister, she wouldn't have noticed. Maggie reached for her wine, and as she turned, the patch of irritated skin near her hairline seemed more pronounced. She immediately smoothed her hair forward to cover the area.

'It will be fine. They will take one look at what you have created and immediately understand why you have been nominated. What about the ceremony itself? What does the gala involve?'

Daisy made a grimacing face and visibly shuddered. It communicated her feelings about formal events with crystal clarity. 'I really only skimmed that part. Me sitting in a room full of retail professionals makes me want to hide under my duvet forever. I hate stuff like that, as you well know.'

'At least you'll have Miles. Remember that time you came to that event with me? You hated every minute of it.'

Annabelle nodded. 'We will make sure you look absolutely spectacular. Between Maggie and me, we can sort everything from your dress to your accessories. You will walk into that gala looking like you belong there, so at least you won't have to worry about that.'

Miles's brother sprang to mind and Daisy felt a huge wave of love for Maggie and Annabelle. She felt very lucky to be sitting surrounded by people who had her back. She laughed as she looked down at her jeans and floral shirt. 'My wardrobe does not run to gala-appropriate formal wear. I'll leave that until later. It's ages away.'

Annabelle swished her hand back and forth. 'Leave it to us. We can all go shopping. It will be lovely to have an excuse to get you properly dressed up.'

Daisy shook her head. 'Yeah, I'm not going shopping, Bells. I'm an outfit shopping free zone. You both know that.'

Annabelle nodded. 'I'll have an online sesh.'

Daisy suddenly felt emotional. 'Thank you for believing in the bookshop and for believing in me, even when I did not particularly believe in myself.'

'Always. That's what sisters are for.'

Maggie raised her glass. 'To the award-nominated bookshop owner and my fave little sister.'

Daisy laughed as their three glasses clinked and as she sat there in Annabelle's perfect kitchen, she felt so very much loved, happy, content, a bit nervous about the gala and the nomination, but overall, life was good. Little did she know things were going to change.

9

Daisy pushed open the back gate with the toe of her boot and nudged it shut with the other as she made her way in from the lane behind the bookshop. Her arms were full with a long, awkward box from the post office and a bag of cinnamon buns from the bakery, which smelt, quite frankly, so divine she'd considered tucking into one in the lane. After depositing them in the kitchen, she made a pot of tea and went through to the shop to check that her final preparations for the Independent Alliance inspectors were in order. Not that she had really done anything differently from a regular day, but still. She'd decided that they either liked what she did or they didn't. She'd been in a lot worse predicaments in her life than worrying about whether some fancy pants people from organisations liked her little shop or not.

However, lots of locals and other shopkeepers along the laneway had pulled out the stops and decided to spruce everything up a bit once they'd heard about the impending visit. Outside the front of the bookshop, Pete had added extra rows of bunting all the way along the street, the pavements had been swept and the panes on the bookshop were sparkling from a big clean.

As Daisy got to the front door and pushed the inner cage door back into its casing, she could see that someone had taped a little flyer wishing the bookshop good luck to the display case near the door. Two small crates of flowers had been left on the doorstep with a note from Roy from the council wishing her good luck and across the road, Nel, the bus driver, gave her a thumbs-up from behind the wheel and tooted her horn twice as she went past. Daisy waved back and smiled as a lovely little warm feeling rolled through her. Pretty Beach had her back at least.

Juliette, the local midwife, in her work uniform, hurried along the pavement with a little posy of flowers in her right hand. 'Hiya! It's the big day! I thought I'd pop these in on my way past. They're from all of us at the surgery. Good luck, Daise. Hope it goes well!'

Daisy kissed Juliette on the cheek. 'Oh my gosh. Everyone has been so supportive already. You lot really are the best.'

Juliette handed over the flowers and nodded at the shop front. 'It looks amazing. All of it. I just walked past Holly's and she's set up a whole display in her window with a stack of books and one of your bags front and centre. Everyone's really rooting for you.'

Daisy laughed. 'I keep saying it's only a nomination, not the Nobel Prize for literature, but no one's listening. Seriously, though, I'm touched. Everyone's been so kind.'

Juliette tutted. 'You deserve every bit of it. Honestly, it's been the talk of the waiting room all week. I must've heard your name mentioned ten times yesterday alone. Even old Mr Hammond was saying he thought it was good. He reckons you ought to go full Hollywood, whatever that means.'

'He's going to be sorely disappointed when he sees the pictures of me in one of Annabelle or Maggie's castoffs.'

'He said as long as there's a photo in the parish newsletter, he'll be happy.'

Daisy chuckled and tucked the flowers into the crook of her elbow. 'Tell him I'll do my best.'

Juliette looked at Daisy with raised eyebrows. 'Honestly, Daise. It's not just the shop, it's the whole thing. You've made a place people feel better for having visited. I've sent new mums here when they're going stir crazy at home. I've come in myself after a twelve-hour shift and sat in the corner with a cup of tea and a biscuit and felt like an actual human again. It's more than a bookshop and we all know it.'

Daisy blinked and didn't really know how to take the compliment. 'You're going to make me cry before they even get here.'

'Too late to start pretending you're not sentimental. We all are. That's the whole point of this town and why I loved it here right from the word go. You either love it or you hate it, as they say.'

'I love it, which is why you can hardly ever get me to leave.'

'You and me both.' Juliette smiled. 'Right, I'll love you and leave you. I've got a wriggly three-day-old to attend to, or about ten of them actually and I have to pretend I know what I'm doing. Good luck, lovely. We're all rooting for you.'

'Thanks, Juliette.' Daisy gestured to the little posy of flowers. 'Tell everyone at the surgery I said thank you, too.'

'Will do.' Juliette waved as she headed off, then turned back for a second. 'And don't forget to breathe. You'll walk it.'

'I'll try.'

As Juliette disappeared around the corner, Daisy turned back to the bookshop, flowers still tucked under one arm, heart full, and wondered what on earth she'd done to deserve such lovely people in her life. She shook her head at her funny, ridiculous, sometimes way too nosy, loving town. It had tucked her in and made her feel safe just when she'd needed it. When she was expecting a group of sharp-eyed, clipboard-wielding assessors from some bigwig retail board. As she pottered around, butterflies made themselves known in her stomach and she kept seeing things in her mind's eye. Judges standing in the doorway, looking around, their faces unreadable as they rolled their eyes at her thrown-together mix of fairy lights and secondhand furniture.

A knock on the glass startled her and she turned to see Dimitri, one of her mum's friends, holding up a paper bag. He pushed the door open. 'Morning, Daise. We thought you might need a bit of luck. I have been told to deliver these with a dose of good Greek lucky vibes.'

Daisy chuckled. 'Ooh, thank you. What have I got from Lottie?'

'Homemade shortbread topped with edible sprinkle flowers from the garden. Don't try one because you won't stop. Lottie said to put them out and they will sweet-talk the judges.'

Daisy peered under a tea towel, widened her eyes and joked. 'Thanks, Dimitri. You really know how to spoil a girl.'

Dimitri winked and tapped the side of his nose. 'The whole town's talking about this. Don't mess it up now, will you? This shortbread will win anyone over.'

Daisy laughed and Dimitri left, the bell jangling again as the door swung shut. She placed the gorgeous shortbread on the counter, carefully took off the tea towel and glanced out at the street as the bunting fluttered and the hanging baskets swayed in the wind and wondered what the inspectors would think. She loved her funny little community and not-quite-perfect shop. Her active goal right from the word go had not been about identical shelves and staff in uniforms. She'd wanted mismatched mugs, lots of lamps, groups of nattering mums on the sofa, wingback chairs and fairy lights and a whole big dollop of cosy. So far, she'd achieved it on so many levels, it wasn't even funny.

Just as she was finishing making some tea for someone who was sitting in the chair near the library trolley, she saw a couple of women peering in the window. She could hear them oohing and ahhing, although their voices were muffled. Swallowing, Daisy adjusted her hair and picked up her iPad. She didn't know how an iPad was going to help her, but it made her feel official. She didn't have anything on it of consequence, but it gave her something to hold, as she gulped and tried to feel, act and *be* normal. Feeling like a fish out of water, she stood awkwardly and waited; the fairy lights glowed, the flower-topped shortbread looked fabulous and the bell jangled as the judges walked in.

The women stepped inside and on taking them in fully, they weren't what Daisy had expected at all. No sharp suits, stern expressions or efficiency. The taller of the two had a mass of artfully dishevelled silver hair and a bright scarf knotted at her neck. Smart casual with tailored trousers and a beautifully cut jacket, she looked friendly and not very scary at all. Next to her, a woman with a bob of bright copper hair in a cashmere jumper in soft sage green and a pair of well-worn leather boots beamed from ear to ear. Both of them carried smart, but not overly corporate, tote bags and overall, the aura of them both was pleasant. Thank heavens for that.

'Hiya,' the silver-haired woman announced. 'You must be Daisy. I'm Jane, and this is my colleague, Susie. We're from the Alliance. We're a bit early. Is that okay? Gosh, it's lovely in here! We are absolutely thrilled to be here. We have been swooning online and outside.'

Susie beamed, a genuine, wide smile that crinkled the corners of her eyes. 'Thrilled doesn't even begin to cover it. I've been looking forward to this visit for weeks, ever since I saw the initial nomination submissions. How exciting! We have been so looking forward to visiting your wonderful shop and Pretty

Beach. Honestly, anyone I mentioned it to said I'd love it. They weren't wrong.'

Daisy was clinging to her iPad for dear life. She'd braced herself for clinical efficiency, not a couple of friendly women who looked like any of her other customers. 'Hello. Welcome to The Bookshop Pretty Beach.' Daisy wished she hadn't said it like that and inwardly cringed.

Jane looked around at the twinkling fairy lights, the cosy nooks and the overflowing bookshelves. 'Oh, it's even better than Instagram! Hold on while I pick my chin up off the floor. I just fell in love.' She inhaled deeply and closed her eyes and then did a funny shaking movement and wrinkled her nose. 'Fabulous! Books, coffee, and is that… lavender? Absolutely divine, all of it. It's like stepping into a perfectly curated yet not dream. Do you take overnight guests?'

Susie nodded vigorously and made a beeline for the wingback chairs in the corner. 'This is precisely what we mean when we talk about creating an experience, isn't it, Jane? So many of the places we've been to are sterile and devoid of personality. This, this is something else. I knew it wouldn't disappoint. I knew it! Oh, my actual gosh, look at the library ladders. Let me at them already.'

Daisy heard herself saying things she hadn't rehearsed. 'I just worked with what I had and tried to make the place, you know, cosy.'

'You have achieved that and then some.' Jane's gaze lingered on the wingback chairs and the library trolley laden with books and flowers. 'Those chairs look utterly inviting, and that trolley is a triumph. Where on earth did you find it? You don't see many of those these days.'

'Facebook Marketplace, believe it or not,' Daisy confessed.

'Really? The eye you have for mixing and matching. The vintage rugs, the lamps, the throws, every single thing is just…'

Daisy felt her cheeks flush. She'd spent countless hours on

her hands and knees getting rid of the dust and years of grime in the place. She'd spent late nights crafting the atmosphere out of nothing but a lot of hope and castoffs. To hear it articulated by these women, supposed arbiters of retail excellence, was quite unreal. She sort of shook her head and blinked rapidly. All thoughts of trying to sound business-like and professional flew up the nearest chimney and out to sea. Visions of when she'd first set eyes on the floor-to-ceiling pigeonholes loaded with her uncle's junk and the sinking feeling of how much work there would be filtered in front of her eyes. 'I just, errr, tried to make it somewhere I'd like to spend time by myself.'

Jane chuckled. 'That is precisely why it works. Authenticity is a rare commodity. So many chains attempt to replicate this sort of atmosphere, but it invariably falls flat with dreadful, lonely, cheap sofas shoved into lost corners. One can always tell when it's been manufactured.' Jane paused by the display table and picked up one of Daisy's cards. 'Ask Daisy for her thoughts? Oh yes, oh yes, yes. What a little find this is. Delightful is the word I am using on my form. Gorgeous, too.'

Daisy gestured to the card. 'I like to be able to talk to customers about them, tell them if they live up to the hype or not.'

'And do they?' Susie asked, now peering at the library trolley laden with books. 'Live up to the hype, I mean?'

Daisy coughed. 'More often than not, they do not, no, if they're, well, sorry I shouldn't really speak out of turn but, umm, some of the publishing houses are, yeah, a machine. A bit of a juggernaut backed with huge social media campaigns and marketing budgets. Say no more. It's like they're all in this clique, too. I'm learning more about it as I go. They beef each other's books up with comps and suchlike. I mean, look at the controversy around that book about the couple who walked around the country that was turned into a film. Case in point.'

Jane tapped the card. 'Right, yeah. That honesty is what sets you apart. It's not about pushing product, is it? Well, it is for those awful big corporations. It's about building relationships and trust, like in the old days when high streets actually meant something in our country and goodness knows we need to revitalise them.'

Susie pulled a book from the trolley. 'I think I could sit here all day.'

Daisy felt her shoulders drop as she sighed in absolute, joyous, utter relief. She remembered the shortbread Dimitri had dropped off, sitting on the counter. 'Would either of you like a cup of tea? And there's some shortbread. Homemade, with flowers on top.'

Jane chuckled. 'An offer I cannot turn down any day of the week, even though I am currently attempting to do keto.'

Susie settled into one of the wingback chairs. 'Pure bliss, Jane. Pure, unadulterated bliss. Shame we're actually here with a job to do.'

Daisy went to make the tea and thought about the early days and how her desperate attempts to make ends meet had been the driving force behind her getting her act together and making the bookshop work. She thought about the sheer effort she'd poured into the place and how, now, although it was more than breaking even, she still cleaned cottages and worked for the bakery in the evenings to keep her ship afloat. All very strange because these two women, from some grand independent retail alliance, were not just approving, but one hundred per cent gushing. Tripping over themselves to give her praise. It was all so very unexpected, she felt almost as if she was spinning.

As she made the tea, she watched as Jane got a laptop out of her bag and started to tap away. Susie held her phone up and took a few photos and gave Daisy a thumbs up. Daisy smiled and felt as if all of her Christmases had come at once. She was doing so very well. It had been a long time coming, that she knew for free.

10

Daisy was sitting in her car outside the school, waiting for the girls to come out. Rain lashed down against the front of her car and she realised that she was going to get very wet. She was also well aware that the hop from the school gates to the car would most probably be an eventful one. Evie would complain if any of her items got even a single drop of rain on them. Margot would then most likely weigh in with her opinion on rain, which would upset Evie and possibly, if Evie was tired enough from the demands of the day, start the rumblings of a complete and utter meltdown. Just another day on the school run with the twins.

As the wipers battled against the downpour, brief glimpses of hurrying parents went past as water sheeted across the glass. Raining cats and dogs wasn't the word for it: Pretty Beach appeared as if it was in the middle of a rain bomb. The afternoon had turned miserable while Daisy had been in the bookshop, dealing with a delivery of new stock and a customer who'd wanted to discuss the entire contents of the historical romance section in exhaustive detail. She'd left Miles in the shop while she did the school run and hadn't factored on the heavens opening as she drove in the direction of the school. Through the rain-streaked passenger window, she could see parents huddled under the shelter of the school's entrance porch, a small forest of umbrellas and coat hoods up against the weather. All clearly more weather aware than she had been and getting thoroughly drenched by good old Blighty weather in the name of maternal duty.

Another parent dashed across the car park with a coat held over their head, clearly having made the same miscalculation about the weather that Daisy had had. At least she wasn't the only one who'd been caught off guard by the sudden downpour. The morning had been overcast but dry, giving no indication that the afternoon would bring cats and dogs from above. Rummaging through the glove compartment in search of anything that might serve as emergency rain protection, she found an ancient pink child's baseball cap and a crumpled carrier bag from the supermarket.

Daisy took a deep breath, pulled her jacket hood up as far as it would go, and opened the car door. The rain immediately trickled down her neck and started to soak through her jeans in the thirty seconds it took her to cross the car park. By the time she reached the school gates, she was already damp, and the twins hadn't even appeared yet. As teachers organised the exodus of children as the rain poured, Daisy squinted to try and see her girls. She spotted Margot first, her little blonde plaits visible in the crowd of children gathering under a covered walkway that led from the classrooms to the playground. Evie appeared a moment later, clutching her school bag protectively against her chest and a look of dismay on her face as she eyed the rain.

'Mummy!' Margot called out as she spotted Daisy among the other parents. 'It's raining really hard! I thought you said Miles was picking us up today. Evie is going to get wet! She hates that!'

Daisy chuckled to herself at the mention of Miles. Not that long before, the notion of someone other than one of the Henley women collecting the twins from school would have been preposterous. Now here was Margot mentioning Miles as if he'd been in her life forever. Secretly, Daisy loved how that felt. 'I can see that, sweetheart,' Daisy called back, as she moved towards the girls while trying to keep her hood from blowing off in the wind. 'Come on then, let's get to the car as quickly as we can.'

Evie's face crumpled. 'My reading book will get wet! And my jumper! And everything!'

'We'll run fast.' Daisy knew that running with the twins and their bags in heavy rain was very optimistic and not at all realistic. 'I've got the car right here, we'll hardly get wet at all.' She outright lied in an attempt to placate Evie. However, as evidenced by the fact that she was already thoroughly soaked just from the brief journey from car to school gate, she didn't hold up much hope of Evie not getting wet. Let the meltdown begin.

'I don't want to get wet,' Evie's tone meant trouble was brewing. 'Can we wait until it stops?'

Daisy glanced up at the sky, which showed no signs of clearing anytime soon. If anything, the clouds looked darker and more determined than when she'd first arrived. 'I think it might rain for quite a while, darling. We're better off getting home now.'

'But my bag! I hate rain on my stuff.' Evie protested.

Daisy pulled the crumpled carrier bag from her pocket. 'We'll put your school bag inside this to keep it dry.'

Evie appeared slightly satisfied about her precious belongings not getting wet. Margot, meanwhile, was bouncing on her toes with excitement at the prospect of running through the rain.

'Can we jump in the puddles?' Margot asked. 'When Miles

picked us up before, he let us walk in the puddles by the duck pond.'

'Absolutely not. You had your wellies on that day with Miles,' Daisy said firmly as she noted the mention of Miles again. To be honest, both girls were pretty taken with him. Worked for her. They weren't the only ones. 'We're going straight to the car with no puddles. I don't want your school shoes getting wet.'

Margot complained. 'Puddles are the best bit about rain.'

'Puddles make you wet and cold and muddy,' Evie noted as she gripped Daisy's hand tightly.

Daisy could see that a debate over rain and puddles would not end well. 'Right, here's what we're going to do. We're going to count to three, then we're all going to run to the car together. No stopping, no puddles, no complaining. Ready?'

Both girls nodded, though Evie looked doubtful.

'One.' Daisy checked that both twins had secure grips on their belongings. 'Two...' She didn't bother with three. Instead, she grabbed both girls by the hand and started moving towards the car park at the fastest pace their little legs could manage as the rain pelted down. They covered the distance to the car in what felt like record time, but all of them were wet, Evie was grizzling and Margot dropped her book bag. Getting the girls into the car while simultaneously trying to prevent their school bags, lunch boxes, and hair from getting wet wasn't easy. By the time they were all safely inside with the doors closed, Daisy felt like she'd completed some sort of extreme parenting challenge.

'Ahh, rain is fun,' Margot announced.

'It was horrible,' Evie countered as she checked her school bag. 'Everything's wet and yucky. I hate rain getting on my stuff.'

'Everything's fine. We don't say "hate," remember?' Daisy started the engine and turned the heating up to maximum. 'A tiny bit of rain never hurt anyone.'

'What if my reading book is soggy? I can't bring back a soggy book.'

'It will be fine, sweetheart. The rain won't have made it through your book bag.'

As they pulled out of the school car park and joined the slow procession of other parents making their way home through the rain, the windscreen wipers continued their losing battle against the rain as they drove through Pretty Beach's narrow streets towards home. At least the bookshop would be warm and dry, Miles would probably have made tea, and there would be biscuits and the promise of a cosy evening ahead. Pulling into the lane behind the bookshop, the rain still drummed against the roof of the car and Evie was not a happy bunny. Daisy felt her phone buzz in her pocket. She parked carefully while the twins gathered their belongings in the back seat, both of them chattering

Daisy turned off the engine. 'Right then. Let's make another run for it, shall we? Straight through the back gate and into the kitchen.'

'Can we have hot chocolate when we get inside?'

Miles appeared at the back door as they approached, clearly having heard the car and held it open while they all piled through into the dryness of the kitchen.

'Successful rescue mission?' Miles asked as he helped Evie.

'Eventually.' Daisy ran her hands through her hair. 'I think we're all going to need dry clothes and something warm to drink.'

Miles smiled. 'Hot chocolate's already on. I thought you might need it when I saw how hard it was raining. It pelted it down just after you left.'

'You're a genius.' Daisy kissed Miles on the cheek as she passed.

Margot made a funny face at Miles. 'Mummy forgot an umbrella. You have spare ones in your car, don't you?'

'I do.'

Daisy rolled her eyes. 'You have spare umbrellas and you let people splash in puddles, too. Girls, get yourselves upstairs and into dry clothes.'

As the twins thundered upstairs, Daisy had a chance to check her phone properly. The message that had pinged as they were getting out of the car was from an unknown number, but the sender had identified themselves clearly enough in the text.

Jane: *Hi Daisy, this is Jane from the Independent Retail Alliance. I hope you don't mind me texting directly - I got your number from our initial correspondence. Susie and I wanted to let you know that we've submitted our assessment report following our visit, and we couldn't be more impressed with what you've built at The Bookshop Pretty Beach. Also, we just had a lovely time. Thank you for having us.*

Daisy beamed, sat down on one of the kitchen chairs and continued reading.

Jane: *The report has gone to the judging panel with our highest possible recommendation. We loved the feel of the bookshop! Authentic community connection, thoughtful curation, and the sort of customer experience that simply can't be replicated by corporate chains.*

Miles was stirring milk and chocolate powder in a saucepan. 'What's that?'

'It's from the alliance women who visited. They've submitted their report.'

'And?'

'And they seem to think it went rather well.'

Miles turned from the stove. 'Rather well?'

Daisy read the rest of the message aloud.

'That sounds more than rather well. That sounds like they were completely charmed by the whole operation, which is not surprising because everyone is.'

Daisy scrolled down and read. 'Everything was lovely from the moment we arrived - the bunting, the flowers, the shortbread, and the community feeling when people popped in and out. This is exactly what independent retail is about.'

Miles read over her shoulder. 'They're basically saying you've created the perfect independent bookshop. Go, Daise.'

'You have to laugh. I bought most of the furniture from Facebook Marketplace and balancing the books is still a skill I am yet to conquer.'

'That's exactly why it works. You created something genuine instead of trying to copy what you thought a bookshop should look like. Love it.'

Jane: *The judging panel will make their final decision, but Susie and I both feel confident that The Bookshop Pretty Beach represents the very best of what independent retail can achieve. Whatever the outcome, you should be enormously proud of what you've built. We'll be in touch soon with more details about the ceremony. With warmest regards, Jane.*

'Blimey, I might actually win,' Daisy said quietly, as if saying it too loudly might jinx everything.

Miles frowned. 'Of course, you might win. Why does that surprise you?'

'Err, because this time last year I was scrubbing floors in other people's houses and wondering if I'd ever manage to make the bookshop profitable. Winning awards wasn't exactly on my list of realistic goals. Not that I had any goals...'

Miles rescued the hot chocolate just as it was about to bubble over. 'Well, you do now.'

'I suppose I'd better go and sort out whatever crisis is developing upstairs, and then we can all have hot chocolate and I can try to get my head around the idea that I might actually know what I'm doing after all.'

'You definitely know what you're doing. You've just been too busy doing it to notice how good you are.'

As Daisy headed upstairs to negotiate a dispute from the

bathroom, she shook her head as it slowly dawned on her that perhaps, her little bookshop really was something special after all. Not only that, maybe *she* was, too.

11

Daisy had collected the twins from school and was walking back through Pretty Beach with Miles when he suggested they do a little detour and take the long way home via the Old Town. The twins were chattering away about something that had happened at lunch involving a dropped sandwich and a seagull, and Daisy was only half-listening. Something was off with Miles and she couldn't work out what. Over the previous few weeks, he'd been quiet, quite frankly irritable, and Daisy had spent a good amount of her brain power trying to work out why. Rather than just ask him, she'd skirted around the issue and hoped it would go away. Head in sand sprang to mind. It was now increasingly evident that it hadn't gone away, far from it. He had been fine when he'd met them at the school gates, greeting the twins happily and asking about their day, but as they had gone ahead, he'd not really said a lot at all. His whole aura was not great and suggested he had things on his mind.

As they reached the junction where they would normally turn left towards the town and the bookshop, Miles pointed. 'Shall we go up through Strawberry Hill?' I thought we could have a look at that house you mentioned, the one Julie told you about a while ago.'

Daisy glanced at him and felt a bit wary. There was something in his tone that sounded odd. 'If you want to. Though I am not sure there will be much to see from the outside. I haven't heard anything else about it.'

'Can we go to the sweet shop?' Margot butted in, having apparently tuned into the conversation at the mention of a different route home.

'We'll see,' Daisy replied automatically.

They turned up the hill that led towards the Old Town and nothing was said for a bit as the twins skipped ahead and then circled back and dawdled here and there. A lovely afternoon, crisp and clear, looked back at them and Pretty Beach was living up to its name. All gorgeous old bricks, flower wreaths on front doors, higgledy piggledy slate roofs, gardens full of beautiful shrubs and wonky chimney pots jutting up into the sky.

'I have been thinking more about what we talked about on the funicular,' Miles said once they were far enough behind the twins that their conversation would not be overheard. 'About making things more permanent between us.'

Daisy swallowed and she felt her stomach tighten. *Here we go.* She took a packet of wine gums out of her pocket and popped in a red one. 'Have you?'

'I know you said you needed time to think about it, but I keep coming back to the same conclusion. We work well together, the girls are happy, and I think we could build something really good if we, well, you, really, stopped being so cautious about it all. I'm not getting any younger, Daise.'

They passed a row of Victorian terraced houses, their front gardens bright with colour and their windows reflecting the sun. Daisy had walked the route hundreds of times over the years, and she adored the Old Town, but Miles and his aspirations to buy a house and make things permanent between them threw her. For someone who had spent years chasing a forever home and being settled, her feelings were hard to understand. Least of all to her. Her voice was a tad on the defensive side. 'I thought we had agreed to leave it for now. The house hasn't even come up for sale, anyway, so it doesn't really matter.'

'We did, but that does not mean I've stopped thinking about it.' Miles flicked the palms of his hands up and sounded reasonable and as usual pragmatic, but his tone was laced with edginess. 'I love you, Daise. I want us to be a proper family.'

Evie called out from ahead of them, having discovered something interesting in a front garden. 'Look, Miles! That dog is enormous.'

Daisy was grateful for the distraction as they caught up with the twins, who were admiring a particularly large old Labrador who was sunning himself on a patch of sunshine on a porch. The Labrador opened one lazy eye and closed it again as if he were well used to being admired by passersby.

'He looks like a teddy bear.' Margot observed.

'Teddy bears are fluffier,' Evie corrected.

Margot shook her head. 'No, they are not! Grandma's teddy bear from when she was young is not fluffy.'

'Shall we keep walking?' Miles suggested.

They continued up the hill, past a small parade of shops that served Old Town residents and a narrow lane that led to one of Pretty Beach's lovely old churches. Daisy tried to steer the conversation to what was going on with the nomination, but Miles clearly wanted to continue his thought process.

'The thing is, I do not see the point in continuing to maintain separate households when we spend most of our time together anyway. It seems like a waste of money and energy, and it sends the wrong message to the girls about the level of commitment we have to each other. Plus, I am *sick* of that tiny flat.'

'What sort of message?'

'That this is temporary. That I am just someone who comes and goes rather than someone who is properly part of their lives.'

They reached the turning that led towards the church, and Daisy could see the house that Julie had mentioned in the distance. A tall Victorian villa with bay windows and a small front garden, exactly the sort of property that would cost a fortune and require serious commitment to maintain.

Miles followed her gaze. 'Is that it?'

'I think so.' Daisy nodded as part of her regretted having mentioned the house to him in the first place.

They walked closer, and Daisy remembered walking past the row of houses to and from school. It was solid, pretty, in need of a bit of love, and to be quite honest, right up her street. It also spoke of serious money and long-term thinking.

'Well, would you look at that? It's perfect from the outside anyway.' Miles nodded.

'Is it?'

'Look at it. Three storeys, plenty of space and that garden would be brilliant. Plus, it's in the Old Town, which you have always said is the nicest part of Pretty Beach.'

The twins had run ahead to peer through the gate, and Daisy could hear them discussing whether the front door was blue or green and speculating about whether a cat flap in a tiny low side door was for the cat who was sitting on the top of a neighbouring fence.

Miles took a picture. 'If it goes up for sale and we like it, we could put in an offer.'

Daisy shook her head, not sure where the "we" was coming from. She had just about got her head above water with the bookshop; she certainly didn't have anything like the finances for a house. It was so preposterous that it was actually laughable. The conversation was moving too quickly for Daisy to process properly. One minute they had been talking about making things more permanent in abstract terms, and now Miles was talking about viewing houses and making offers as if it was already decided. Something very odd was going on with him and her. Daisy couldn't compute whether she liked it or not. 'Hang on. This is all moving a bit fast, is it not?'

'Is it? The girls already think of me as part of the family. How much longer do you want to wait before we make it official?'

Daisy hoped Miles didn't clock the edge of panic creeping into her voice despite her efforts to stay calm. 'I don't know. I just know that buying a house together feels like a very big step. Enormous.'

'It *is* a big step, which is precisely why I want to do it.'

The twins were sitting on a bench on a small green space opposite, where it had been placed to take advantage of the view down towards the harbour. Daisy watched them and tried to work out why the prospect of living in a beautiful house with a man she loved and children who adored him wasn't making her jump up and down with glee. 'Let's, umm, think about it.'

'I know that I love you and want to build a life with you, and that has to count for something.'

Daisy looked at the house again, squinted and tried to imagine herself living there with Miles and the twins. The rational part of her mind could see that it would be lovely, that the girls would thrive in a place with so much space and such a good garden and that she and Miles could be gloriously happy. The sensible part of her, the part that had learned to be cautious through hard experience, was sending up warning signals, red flags and alarm bells all over the show. 'It's not even up for sale, but I need to think about it for a long time.'

Miles swore and not just once. 'Why?'

'Because it is *complicated*.' Daisy felt increasingly defensive about her reluctance to commit to something that probably looked straightforward from the outside. 'It's not just about us, it is about the girls and their stability. Sorry, I know you think I'm selfish, but for me, they come first. End of story.'

'What are you saying?'

Daisy was well aware that she was being over-the-top cautious. However, she could not articulate her fears without sounding either paranoid or unreasonably pessimistic. How could she explain that she'd learned not to trust good things to last, that she was waiting for disaster, that she was terrified of building her life around someone else's presence only to have them decide they wanted something different? Or to jump off a cliff on the end of a bungee rope. Her voice sounded small and lame. 'I don't know.'

'So what do you want to do? Keep things exactly as they are indefinitely?'

'Maybe.' Daisy knew as soon as the word left her mouth that it was not a realistic answer.

'Right. Okay, so I just wait until *you* decide. I like being in limbo, not. No change there, then in our relationship. What Daisy wants, Daisy gets.'

'Miles!'

'Sorry.'

The twins had discovered something interesting near the bench and were calling for them to come and look. Daisy was grateful for the interruption. 'What have you found?'

Margot was holding up a piece of driftwood. 'A really good stick. Look, it is shaped like a snake.'

Evie looked at Daisy with wide eyes. 'Can we take it home for the nature table?'

'Yes, you can.' Daisy was barely paying attention to the twins' latest treasure. Her mind was processing Miles's words about keeping him in limbo and being unfair to everyone involved. They began walking back down the hill towards the main part of town, the twins running ahead with their stick and debating what they were going to do with it once they got home.

Miles picked up the conversation. 'I'm not trying to pressure you.'

'I suppose I have been taking it one day at a time.'

'That is fine for a while, but at some point you have to start making actual decisions about what you want your life to look like.'

They had reached the bottom of the hill and were approaching the turning that would take them back towards the bookshop. 'The girls will be getting hungry. I should probably start thinking about tea.'

Miles shook his head and did *not* sound happy. 'Don't deflect by using them. You always do that. We are not finished talking about this.'

'I know, you've made that abundantly clear.'

∽

It was hours later, the twins were tucked up in bed, and Miles was standing, stirring a pot of Brazilian garlic rice. Daisy had had a long bath, washed her hair and had her soft clothes on. She was sitting at the kitchen table with a glass of gin and elderflower tonic, sipping and chatting with Miles.

Miles raised his eyebrows. 'Any further thoughts on what we spoke about before? Did you mull it over in the bath?'

Daisy shook her head. She had done nothing of the sort. In fact, she'd shoved it in a box labelled "Too Hard", slammed the lid and put it to bed, hoping not to open it again for a good few weeks or months. 'Not really.'

'Oh, okay. Any reason for that?'

'It is all a bit too much right now.'

'Too much how?'

Daisy snapped. 'Just too much! I cannot think about houses and moving in together and making everything official when I have got a dozen other things to worry about.'

'Here we go.'

'You keep bringing this up and *not* getting the message. It's like you're trying to start an argument. I want things to stay as they are for now.'

Miles did not back down. 'For how long?'

'I don't know. Until I can get my head around it all without feeling like I am going to have a panic attack every time someone mentions the future.'

'Panic? What? Panic attack! Where has that come from? Since when?'

Daisy had never properly told Miles about the anxiety, panic-like occasions that often slammed into her when she was in bed. She backpedalled like a mother. 'Not actual panic attacks. Just that feeling like everything is moving too fast and I cannot keep up. Not that long ago, I was worried about paying my rent, then it was all about keeping the bookshop afloat, and now you are talking about buying Old Town houses and planning our future as if it is all decided. Miles, it *is* quite overwhelming.'

'It does not have to be decided.'

'But you do not want to take as long as I need. You want me to make a decision and you are getting frustrated because I keep saying I need more time.'

'I'm frustrated. I cannot work out what you are so afraid of.'

'I am not afraid,' Daisy said automatically, though she knew this was not true and suspected that Miles knew it too. She looked through the kitchen door, across the little hallway and into the bookshop and took in all the familiar details that made it feel like home. The mismatched furniture, the library ladders, the fairy lights that had multiplied over the months until they twinkled from every corner. She'd built the space from nothing, from the ground up and had created something that worked through trial and error and sheer determination. The thought of changing anything made her feel edgy. She just didn't know how to put it into words. It had been the same way since the anxiety thing had first arrived in her world. When it wasn't there and she was thinking straight and being rational, it made no sense. The other times it did. 'We might spoil what we already have.'

'Why?'

It was a fair question, and Daisy considered the various answers she could give. She could talk about her experience with the twins' dad and how quickly, whether good or, quite frankly, exceedingly bad, things and people could disappear without warning. She could mention the years of financial insecurity and constant moving that had taught her not to get too attached to stability, anyone or anything. She could explain about the anxiety that every now and then slammed on top of her head. Instead, she tried to deflect and lied through her teeth. 'Oh, look, sorry. I'm just tired, and when I'm tired…'

Miles shook his head and stirred the rice. 'Let's leave it. You clearly don't want to talk about it. Thing is, Daise, this relationship isn't all about you.'

Daisy swallowed. Maybe she *was* selfish. Maybe it *was* all about her. Maybe she *was* being unreasonable. Maybe that would have to do.

12

It was the following Monday. Miles had stuck to his word and said nothing else about the permanency or lack thereof of their relationship. Daisy had kept the lid on the box locked. In fact, she'd added a padlock and left it alone.

Maggie had called saying she'd taken the day off work and needed a walk and some fresh air. That was the first red flag that Daisy had seen in no uncertain terms waving itself right in front of her eyes. Firstly, Maggie never took random days off, and secondly, she didn't say things like she "needed a walk". The second red flag with an accompanying alarm bell was that something in Maggie's voice had sounded different from usual. Daisy was right away, out-of-the-gate, concerned. She could not quite put her finger on what it was with Maggie, but she didn't like it one iota. Not at all. It wasn't that Maggie had sounded upset exactly; it was more that she'd sounded like someone who was trying very hard to be normal and not quite managing it. Someone who, to Daisy, didn't sound like her older sister. A horrible feeling in Daisy's stomach told her that things were not all roses in Maggie's world and that she was about to find out.

They met at the top of the steps that led down to the beach, not far from where the coastal path made its way past the beach huts and around the bay towards the duck pond. Maggie was already there when Daisy arrived. Standing with her hands in her pockets and looking out to sea, all the red flags that had been waving when Daisy had heard Maggie's voice jumped up and started to go ballistic.

Daisy was slightly out of breath from having walked quickly from the bookshop. 'Sorry, I'm a bit late. I had a call from a customer who could not decide between three different crime novels and needed a full consultation. I couldn't get her off the phone.'

As Maggie turned around, Daisy noticed that Maggie looked tired. Not just every day tired like the rest of the world, but sort of grey-tired and very, very lacklustre. As if someone had stood in front of her with a paintbrush, dipped it in a little tester pot of grey wash paint and brushed it down her face. 'All good.'

Daisy was more than certain that things were not good. She stayed quiet and followed behind Maggie as they walked down steps towards the beach alongside worn, old, weather-beaten wooden railings. The beach was weekday quiet, the sea calm, the breeze light and a few sailing boats floated past in the distance.

'How are things with you?' Maggie asked. 'Any news on the award thing?'

Daisy studied Maggie's profile and noticed things that made her feel very, *very* uneasy. She looked saggy and there was something around Maggie's left temple, the same patch of irritated skin she had noticed at Annabelle's house. It now looked more pronounced despite what appeared to be careful makeup application. 'They said they would be in touch, but nothing concrete yet.'

'Good, that it is moving forward.'

'I know, it's exciting.'

They walked along the edge of the water, where the sand

was firm and easy to navigate and the beach huts painted in the traditional pastel Pretty Beach colours stretched away to their left. Most of them were closed up, their doors secured with padlocks and their little verandas cleared of deckchairs and windbreakers that appeared during the summer months.

Maggie gestured towards the beach huts with an odd forced cheerfulness. 'Do you remember when we used to pretend they were our houses and we would move from one to another depending on what colour mood we were in?'

Daisy internally shuddered. Maggie was reminiscing: things were bad. She played along. 'I remember you always wanted the blue one because you said it matched your eyes,' Daisy chuckled.

'Did I really say that? How vain of me.'

'What's changed?' Daisy teased.

As they walked, a couple of dog walkers said hello, a woman jogged past, but mostly the beach was quiet and there wasn't much going on at all. The only sounds really were the waves and the odd seagull here and there. It felt to Daisy as if Maggie was trying to make conversation. Daisy couldn't get her head around it.

'How are things with Miles?'

'Complicated. He wants us to move in together, and I keep finding reasons to put off making a decision about it.'

'What sort of reasons?'

'The usual ones. What if it does not work out? What about the girls? What if we are better as we are, rather than trying to make it more official? Blah, blah, blah. I'm weird, yes, I know. Apparently, I'm selfish too, but it is what it is.'

Maggie nodded, pressed her fingers against her temple and didn't sound that interested. 'He said you are selfish? Right. Those *are* reasonable concerns, I suppose.'

'Am I just being pathetic and scared of commitment?'

Maggie sighed and tutted as if she was simply too tired to

bother. 'You are a bit. I mean, you have been through a lot with the twins, though.'

Daisy didn't know what to say. Maggie was clearly in no mood to discuss her relationship, even though she'd been the one who'd brought it up. They'd reached the far end of the beach where the path either went up or they could turn off and follow it as it curved around towards the duck pond. Maggie made as if to turn and Daisy followed. The transition from sand to grass was marked by a low sea wall where people often sat to eat fish and chips or just watch the world go by. The wall was empty except for a single seagull and a woman who was sitting with her phone in one hand and pushing a pram slowly back and forth with the other.

'Shall we sit down for a bit?' Maggie suggested and headed towards the wall without waiting for an answer.

They settled themselves on the sun-warmed stone wall and looked out at the view back across the beach towards the town. Pretty Beach looked gorgeous; all pastel-coloured buildings climbing up the hillside, the odd church tower here and there, the trees and chimney pots of the Old Town vying for space in a jumble of loveliness.

'Actually, there was something I wanted to talk to you about.'

Bang, there it was. Daisy braced herself. 'Right. What sort of something?'

Maggie looked out at the water as if she was trying to work out how to phrase whatever she needed to say. When she did speak, her voice had a carefully controlled tone. It was the sort of tone people used when they were trying to sound casual about things that were the complete opposite. 'I had to go to the doctor about this thing in my head.' Maggie touched the irritated patch near her temple. 'This bit here has been bothering me for a while.'

Daisy felt her stomach drop. 'What thing? What sort of bothering you?'

'Just not healing properly and getting a bit bigger rather than smaller. Going away and then coming back again. You know how these things are supposed to get better on their own, but this one wasn't playing by the rules.'

Daisy's mind raced ahead to all the possible implications of skin problems that didn't heal properly and doctors' visits.

Maggie's voice was *very* odd. She was clearly trying to sound casual as if she was forcing herself not to appear concerned. It didn't work; she sounded happily strangled. 'Anyway, the doctor thought it would be sensible to have it looked at properly, so I had a little biopsy done. Nothing dramatic, just a quick procedure to check what sort of skin thing it actually was, is.'

The word 'biopsy' hung in the air. Daisy had heard the word before, in contexts that hadn't ended well, and the casual way Maggie discussed it didn't fool her for a second. Her head swam and she felt as if she'd turned into a statue of concrete sitting right there on the wall. She tried to sound both concerned and unconcerned at the same time. It didn't work. Attempting to match Maggie's matter-of-fact tone, her brain screamed questions. 'When did you have this biopsy?'

Maggie shook her head and made a funny little movement with the fingers of her left hand. A sort of flick of dismissal, together with nervousness. 'A few weeks ago or something. The results came back, which is why I wanted to have a chat with you about it all.'

'What did they say?' Daisy could see that despite Maggie's attempts to sound breezy about the whole situation, there was genuine worry in her eyes. She edged closer on the wall and peered at Maggie's temple.

'They said it might be something, I can't remember the name, but it was dodgy, apparently the most common and least dangerous. I'm not going to say the word, but you know what I'm talking about.'

Daisy's world started to spin very, very fast as the words hit her like a physical blow, even though Maggie had immediately followed them with reassurances about whatever the thing was, being common and not dangerous. The thought of anything being wrong with Maggie made Daisy feel sick to her core. 'I don't know what to say. This is a bolt from the blue.'

'I'm fine,' Maggie said quickly, clearly recognising the panic that had started to show on Daisy's face. 'The doctor said it was basically the skin equivalent of a minor nuisance rather than anything properly scary. It just needs to be removed, and then that will be the end of it. Yeah, so that's it. I go in and get it out. It will be over and done very quickly.'

Daisy gulped, closed her eyes for a second and tried not to sound panicked. 'Removed how?'

'They need to cut out the affected area and stitch it up and Bob will be my uncle. The doctor said it was one of the most routine procedures they do. Apparently, they do it to men's foreheads every day of the week.'

Daisy stared at Maggie and tried to process the information and work out why Maggie talked about it as if they were discussing something as mundane as having a tooth filled. 'How long have you known about this?'

'I'd been aware of the thing on my head for ages, but I only got appropriately worried about it recently when it started changing size and texture and then the biopsy...'

'Ages!' Daisy could hear her voice getting higher and more strained despite her efforts to stay calm. 'You've been walking around with a potential skin cancer for ages and you didn't think to mention it to anyone? What the actual?'

'We live in England! Obviously, I didn't think it was anything like that. I didn't want to worry people unnecessarily, which is why I just got on with it and had it done privately in town.' Maggie's tone was defensive. 'It wasn't definitely anything at that point, just a thing that was being a bit stubborn about healing. I thought it was eczema.'

Daisy shook her head over and over again. 'But you were worried enough to go to the doctor.'

'Eventually, yes.'

'And you had a biopsy and you didn't tell anyone. I can't even...'

'I thought it made sense to follow professional advice. I didn't want to worry anyone and have people make a fuss over nothing.'

Daisy stood up from the sea wall and started pacing along the grass verge. Her mind raced with questions and concerns. She felt very, very scared and even more protective. 'What else did the doctor say? Will you need follow-up appointments after the removal or what?'

'Daise, please sit down. You're making me nervous with all that pacing around. Honestly, it's completely routine. In and out, that's it.'

Daisy stopped pacing but didn't sit down. Instead, she stood in front of Maggie with her hands on her hips. 'I'm making *you* nervous! You just told me you've got something that could be bad and you're worried about me making you nervous? I mean, really?'

Maggie sounded as if she'd rehearsed an explanation. 'It just needs to be cut out and then it will be gone forever.'

'But it's a type of cancer? Sorry, Mags, I'm saying the word.'

'Technically, yes, but the doctor said it wouldn't actually make me ill. Not now it's been found, anyway.'

Despite Maggie's attempts to make light of the situation, Daisy could see the worry lines around her eyes and the way she kept touching the affected area as if it caused her discomfort. The makeup that she'd clearly applied to try to disguise the problem wasn't managing to do its job. Everything about Maggie's posture suggested she was more concerned than she let on. Daisy couldn't seem to get a hold of herself as the bottom dropped out of her world. 'When is it?' Daisy sat back down on the wall and folded her hands tightly in her lap.

'They said they would call me with an appointment within the next couple of weeks. It would depend on availability and how quickly they could fit me into the schedule.'

'Right, so we need to work out who is going to drive you to the hospital and bring you home afterwards, and whether you will need someone to stay with you and what sort of time off work you will need to take.'

Maggie shook her head. 'We don't need to work out anything of the sort! I'll be in and out in a day. I'm perfectly capable of organising my own medical appointments and recovery arrangements. I wanted to tell you because I don't want Mum to know.'

'What? Sorry, nope, I am not being part of that! You don't want Mum to know! Don't be ridiculous, Mags.'

'I thought you might say that.'

'You don't get to make that decision now you've told me.' Daisy watched a small fishing boat make its way across the bay towards the harbour.

'I wanted to talk to you first because, well, what with working with Bells and Mum, I thought if you know, you can, I don't know, help me not to have to tell them.'

Daisy made a face and slowly shook her head from left to right. 'That is not a good idea and I am *not* happy to be part of it.'

'Honestly, it's not that big a deal.'

'Honestly, it's a *very* big deal.'

'Fair enough, but not the sort of big deal that requires emergency family meetings and elaborate care rotas and people treating me like I'm made of glass.'

Daisy could see the logic in what Maggie said, but she wasn't happy about it at all. She immediately wanted to step in and fix everything. It was the same protective instinct that had driven her to move heaven and earth to create stability for the twins, and she could feel it kicking in now with the same intensity. 'So what happens after it's removed?'

'They check all the affected tissue and monitor the healing process and then I would get on with my life as if nothing had happened.'

'And there is no chance of it spreading or turning into something more serious?'

'The doctor said she couldn't guarantee that, but once it was removed, that would be the end of the story for most people. The results will, well, you know...'

'But you would need to be more careful about sun protection and regular skin checks and that sort of thing?'

'Probably, yes. It's not a big drama, Daise.'

It was *such* a big drama. Daisy felt slightly reassured, but she struggled to accept that Maggie had dealt with the uncertainty and worry on her own without telling anyone in the family. 'I wish you'd said something earlier. Even if it was just to have someone to talk to about being worried.'

'Daise, it's nothing. You know how I am about medical stuff. I wanted to wait until I had actual facts rather than sharing vague anxieties about things that might turn out to be nothing. I hate it when people make a fuss. I am fine.'

'But it's not nothing, is it? You are not fine. Mum *has* to know.'

'I didn't want anyone to drive themselves mad with worry about something that really was going to be fine. It's a minor procedure.'

They stood up from the wall and began walking towards the duck pond. When they reached it, the water was dark and still and several ducks floated serenely on the surface. A wooden bench had been positioned at the edge of the pond to take advantage of the view. Daisy and Maggie settled themselves on it without saying much at all. Daisy stared at the wings of a duck and tried to work out what in the world she was going to do about Annabelle and Susannah not knowing. One thing was for sure: there was no way she was going to be part of it. She'd give Maggie a bit of time and then say that the others had to know.

'Do you remember when we used to come here as children and try to work out which ducks were which? The twins were doing that the other day when we walked down here with Mum.' Maggie laughed.

Daisy felt irritation run through her from top to bottom. Maggie had apparently decided that they'd talked about her health enough for one afternoon. Deciding to take Maggie's lead, she forced herself to chuckle. 'I remember you always insisting that you loved wonky tail feathers.'

'I liked the idea that they were individuals with personalities rather than just generic ducks.'

They sat watching the ducks for a while and Daisy had to fight not to say anything. The rational part of her mind tried to accept Maggie's words that it was all indeed minor and an easily treatable condition, but the emotional part reeled from the shock of hearing the implication of what it might entail being applied to someone she loved.

'Are you scared?' Daisy asked eventually.

'A bit.'

'Right.'

'I'm worried about potential scarring, though the doctor said they would do their best to minimise that and that it would probably fade significantly over time.'

Daisy felt as if scarring was the last of Maggie's worries. 'Well, you would still be beautiful regardless of whether you had a small scar near your temple.'

'You have to say that because you are my sister.' Maggie leaned back against the bench and looked up at the sky. 'I feel better for having told you.'

'Good…'

'I hate appearing vulnerable or needy. It's a Henley thing.'

'I know you do.' Daisy checked the time on her phone. 'I should probably head back. I need to collect the twins from Mum's house and start thinking about tea.'

'Yep. Promise me that you won't spend the next few weeks worrying about this constantly and imagining worst-case scenarios that aren't going to happen.'

'No, come on, I can't promise not to worry.'

'That was probably the best I was going to get from you, wasn't it?'

'It was.'

They got up and started walking and reached the top of a set of steps that looked out over Pretty Beach. The town spread out below them, looking exactly as picturesque and peaceful as it always did. Oh, how deceptive appearances could be. Daisy felt sick, sad and frightened, despite Maggie's assurances that it was all a minor thing. It was funny how everything could look perfect on the surface sometimes, as underneath things were far from smooth. Every now and then, complicated life things popped their head up with developments letting you not forget who was in charge. They always, always, always reminded you that nothing *ever* stayed the same. Daisy knew the feeling all too well.

13

Daisy was right up the top of the chandler building at the very front of the attic room. With a cup of tea beside her, she'd started on sorting out and, with luck, clearing yet another box of Dennis's things. Despite having added lots of his books to the shop and what felt like many hours of going through his stuff, truthfully, she'd hardly even made a dent in his junk. Piles and piles of it were still everywhere and sometimes it felt as if it were somehow multiplying by the day. Susannah had noted that he was borderline a hoarder and had told Daisy that slow and steady wins the race. Therefore, every time Daisy had had a spare half an hour or so, which wasn't very often, she'd gone up and cleared one small section. A strange mix of monotony, secondhand decluttering and a cathartic feeling all at the same time.

Tucked up at the top of the building in the warm, outside it felt as if there was a storm brewing. Daisy could smell and feel it in the air. Wind rattled the attic windows with a dogged persistence and even the way the sound from the ferry horn travelled told Daisy that things out at sea were whipping up trouble. As she listened to the window rattling away to itself, she drank her tea and shook her head at all the clutter and paraphernalia around her. Dennis had clearly been a man who never threw anything away, that fact wasn't in doubt. She didn't know too much about the falling out between him and Susannah but she did know he was a hoarder of books and published works. The man had been in possession of a serious book loving habit. The evidence surrounded her in towering stacks of paperbacks, hardcovers, and what appeared to be every literary magazine published between 1970 and 2010. She'd found more than a few copies of the same Agatha Christie novel, a collection of recipe books that looked as if they'd never been opened, and enough gardening manuals to stock a small library. Ditto encyclopaedias and special edition comics. Not a bad attic to have when one was a bookshop owner, it had to be said.

As she sat with her legs crossed and sorted through a pile of old Beatrix Potter books, the weather began to take a turn just as she had predicted. Starting with a tap tap at the windows, the rain then started to lash against the diamond-panes and every few minutes, a vicious gust of wind sent something clattering across the roof tiles all along the laneway. Daisy had always been able to smell storms coming in Pretty Beach and this one had the feel that it had been hanging around out at sea for a while. It was the sort of weather that made people want to cosy up with cups of tea and books. Sometimes in the shop, storms and rain meant that she was busy because people often wanted the cosiness of snuggling up in a bookshop by the sea.

As she sorted and tidied a bit more, she went down to the kitchen to make another cup of tea. She'd put her earphones in and was halfway through a podcast about independent bookshops when she'd started to lose concentration as her mind drifted off far away from the podcast and into its own. She kept thinking about everything that was happening in her life; Maggie, Miles and the Old Town house thing, the nomination. Her brain flicked between things and the podcaster's voice. The host was interviewing a woman who'd built a successful chain of boutique bookshops across the north of England. Truth be told, the confident discussion of profit margins and expansion strategies was way over Daisy's head. The woman talked about "brand identity" and "customer experience journeys" as if these were things that every bookshop owner understood instinctively. Daisy was certainly not in the same boat. Sometimes she struggled to remember whether she'd ordered enough copies of the latest bestseller to meet demand and brand identity in Daisy language meant turning on the fairy lights. Daisy shuddered as the woman in her ears droned on about brand. Really, all she had done was throw a few lamps and second-hand furniture around and add a few rugs and a load of books.

She paused the podcast and pulled out her earphones. A girl has to pull the plug when the discussion of quarterly revenue projections comes up. Standing up, she picked up a pile of Penguin classics to go down to the shop, put them on the windowsill and stretched her back as she looked out at the view. Tucked away under the eaves, the attic room with its sloped ceilings and dormer windows looked out over the rooftops of Pretty Beach as it was pummelled with rain. As she put her arms over her head, grabbed her elbows with her hands and stretched her sides, she could see the harbour and glimpses of angry slate grey sea topped with just as grey clouds. Stretching, she pondered; Maggie's news had been playing on her mind all week. Despite Maggie's insistence that the whole thing was routine and nothing to worry about, Daisy had done exactly what Maggie had asked her not to do and had spent several hours researching stuff via Dr Google. Never, *ever* a good idea. Dr Google was full of all sorts of advice from hither, thither and yon. She'd read patient forums where people discussed their experiences with surgery, and while most of the stories had positive outcomes, there were enough mentions of complications and setbacks to feed her anxiety.

The worst part was that Maggie didn't want to tell Susannah or Annabelle until after the procedure was over. She'd made Daisy promise not to say anything, which meant carrying the weight of the secret while trying to act normal around the rest of the family. Daisy had never been good at keeping secrets, particularly ones that involved potential health problems, and the stress of pretending everything was fine was exhausting. There was no way she was prepared to keep the secret. Her plan was to give Maggie another few days and then tell her that Susannah and Annabelle had to be told.

Together with that worry, Miles had been asking her about the house situation all week and she'd been making increasingly feeble excuses about why she wasn't ready to commit to anything. The truth was that Maggie's skin issue had made her realise how quickly things could change and how solid-seeming foundations could shift without warning. If something as basic as good health couldn't be relied upon, really, she had no clue about the future.

She knew her reluctance was frustrating the heck out of Miles, though he'd mostly kept it under wraps, but she'd felt him becoming a tad distant as time passed. Really, who could blame him? Daisy had recognised the signs of someone who was losing patience and she wasn't really sure what the answer was.

Deciding things would work out if she didn't worry about them, she picked up another box and lifted the lid, expecting to find more of Uncle Dennis's eclectic reading material. Instead, she discovered a collection of photograph albums and loose pictures that spanned several decades. The top album was bound in faded red leather with embossing on the cover in gold lettering that had worn away in places. She opened it carefully, very aware that she was looking at someone else's private history, but carried on anyway. The early pages showed a young Dennis with a woman who must have been his partner, though

Daisy had never heard mention of him being married, so she wasn't sure who it was. They looked happy together in the photographs, standing outside various holiday cottages and restaurants, arms around each other's waists, squinting into the camera with unselfconscious smiles. The woman had dark hair styled in the fashions of what looked like the 1960s and 1970s, and there was something familiar about her face that Daisy couldn't quite place.

As she turned the pages, she began to see the progression of their relationship. Photographs showing them looking impossibly young in formal clothes that now seemed very quaint and even more old-fashioned. A whole load of pictures captured them exploring what looked like European cities, feeding pigeons in public squares and posing outside famous landmarks. There were photographs of them decorating the sitting room right below where Daisy was standing - painting walls and hanging pictures, clearly delighted with their domestic achievements. The middle section of the album showed photographs of dinner parties with friends, holidays with other couples, and Christmas celebrations where they wore paper hats and pulled crackers. They looked comfortable together and as Daisy flicked through, she wondered all sorts of things: who the woman was, how close the pair of them seemed, how the old building had seen a happy couple in their prime.

Closing the album, she slotted it carefully in a box and made a mental note to ask Susannah who the woman in the photos was. As she shifted the box, she checked the time on her phone as the storm showed no signs of abating, and she realised that she had been in the attic with her tumbling thoughts for most of the afternoon. Heading back down to the kitchen with a pile of books in her arms, she popped the kettle on as the storm battled the coast.

Making herself a cup of tea, she then stood at the window watching the wind and rain as she stood by the interior door to the bookshop. The pavement was almost invisible through the sheets of rain, and she could see people hurrying along the laneway with their heads down and coats pulled tight against the weather. It was the sort of afternoon that made you grateful for warm, dry spaces and the luxury of staying indoors.

Her phone buzzed with a message from Miles.

Miles: *Hope you're okay. This storm is mental. Any damage to the shop?*

Daisy: *All fine here. Just watching it. The bookshop is lovely and cosy with all the fairy lights on. Makes the storm feel quite dramatic from inside.*

Miles: *Good. The storm came in up here, too. It's all over the news. Mum's flat is getting battered, but she's fine. She says it reminds her of being on a ship, lol.*

Daisy: *Ha! That's one way to look at it. How are you both holding up?*

Miles: *We're good. Just having tea. I'm a bit worried about you, tho.*

Daisy: *Don't be. The twins are at mum's, so I'm just pottering about with a cup of tea. The old building is solid as a rock. Takes more than a bit of wind and rain to rattle it. She suggested they stay there...*

Miles: *Oh, right, okay. How about I hop on the train then??? Mum is fine.*

Daisy: *Definitely. The weather shouldn't affect the train, should it?*

Miles: *I don't think it can blow a train off the track.*

Daisy: *Will your mum be OK?*

Miles: *Yes, she said she wants to get rid of me so that she can watch Vera, so she'll probably be pleased to see the back of me.*

Daisy: *Funny. Great, looking forward to a cosy night in with you.*

Miles: *Me too. Love you.*

Daisy: *Love you, too. Stay safe and dry. Text me when you get on the train.*

14

Daisy pulled her wax jacket tighter around her as she stepped out of the front door of the bookshop and right into the ferocity of the storm. There are storms and then there are Pretty Beach storms. The little town by the sea seemed to do just about everything better than anything and anyone else, including getting ravaged by wind and rain coming in off the sea. As the wind hit her, Daisy immediately gasped, blinked rapidly and put her head down. It was so fierce it nearly knocked her sideways. Daisy, old-school Pretty Beach-er as she was, had experienced howling coastal storms many times before and she could tell that it was getting worse by the minute. Rain lashed down in sheets that made it almost impossible to see more than a few feet ahead and the noise was extraordinary. Wind howled around the buildings as if it were alive and furious with everything in its way and bunting flapped like crazy overhead. Pretty Beach was taking a battering and didn't it know about it.

Making her way carefully along the laneway, she kept close to the shop fronts for shelter and hustled along trying to avoid the puddles. Her car was parked just around the corner from the bookshop and even that short distance felt treacherous as the rain poured and the wind battered. A dustbin had blown over outside the bakery and was rolling back and forth across the pavement with a horrible clatter. Someone's hanging basket had torn free from its bracket and lay smashed on the ground, soil and flowers scattered everywhere. Daisy was on her way to pick Miles up from the station and was now wondering if he would have been better off staying put with his mum.

The car felt as if it was rocking as she got in and turned the engine on. Daisy gripped the steering wheel and took a deep breath. The car, of course, wasn't rocking; it was just that outside the trees, signs, and just about everything around her felt as if they were moving. As she turned on the engine, the windscreen wipers could barely keep up with the rain and she had to lean forward to peer through the glass. She'd driven in bad weather many times before when coastal storms had hit Pretty Beach, but this storm had suddenly taken a turn for the worse and felt dangerous.

The journey to the station didn't normally take long, but as she crawled along at walking pace, she shuddered. A few tree branches had come down here and there and most sensible people, her not being one of them, had clearly decided to stay off the roads and the streets were almost empty. Even the ferry had stopped running, according to the electronic sign at the harbour, which flickered intermittently as the power supply struggled against the storm. By the time she reached the station car park, Daisy's hands were shaking as the driving conditions felt genuinely hazardous. She parked as close to the station entrance as she could and sent Miles a quick text to let him know she'd arrived. Deciding to go inside, she braved the rain and walked in to see a few other people doing the same thing. As she stood peering in the direction of the platforms to see if she could see the fast train, she could hear the storm raging outside. The station roof creaked ominously and where rain was leaking through the roof in front of her, it fell in drips into a bucket that someone had placed strategically near a whiteboard notifying customers of delays to service because of the storm.

After the fast train pulled in, Miles appeared a few minutes later, along with lots of other passengers, his hair damp and jacket soaked just from the short walk from the platform to the waiting area. He kissed her quickly and they both headed for the exit without lingering.

'Christ, it's wild out here,' Miles said as they reached the car. 'The train was delayed because of fallen trees on the line. I wasn't sure it was going to make it through at all. None of this was going on when I messaged you earlier! It's madness. I should have stayed where I was.'

'I know. I'm not sure we should be driving in this.' Daisy started the engine anyway and the journey back was even worse than the drive to collect him. The wind had picked up further, and debris was flying around everywhere. A shop sign had torn loose somewhere and went cartwheeling past them down the street. Daisy had to swerve to avoid a branch that fell from a tree just as they drove underneath it.

'Maybe we should pull over and wait it out.'

'Where? There's nowhere safe to stop.' Daisy kept her eyes fixed on the road, what little she could see of it through the rain. 'We're better off getting back to the bookshop. At least there we'll be properly indoors then. Let's hope the power doesn't go out.'

They made it back to the laneway and just as Daisy turned off the engine, a tile from somewhere high above smashed onto the pavement just a few feet from the car. They sat for a moment, neither of them speaking, listening to the storm rage around them.

'Right, we need to leg it as quickly as we can.'

They ran for the back gate of the bookshop, Miles's

overnight bag clutched against his chest, both of them soaked within seconds despite the short distance. Daisy fumbled with the key as the wind tried to tear the gate out of her hands, and they stumbled into the relative shelter of the back garden. Inside, she slammed the back door and everything felt suddenly calm and safe. Looking through to the bookshop, the fairy lights twinkled peacefully, the radiators ticked with warmth, and from inside, the storm didn't sound anywhere near as bad. Daisy leaned against the door and let out a whistling breath.

'I'm not going anywhere tonight,' Miles said, shaking water out of his hair. 'That's the worst weather I've ever driven in, and I wasn't the one driving. How did this turn so bad, so quickly?'

'Good. I don't want you going anywhere.' Daisy hung up her coat and put the kettle on. 'I've never seen a storm hit so fast. Usually, they blow themselves out before they get this far.'

Miles took a bottle of beer out of the fridge, offered one to Daisy, flipped off the lids and checked his phone as they walked through into the bookshop. With the blinds pulled half down, the building felt solid, but the wind put every window and door to the test.

Daisy nodded at Miles's phone. 'What did your mum say? How is she coping with it up there?'

'She said it was quite exciting, actually and that it reminded her of storms she used to watch from her parents' house when she was young. She's got plenty of food and candles if the power goes out, so she'll be fine. Her plan is to settle down with Vera.'

'And the flat? No damage?'

'No, it's not anywhere near as bad up there. She said that a few plant pots blew over on the balcony, but nothing major. Those old buildings are built to last.'

'I'm glad you're here now. What a palaver.'

'Me too. I was genuinely worried we weren't going to make it back in one piece.'

'I was, too, to be honest. I haven't seen a storm like this for a while.'

Outside, something large crashed to the ground with a sound that made them both jump. As Daisy jumped up and looked out, it was one of her hanging baskets which was in the middle of the entrance. 'Oops, I should have brought them in earlier.'

'Climate change, you reckon?' Miles asked.

'Don't know. We do get hotter summers, wetter winters, storms that come out of nowhere and knock everything sideways.'

'Makes you appreciate having an old building like this. I bet this one has seen a few storms in its time.'

Daisy looked around the bookshop, at the thick walls and deep-set windows that had been built long before anyone worried about energy efficiency or modern building regulations. 'Yes, I suppose so.'

'Do you need to call your mum to check that the twins are okay?'

'She just messaged me. They're fine.'

'Then there's nothing we can do except wait for it to pass.'

'Yep, how happy am I that I got one of Deepa's curries out of the freezer earlier?'

'You, Daisy Henley, are a good woman.'

Daisy giggled. 'I am.'

The lights flickered for a moment, and Daisy raised her eyebrows. 'Deepa makes the best lamb curry in Pretty Beach. She gave me three portions last week when she came in to buy a book. I like how the Pretty Beach way works. I not only get paid to sell books, I get extras by way of food.'

Miles leant against the worktop. 'I'm starving after that journey. How and why do storms make you more hungry?'

'No, I think that's just a Miles thing.'

Daisy put the curry in the microwave and pulled a bag of

naan bread from the bread bin as the wind blew in the chimney and rain blasted against the windows. Inside, it sounded distant, muffled and actually quite nice. 'I love nights like this. Not the terrifying drive to collect you, but being inside when the weather's doing its worst outside.'

The microwave pinged and Daisy stirred the curry before putting it back for another few minutes. Steam rose from the container and filled the kitchen with the smell of cumin and coriander. She opened a bottle of wine and poured two glasses.

'To surviving the storm.' Miles clinked his glass against hers.

Maggie went through Daisy's mind. She hadn't told a single soul and was not happy about it. She nearly gave in to the temptation of sharing Maggie's news with Miles, but didn't go through with it. 'To surviving lots of things.'

About fifteen minutes later, they were very cosily sitting in the kitchen at the little table with the curry between them and naan bread that had just come out of the oven. Outside, the storm continued to rage, but inside, everything felt perfect. The shelves Pete had put up with the copper rail underneath looked lovely. The duck egg blue paint on the cupboards had transformed the whole room and the little table felt almost as if it was a friend. All of it felt oh-so settled, cosy and just right. 'How funny. You and I here eating curry while a storm rages outside. What if we hadn't met?'

'I was meant to have ice cream chucked at me by an identical twin.'

'Sometimes I look around and can't quite believe it's real. That this is actually my life now.'

Miles shovelled in another forkful of curry. 'It's real. You made it happen.'

'With a lot of help. Mum letting me live rent-free. Annabelle and Maggie donating half their furniture. Pete doing all the DIY. Holly and Xian saving us from GayesBooks. The whole town rallying round when I got nominated for that award. You. Yeah, good people.'

'You did the work. You opened the shop and made it welcoming and built up the customer base. You can't take credit away from yourself.'

Daisy sipped her wine as a strong gust of wind rattled the windows. She thought about all the people who had lived in the same rooms over the years. Uncle Dennis with his mysterious girlfriend. Other families and couples who had weathered storms and got on with the business of living. 'I feel very lucky.'

'You deserve to feel lucky.'

'The twins are happy. The bookshop is working. You're here. Everything feels as if it's in the right place.' Daisy gulped as she thought about Maggie; that for sure wasn't in the right place.

'Yep.'

Daisy nodded. 'Which is why I don't want to change anything.'

'You've said. What about the house situation? Have you thought any more about that?'

Daisy had been wondering when Miles would bring it up again. She kicked herself for triggering him, took another mouthful of curry and considered her answer. 'I think we should look at a place if one comes up, but I don't want to say that we'll, you know, move in.'

Miles put down his fork. 'Right.'

'I haven't changed my mind, but sitting here tonight and realising how good this feels and how right it all seems makes me happy. I need to look at celebrating what we've got.' Daisy gestured around the kitchen.

'You're not just saying it because the wine and the storm have made you sentimental?'

The lights flickered again and they heard a bang somewhere in the distance. 'I should check that the girls are okay at Mum's,' Daisy said as they cleared the plates.

'Text her. Then we can just settle in for the night.'

Daisy sent a quick message to Susannah and got an immediate reply saying that all was well and the twins were fast asleep. They had watched the storm from the sitting room window until bedtime and thought it was better than anything.

'All fine. Mum says they were disappointed when the power didn't go out because they wanted to have an adventure with candles and Mum's torch on her phone.'

'Funny. Yeah, it's been nice; curry, wine, and not making decisions about the future. What more could you want?'

Daisy swallowed. She wanted Maggie to be okay and to actually be able to offload to someone about it. 'Nothing. Absolutely nothing at all.'

15

The morning after the storm, Daisy was standing outside the bookshop with a broom in one hand and a dustpan in the other, surveying the damage. Pretty Beach had taken quite a battering, it had to be said. The laneway was strewn with bits of roof tiles, broken plant pots and soggy bunting that had torn free from its moorings. One of the shop's hanging baskets lay in pieces near the front door, a sorry mess of mud and broken stems. At least the shop windows were intact, and overall, there had been little damage except for a cracked pane in the lean-to conservatory from a fallen branch. She swept up the worst of the debris and dumped it in a black bin bag. The bookshop itself had weathered the storm well enough. A few roof tiles had shifted and would need attention, but nothing that couldn't wait. The fairy lights in the window had survived intact, which felt like a small miracle given how violently everything had been shaken about.

Holly emerged from the bakery with a broom. 'Morning, Daise. What a night that was. Any damage your end?'

'Nothing major. Lost a hanging basket and some tiles, but we got off lightly.' Daisy gestured at the mess around them. 'It could have been a lot worse.'

'Tell me about it. We've got half a tree in our back garden and the power was out until about an hour ago. Still, at least everyone's safe.'

'Yeah, it was a big one.'

'See you later. Have a good day.'

Daisy had just finished sweeping when her phone buzzed in her pocket. She pulled it out and frowned at the message.

Annabelle: *Morning. I'm coming over in about twenty minutes. Need to chat about something important.*

Daisy: *Yes, I'm here. Just clearing up storm damage. Everything okay?*

Annabelle: *Not really. It's about Mags. See you shortly.*

Daisy stared at the messages and felt her stomach and just about everything else drop. This was exactly what she had been dreading. Somehow, Annabelle had found out about Maggie and was coming over to demand explanations. The secret that Maggie had been so determined about was going to come crashing down around all of them, which is why Daisy had never wanted to be part of it in the first place. She snatched a packet of wine gums and put two yellow ones in her mouth at once.

Going back inside the bookshop, she put the kettle on and shook her head. If Annabelle was coming over for a serious conversation about family medical issues, tea would definitely be required. Twenty minutes later, Annabelle's car pulled up outside and Daisy watched as she got out and picked her way carefully across the pavement, stepping over the worst of the puddles. Even first thing in the morning after a major storm, Annabelle managed to look put-together.

'What a mess.' Annabelle tutted as she reached the front door. 'The whole town looks like it's been through a blender. We haven't had a storm like this for ages.'

'It could have been worse; at least nobody was hurt or at least not that we know about yet.'

Daisy locked the door behind her. 'Tea?'

'Please and maybe something stronger if you've got it.'

Daisy swallowed, now convinced that Annabelle knew what *she* did.

Annabelle didn't waste any time getting to the point. 'Maggie called me last night, after the storm had calmed down a bit. She told me about the biopsy and the surgery. She said you already knew.'

Daisy nodded, as relief that Annabelle knew flooded through her. 'She told me and made me promise not to say anything to anyone.'

'Why? Why would she do that, Daise? I'm so cross with her for not telling me!'

'I know. She didn't want people to worry unnecessarily. She said it's routine and minor and would be over and done with before anyone had time to get worked up about it. She didn't want it to affect work. I told her I wasn't going to be part of it and then I didn't know what to do.'

'And you believed that it's minor?'

'I wanted to believe it. She was very convincing about the whole thing being no big deal.'

Annabelle leaned back in her chair and rubbed her neck. 'She was convincing with me, too. Very matter-of-fact about the whole thing. Come on, they're taking a chunk out of her scalp. I could tell she was more worried than she was letting on, though.'

'What made you think that?'

'The fact that she called me late on a stormy night to discuss medical procedures. That's not exactly normal behaviour for Mags.'

Daisy agreed with the assessment. 'What exactly did she tell you?'

'That she'd had a biopsy done a few weeks ago and the results had come back. She said the doctor had told her it was the most common and least dangerous type, but that it needed to be removed to prevent, well, you know...'

'That's more or less what she told me.'

'She also said that you were the only other person who knew about it and that she didn't want to tell Mum until after it was over. That is so ridiculous! How can Mum not know?'

Daisy winced. That was the part of Maggie's plan that she was not happy about. Keeping secrets from Susannah felt wrong on multiple levels. 'I tried to talk her out of that. I said Mum would want to know what was going on. Logistically, it's impossible anyway...'

'What did she say?'

'That Mum had enough to worry about without adding minor medical procedures to the list and that if she told Mum, then Mum would insist on being involved and making a fuss.'

Annabelle made a face and nodded. 'Which she would.'

'Exactly. You know what Mum's like with medical stuff. She turns into a one-woman army of concern and casseroles.'

Annabelle smiled at the description. 'Spot on. She does like to take charge when anyone's unwell.'

'Maggie said she just wanted to get it over and done with quietly, then tell everyone afterwards when there was nothing left to worry about. I can see her point.'

'And what do you think about that plan?'

Daisy had been wrestling with that question ever since Maggie had first told her. On one hand, she could understand the impulse to keep family drama to a minimum, especially for something that was supposedly routine and minor. On the other hand, it felt totally wrong to exclude Susannah from something that concerned one of her daughters. All she'd been able to think was what if it had been one of the twins keeping things from her. 'I think it's an absolutely *enormous* mistake, but it's not my decision to make.'

'Isn't it, though? I mean, if something went wrong and Mum found out afterwards that we'd known about it and hadn't told her, she'd never forgive us. I know I would feel the same. I actually think it's quite mean of Mags.'

That was exactly the scenario that had been keeping Daisy awake at night. The thought of having to explain to Susannah why they had kept her in the dark about Maggie's medical treatment was not a pleasant one. 'I know. I've been worrying about that twenty-four-seven. At least, she's told you now.'

'There are just so many reasons why not telling Mum is a bad idea. What if it doesn't go as smoothly as expected? What if there are complications or the recovery takes longer than planned? What if, I don't know, they don't get all of it, or it shows something else and she has to have more done? Then we have to tell this whole lie to Mum. That will not be good.'

'Maggie said it was routine. In and out.'

'That's what they always say, but routine procedures can still go wrong. Even if everything goes perfectly, Mum's going to know afterwards. Maggie is being selfish and ridiculous.'

Daisy hadn't thought about the practical aspect of the cover-up. Maggie would presumably have some sort of dressing or bandaging after it was done. 'What do you think we should do?'

'We need to convince Maggie to tell Mum herself.'

'And if she refuses?'

Annabelle weighed up the options. 'Then I think we tell Mum ourselves. As gently as possible, with lots of emphasis on how minor and routine it all is, but we tell her nonetheless.'

'Maggie won't be happy.'

Annabelle swore. 'She'll have to suck it up. Mum will never forgive us if we let her find out some other way.' Annabelle was adamant.

Daisy knew that Annabelle was right. Susannah had very strong feelings about family loyalty and mutual support and the idea that her daughters might keep medical secrets from her would be *deeply* hurtful. 'They said they'd call with an appointment once they had a slot available. So we've got a bit of time to work on Mags.'

'She didn't want to discuss it any more than absolutely necessary.'

'That could just be her way of coping with being worried about it.'

Outside, the cleanup from the storm continued as people emerged to assess the damage and start the process of getting back to normal. Through the window, Daisy could see Holly sweeping debris from outside the bakery. A few other shop owners had emerged to assess storm damage and there was a general sense of people pulling together to get their little corner of Pretty Beach back to normal.

'There's something else.' Annabelle sighed and narrowed her eyes.

'What?'

'I don't think this is the first time she's had concerns about her skin. When I really thought about it last night after we came off the phone, I remembered her mentioning ages ago that she'd had a mole checked out. A couple of years ago. She made it sound routine at the time, but now I'm wondering if there's been a pattern of problems.'

'Did you ask her about that?'

'I tried to, but she changed the subject. She said it was completely unrelated and that I was overthinking things.'

'Which could be true.'

'Or it could be that she's been dealing with these concerns for longer than she's admitted to any of us and that it's more serious.'

Daisy closed her eyes. All of it was *exceedingly* unsettling. The family had always been close and supportive of each other through difficult times and the idea that one of them might have been struggling in silence went against everything they believed about looking after each other. 'What do you think we should do?'

'I think we need to have a proper conversation with her. All cards on the table. Find out exactly what's been going on and how long she's been worried about things.'

Daisy could see the logic as clear as day, but Maggie was a tricky old kettle of fish at the best of times. She had always been the most independent of the three sisters, the one who preferred to solve her own problems rather than asking for help. 'She's going to hate us for interfering.'

'Whatever. If something serious is going on and we don't do anything about it, we'll never forgive ourselves.'

'And Mum will never forgive us either.'

'Exactly.'

'Why do you think she suddenly decided to tell you?'

'Who knows? She's starting to accept that she needs support, or, I don't know, it could also mean that she's more scared than she's letting on.'

Daisy knew that when it came down to it, there was really no choice to make. Susannah's feelings had to take priority over Maggie's desire for privacy. 'I think we already know what we have to do. Mum has to know.'

'I think so too. The question is whether we can convince Maggie to do it herself or whether we have to take matters into our own hands.'

'Let's try talking to her first. One more proper conversation where we explain why keeping Mum in the dark is a bad idea. If that doesn't work, we tell Mum ourselves and deal with the consequences.'

Annabelle shook her head slowly and exhaled dramatically. 'I *hate* family drama.'

'So do I.'

16

Daisy was sitting in Maisy's coffee shop opposite Annabelle, both of them nursing cappuccinos and a large slice of carrot cake sat in between them. The intention of the carrot cake and sugar overload was to make them feel better. It hadn't really worked. The cake and the sugar hit had let them down. They were sitting discussing the Maggie situation.

The pair of them had confronted Maggie with the fact that they were very unhappy about Susannah not knowing about the surgery. Eventually, with much toing and froing, Maggie had come round. After a lot of complaining, she'd given in and told Susannah what was going on. The fallout had not been pretty. There had been ensuing phone calls and visits from Susannah who, just as Maggie had predicted, went full throttle into crisis mode. This, of course, was exactly why Maggie had not wanted to tell her in the first place.

Daisy sliced a piece of carrot cake off and popped it into her mouth. 'At least Mum knows now. I couldn't stand the fact that all three of us knew but she didn't. It was bad enough when it was just me, but there was no way I was going to keep that secret. It didn't bear thinking about.'

Annabelle nodded. 'Exactly. There was no way that Mum wasn't going to find out anyway. I mean, you can hardly have skin removed from your scalp without anyone noticing, can you?'

Daisy rolled her eyes. 'Precisely. Though, actually, if anyone could've pulled it off, it would've been Maggie.'

Annabelle shook her head. 'Nah, not even Maggie could have hidden that from Mum.'

'Knowing Mags, she would have pretended to go on holiday or something or she would have made up something about having filler....'

Annabelle burst out laughing. 'Actually, I could see her doing that, couldn't you? Yes, you're right.'

'She would have pulled it off, too.'

'The thing is,' Annabelle continued, cutting another piece of carrot cake with her fork, 'Mum's reaction was exactly what we all expected it would be. She's gone into full protective mode and is trying to organise Maggie's entire life for the next six months.'

'I know. When I spoke to her yesterday, she was talking about meal plans and vitamin supplements and whether Maggie should be working.'

'Poor Maggie.'

Daisy sipped her cappuccino. 'Actually, I think she's secretly quite relieved. All that energy she was putting into keeping it from everyone must have been exhausting. It's so much better now that we all know.'

'You think so? She seemed pretty annoyed with us when we cornered her about it.'

'She was annoyed because she knew we were right and she didn't want to admit it. You know what Maggie's like when she's been caught out doing something she knows she shouldn't have done. A leopard does not change its spots. She's always been the same.'

Annabelle laughed. 'Like when we were teenagers and she got caught sneaking back into the house after that party at Rachel Morrison's. She was furious with us for weeks, even though we hadn't done anything except be awake when she climbed through the kitchen window.'

'Exactly. She hates being told what to do, even when what she's being told is sensible and for her own good. I saw her briefly yesterday when I dropped the twins off at Mum's. She looked tired but not as stressed as I expected. I think having it all out in the open is actually helping, even if she won't admit it.'

'What did Mum say when you saw her?'

'She was trying to be calm and practical, but you could see she was in full worry mode underneath. She kept asking if I thought Maggie was eating enough and that she'd known something wasn't right.'

Annabelle nodded knowingly. 'I got three phone calls from her on Monday alone, all asking slightly different versions of the same questions about Maggie and whether we thought she was being honest about how she was feeling.'

'At least she's channelling her worry into practical things like cooking and organising rather than just panicking. Remember when I had the twins and she turned up at the hospital with enough food to feed half the maternity ward?'

'I remember. She'd been up all night making casseroles and soup because she didn't know what else to do with herself. She must have baked fourteen loaves of bread, too.'

Daisy finished her piece of carrot cake and pushed the plate towards the centre of the table. 'The ironic thing is that now Mum knows, I actually feel better.'

'I'm not sure Maggie sees it that way. When I spoke to her this morning, she was complaining about Mum wanting to come and clean her flat and stock her freezer with homemade meals.'

'That sounds exactly like Mum's idea of being helpful.'

'I told Maggie she should just let her do it. It's not like having a clean flat and a freezer full of food is going to hurt.'

'What did she say to that?'

'That she's a grown woman who can manage her own domestic arrangements, thank you very much. But I could tell she was wavering. Sometimes you just have to let Mum do what she has to do.'

'You know what I think the real problem is? Maggie's spent so long being the one who sorts things out for everyone else that she doesn't know how to let other people take care of her.' Daisy noted.

'Exactly. She's always been the organised one, the one with the answers, the one who knows how to handle any crisis..'

'Whereas I am an expert at being a disaster and letting other people rescue me. You're the same…'

'Speak for yourself. I'm excellent at managing my own disasters, thank you very much.'

'Maggie's never learned how to ask for help.'

'You know what the strangest thing about all this has been?'

'What?'

'How it's made me realise how much we all depend on each other, even when we pretend we don't. The idea of one of us going through something difficult without the others knowing about it feels wrong somehow.'

'We might drive each other mad most of the time, but we're a unit. When something happens to one of us, it affects all of us.'

Annabelle raised her coffee cup in a mock toast. 'To interfering family members who love each other too much to mind their own business.'

'I'll drink to that.'

Daisy felt grateful that she wasn't the only one that knew and as if a huge weight had been lifted off her shoulders. Whatever happened with Maggie, at least now they were all dealing with it together rather than trying to manage separately around the edges of a secret. She just hoped and prayed that everything was going to turn out okay.

17

Daisy had a lot on her mind; Maggie's health, the book award and gala event, having a glass panel in the lean-to conservatory fixed after the storm and Miles. She'd been up just as the sun had risen in Pretty Beach, had cleaned both the shop and the living accommodation from top-to-bottom and had done some work for Chloe in the bakery. After whizzing through the school run without any problems concerning forgotten school bags or tears, she was ticking off her jobs list like a pro. She may or may not have also had a good twenty minutes or so sitting on the loo doom-scrolling people with much better lives than hers on Insta. She was human after all.

She was in the kitchen arranging a beautiful bundle of flowers from Susannah's garden in a jug on the worktop when she heard the back gate. She then proceeded to see Miles walking towards the door like a man on a mission. He'd been up visiting Elizabeth, sorting out her streaming services and she hadn't been expecting him until later. He did not look bad. The jeans needed removing.

She unlocked the door, beamed, kissed him and let him in.

'You're early. I thought you weren't coming down until this evening.'

'I caught an earlier train. I needed to talk to you about something before the day got away from us.'

'Right. That sounds ominous. What's up?'

Miles had a serious expression on his face. Daisy liked the face in all its seriousness. In her mind, the jeans were followed by the rest of his garments.

'Nothing's wrong exactly. It's just that something's come up that we need to discuss.'

'Work something or personal something?'

'Work. But it affects everything else, too.'

Daisy squinted. In her experience, conversations that involved phrases like "we need to discuss" rarely ended well. She gestured towards the wingback chairs. 'Shall we sit down?'

Miles sat down and leaned forward with his elbows on his knees. He looked more serious than Daisy had ever seen him, and that included the period when his mum had been in hospital. 'I've been offered an opportunity.'

Daisy nodded and turned her mouth upside down. 'What? An opportunity? Like what? What do you mean?'

'It's a work thing which is significant.'

'That's good news, isn't it?'

'It is. It's to do with that New York start-up I've been working with. We've been brokering this for ages and what with the new American government, it's taken off. Next level seed funding is happening.'

Daisy narrowed her eyes. 'I thought it was in San Francisco?'

'That's part of it, but this is more the financial side.'

Daisy wasn't sure what she was meant to say. She associated seeds with, well, growing stuff in little pots and had precisely zero knowledge of what seeding meant. Nor, to be frank, did she want to learn. 'So, why the look on your face?'

'I'll need to go over there quite a bit. New York.'

Daisy felt the words hit her like cold water. 'Quite a bit? Meaning?'

'Often-ish.'

'What? Like permanently? Is that what you're saying?'

'No, but, well. Yeah, I'd be back and forth.'

'Right.' Daisy stared at the flowers on the table and tried to process what he was telling her. After all their conversations about him buying a house in Pretty Beach, about making things more official between them, about planning a future together, he was now talking about New York. Oh, how much her boat was being rocked. 'When did this come up?'

'It's been going on for a while.'

'Right, and you're only telling me now?'

'I wanted to think it through properly before we discussed it. Work out what it might mean for us and what's going to happen with my mum and, you know, everything really.' Miles appeared uncharacteristically flustered.

The feathers on top of Daisy's head and just about all over her body were ruffled. 'What it might mean for us is that you'd be in New York and I'd be here with the twins and the bookshop. That isn't great. It's not exactly rocket science.'

Miles held up his hands, then rubbed his face and shook his head. 'Look, Daise, when this opportunity first came up, I thought about it and wondered what to do.'

'And now?'

'Now I realise that this job has made me see exactly what I want even more and where I want to be. It's really crystallised everything.'

Daisy frowned. 'I don't understand what you are saying.'

'The flight to New York is seven hours. So, with the fast train to London, it's completely doable. I could be based here and travel when I need to. Other people do it all the time.'

Daisy screwed up her nose. She couldn't even fathom what

he was saying. 'You want to permanently live here and commute to New York? Said no one ever. You've gone mad.'

'I'd only have to go when I need to. Most of the work can be done remotely anyway. It's not the nineteen-seventies where you have to be chained to a desk in an office. The meetings I'd need to attend in person would be signing-off type stuff. You know how much I deal with San Francisco at the moment and that's all via a screen.'

Daisy stared at him. 'You're serious about this.'

'Deadly serious, but there's more to it than just the work arrangement. Having all this come to fruition has really clarified things for me.'

Miles was seriously annoying Daisy. She'd known it was too good to be true that he wanted to be in her world. He was rocking her boat, not making much sense and she didn't like it in the slightest. She gave him the benefit of the doubt. 'What do you mean?'

Miles stood up and walked to the window. 'This opportunity has clarified everything for me. It's made me realise that I don't want to keep renting flats and living in temporary arrangements. I want to buy a house here in Pretty Beach. I'm sick of that flat, to be quite honest. It's tiny and I feel as if I am constantly living out of a bag. I am not putting up with it, whatever you say.'

'Won't going back and forth to New York make you feel like you're living out of a suitcase?'

'Exactly. I want a proper house. Somewhere with enough space for my mum to have her own annexe, if she wants to come down here and somewhere that feels permanent. When people ask me where I live, I want to reply with Pretty Beach, not that I am temporarily renting a flat month to month. I need a place where Mum could move to if she can be persuaded. So I can go off and know she's safe. I need to say that I'm in a real relationship and have an actual base where I belong. I am sick to the back teeth of this. I want to buy something here, whether you're in or not.'

Daisy's heart sped up. 'I see. You want Elizabeth to move here permanently, too?'

'I think she'd like to. I want to give her the option of staying if she wants to. She has no one up there now.' Miles made a wincing face. 'A lot of her friends are no longer with us. She just rattles around in that flat all day now that she's scared to go out.'

'And what about, umm, us?'

Miles turned back to face her. 'I'm ready to stop tiptoeing around what this is. I love you, Daise. I love the twins. I want to be part of your family, not just someone who visits and helps with the school run occasionally. However, if you're not ready, you're not ready...'

Daisy gulped. 'You *are* part of our family.'

'Am I? Because sometimes it feels like you're waiting for me to disappear.'

'I'm not...'

'You are and I understand why. You've had to protect yourself and the girls for so long that it's become second nature. But I'm not going anywhere, Daise. This job offer has made me realise that more than ever.'

Daisy wiped her eyes with the back of her hand. She may have had a fleeting thought about the removal of the jeans right in the middle of it all. 'Isn't that all back to front? How has a job offer in New York made you realise you want to stay in Pretty Beach?'

'Because even though I've been working on this for ages, when it came up it clarified things. It made me realise that you're my home. Not a place, not a job, not even this beautiful town. You and Margot and Evie are what matter to me. Everything else is just logistics.'

Daisy stared at him, not really sure what to do, say, think or feel. 'New York, wow. Pretty Beach to New York.'

'People do it all the time. Come on, Daise. Bells and Maggie go up to the city a few times a week and Maggie is always flying off somewhere or other. It's no different to driving to Scotland in terms of the time it takes. Technology makes it easier than ever.'

'It just feels huge.'

Miles sat down again. 'It's huge for me. I need to stop dicking around in a holiday flat.'

Daisy looked around at the place she'd created for herself and the girls. 'I love this place. It's the first home that's ever really felt like ours.'

'I'm not asking you to give it up. We could keep the bookshop exactly as it is. There are loads of options.'

'You've really thought about this.'

'I've thought about nothing else for ages. You must have noticed.'

'What does Elizabeth think about all this?'

'I haven't discussed the details with her yet, but she's mentioned a few times how much she loves it here and how safe she feels. How she'd forgotten what it was like to walk to the shops without looking over her shoulder.'

'Well, it is safe here.'

'She wouldn't be rattling around in that London flat on her own, worrying about every sound outside because, for sure, that's what it's got to.'

Daisy stood up and walked to the window. Outside, Pretty Beach was going about its morning business. The postman was making his rounds, someone was putting fresh flowers in the display outside the florist, and a cat was picking its way carefully across the wet cobblestones. It was all so familiar and comfortable and safe.

'What is it about wanting to settle down? Before, well, you had your London life when we first met. You were here because of Luke...'

'I was here because I was already feeling antsy and wondering what life was all about. I realised that my London life was just a series of habits and obligations. I had the flat because it was convenient for work. I had the gym membership because it was expected. I went to the same restaurants and pubs because they were familiar. But none of it actually made me happy.'

'And this does?'

'This does. You do.'

Daisy chuckled. 'Me and the girls and all our chaos.'

'Yup, love it.'

'Even with all my neuroses?'

'Not sure about that bit. I want to be more in it with you, not at arm's length.'

Daisy knew he was right. She had been keeping him at arm's length, even as she'd fallen deeper in love with him and thinking about jeans removal a lot of the time. It was a habit born of self-protection, but maybe it was time to break it. Daisy stood up and walked to the kettle. 'Tea?'

'Please.'

'We'll have tea and discuss it some more.'

18

Daisy opened the plastic on a packet of wine gums and thought about the New York situation. Picking out three red ones, she popped them all into her mouth as she sat on the top deck of the ferry, looking out over Pretty Beach. On her way to Newport Reef to pick up ballet shoes for the twins, she was glad to be on the water. She loved being on the ferry. It never failed to ground her with its funny old ways. The way it creaked, bobbed up and down and its lovely old timber had been part and parcel of how she rolled for all of her life. She'd cried on the ferry when she'd heard the bungee jump accident news, remembered trips on the ferry with her mum and sisters when she was a little girl, pushed the twins on in their first pram when they were tiny little bundles of pink blankets and many a time had used its therapeutic properties to fix all sorts of problems in her life. Shame it couldn't be shrunk, wrapped, popped into a bottle and prescribed for health.

As she sat and pondered the whirlwind going on around her, she looked out to sea, sucked on the three sweets and tried not to worry too much about Maggie, the New York thing or how worried Susannah was. Just as she was forcing herself not to get out her phone and fill her brain with more stuff, stuff, stuff, Steven, one of the deckhands, stopped to say hello.

'Alright, Daise! How are you? Long time no see. What's been occurring in your world? I haven't seen you for ages.'

Daisy smiled. 'Hi. Everything and nothing is what's going on in my world. I was just sitting here thinking about how much I love this ferry, when my brain is busy. It always somehow seems to calm me, if you know what I mean.'

'Does that for a person. Why do you think I work here?'

'You're not silly, are you?'

'I am not. I hear you've brought a little bit of prestige to our shores, as it goes.'

Daisy chuckled at the mention of the award and was glad not to have to talk about the horrible things going on in her life. 'I don't know about that.'

Steven bantered. 'It's some achievement if you ask me. Your bookshop is putting us on the map down here in the sticks.'

'It's mad really. I still can't quite believe it happened.' Daisy shifted on the bench and looked out at the water. 'The whole thing has been a bit of a whirlwind.'

Steven leaned against the rail and folded his arms. 'My missus said she saw you on Facebook, was it?'

'Probably Instagram. It's all quite bonkers. Give me a quiet day in the shop any time over it all, but it's good for the shop, so it is what it is. You know me, I'm quite happy here in Pretty Beach doing my own thing.'

'The whole town's talking about it. Pete was saying it's brought loads of new customers in already and Roy from the council.'

Daisy nodded. 'I suppose it has. Actually, now you say it, yesterday I had people coming from three counties away just because they'd heard about the shop because of the nomination. Funny how word spreads.'

'That's brilliant, that is. It's good for business and good for

Pretty Beach as a whole, if you ask me.' Steven checked his watch and glanced towards the front of the ferry 'How are Maggie and Bells? I haven't seen them on the ferry for ages.'

Daisy swallowed at the mention of Maggie. If only she didn't have to tell a little white lie. 'They're both well, thanks.' The fib came out automatically. Maggie was, in fact, facing something that might change everything. Steven asking her with a genuine look of interest on his face made Daisy's stomach lurch. Underneath everything going on in her world - the award, the bookshop's success, and Miles, Maggie's surgery made everything fragile, dodgy, worrisome and very, very uncertain. Mostly Daisy had tried to bury it because at the end of the day, there was nothing she could do and Maggie had been adamant about zero fussing.

'Maggie still doing her thing for the PR business? Always seemed too clever for her own good, that one.'

Daisy's voice sounded strange to her own ears. She hoped Steven wouldn't clock that something was going on. 'She is. You know what she's like. She can't sit still. She's always busy.'

'Bells?'

'Yes, she's well too. They both are.'

Steven nodded. 'That's what we like to hear. Your mum must be so proud. Look at you, Henleys; all three of you girls doing so well, the twins are gorgeous and now you with your award-winning bookshop. It's true what they say about the Henley girls; always winning, isn't that right?'

Daisy played along and chuckled. If only Steven knew how complicated it all was beneath the surface. It had always irritated her a bit how the locals of Pretty Beach assumed that if you had a Henley surname, things were somehow gilded. A lot of the time, especially when she was at school, she'd hated how being a Henley had come with certain expectations, many of which she nearly always failed to live up to, at least in her mind. For a lot of the time, she'd not felt as if her world was gilded in any shape or form and now Maggie's success might be overshadowed by something much more serious. A little bit of the gold on top of the "H" of the Henley name had worn off. No one needed to know that, though. Better to keep up the fallacy. 'Ahh, I don't know about that.'

The ferry lurched slightly as it hit a patch of choppy water and Daisy gripped the rail.

Steven straightened up. 'Right, I'd better get back to it. It's really good to see you, Daise. Next time I bump into you, you might have won that award, if you're lucky. You'll be too fancy to speak to me then.'

'I hope so, thanks, Steven.'

As he walked away, Daisy pressed her lips together and stared out at the horizon, trying to focus on the rhythm of the ferry's engine rather than thinking about Maggie's situation. Pulling out the packet of wine gums, she chose a green one, popped it in her mouth and let it dissolve slowly on her tongue. The ferry chugged steadily towards Newport Reef as she stared at a seagull and crossed her fingers about Maggie. The "H" tarnished a little bit more.

~

An hour or so later, Daisy was in possession of the ballet shoes. The ferry ride and a little nosey and mooch in the shops in Newport Reef had done her the world of good. The sea air and getting away from Pretty Beach for a bit had done wonders for decompressing all the things that had been going on in her brain. She was now sitting in more or less the same position as she had been on the outward journey, but was now going the other way. The captain's voice crackled through the tannoy system, cutting through the ferry's engine.

'Yeah, good afternoon and welcome to the Pretty Beach ferry. Ladies and gentlemen, we will be approaching The

Middles shortly. There's a bit of a swell out here today, so we're expecting some choppy conditions for the next ten minutes or so. Please make sure you're holding on to something secure and mind yourself on the decks. No standing at this point. Repeat, no standing at any time. Thank you for travelling safely with Pretty Beach ferries.'

Daisy gripped the rail in front of her and prepared for a bumpy ride as she watched a couple of tourists get up and go inside. From experience, she knew how rare it was for the announcement to be made and wondered if she, too, should get up and go in. Deciding she'd just stay put, she looked ahead and waited. The Middles was a stretch of water not far from Pretty Beach where the currents met and the seabed rose up, creating conditions that could sometimes turn legs to jelly. Daisy had been through it hundreds of times and as expected, the ferry began to pitch as they hit the first of the bigger swells. She watched the horizon tip and sway and the sea and sky shift up and down right in front of her eyes. A woman sitting on a bench near the stairs gripped the rail and braced herself as her toddler giggled with delight at the movement.

Steven appeared, moving carefully across the deck, checking that passengers were secure. He caught Daisy's eye and grinned. 'Got to love The Middles on a day like this. It's a bit livelier than usual today, eh? We aim to please. Good thing you've got your sea legs, Daise.'

'Just about.' Daisy chuckled as the ferry rolled to one side, then the other and rode the swells. The packet of wine gums slid across the bench beside her and she grabbed it before it fell underneath. The bumpy Middles reminded her of being on the ferry with Maggie and Annabelle. Maggie loved it when The Middles was rough and had always tried to stand at the rail during the worst weather, daring the waves to make her sick and always getting told off by one of the crew. Annabelle had always preferred to sit inside and pretend the motion wasn't happening at all.

The thought of Maggie brought worry flooding back. Here Daisy was, being tossed about on the water with a horrible feeling that Maggie's next few months, years even, were not going to be good. A large wave caught the ferry and sent spray up over the lower deck. Daisy heard someone laugh nervously and felt the familiar mixture of fear and exhilaration that came with being in The Middles.

The captain's voice came through the tannoy again. 'We'll be through the worst of it in just a few minutes now. Thank you for your patience. Please, no standing on the deck.'

Daisy closed her eyes and let the motion of the boat wash over her as the ferry navigated through the next swell. Then, just like that, it began to settle as they moved through the worst of The Middles and into calmer water. She opened her eyes and as the ferry settled, Pretty Beach came into full view ahead of them. The sight of it lifted Daisy's spirits, even when she was worried about other things. The pastel-coloured houses stepped down the hillside, all soft pinks, pale blues and yellows, the tiled roofs created little lines across the landscape and here and there chimneys sent thin wisps of smoke into the air. On top of it all, the lighthouse stood sentinel stark against the sky. Daisy could just make out the line of striped beach huts in the distance and the bunting stretching between lamp posts along the seafront fluttered in the breeze.

Taking out her phone, she scrolled through her Instagram comments and smiled at the messages here and there and a few photos people had tagged her in of their visits to the bookshop. It still felt surreal that strangers were taking pictures in her little shop and posting them online with captions about how magical it was. It wasn't a dream though; it was there for real right on the screen of her phone. She had, at least, done something right in her life. At least the bookshop was going well. As she waited for the ferry to get closer, she dabbled around on Instagram for a bit. Moving to her emails, she scrolled. Same usual old load of rubbish that she really needed to cull; a course she'd shown interest in years before that was emailing her like twice a day, an offer for half price on washing powder and a newsletter from a celebrity in Rome pontificating on how many pairs of ludicrously expensive ballet flats she owned. And delete. Scrolling without a whole lot of enthusiasm, one subject line caught her attention. "Video Feature Request - The Independent Retail Alliance."

Daisy opened the email immediately and read it quickly. The Independent Retail Alliance wanted to know if they could come and film some content for their social media channels about the award and the upcoming gala event. They were putting together a series about independent shops that were making a difference in their communities, and her shop was front and foremost. The email was polite and professional, explaining that they'd only need a couple of hours, if that and would work around her schedule. They wanted to capture the atmosphere of the shop, interview her briefly about the award, and film some general footage of customers browsing and the daily operations.

It was quite the honour but part of Daisy couldn't be faffed. She felt her stomach flutter with nerves. Yikes. Cameras, attention and people wanting to document her little world. It was flattering that the shop was being recognised, but a lot of her didn't want a bar of it. Not a bar. The ferry's engine changed pitch as they approached the harbour, and Daisy could see Steven with a huge coil of rope in his hand preparing to dock. Thinking about the filming thing, she half tutted and half sighed. She'd quite like to just be a little bookshop owner in jeans and a floral shirt minding her business, serving cups of tea and saying hello to people. The award was bringing a lot of attention. She tucked her phone back into her pocket and decided that she'd think about the filming request later. She had a lot on her plate and she needed to process it properly and right at that moment she had normal life at her beck and call: she needed to collect the twins from school, do their tea, etcetera, etcetera, etcetera.

With her brain having lost some of its earlier calmness from the therapeutic properties of riding the waves, Daisy gathered her bag and the ballet shoes and got herself together as the ferry bumped against the wharf. Seagulls called overhead, rigging clanged in the harbour, a dog barked somewhere near the ice cream van, water slapped against the hulls of moored boats, and the creak of the ferry's old timber felt like a friend. The engine cut to idle with a low rumble and Daisy could hear Steven calling instructions as he secured the mooring ropes. Behind her, the woman with the toddler was gathering up toys and promising ice cream if there was no fussing about getting off the boat. The ferry horn gave a small, low blast and Daisy stood with the other passengers as the gangway was lowered with a clunk. The smell of fish and chips drifted, mixing with the salt air and the faint scent of diesel from the engine.

As Daisy stepped off and walked away from the ferry, she inhaled and sighed, loving getting home. Strolling in the direction of the laneway, Pretty Beach wrapped itself around her. The narrow streets with their uneven cobblestones led her past the shopfronts she'd known all her life. The florist was arranging flowers in metal buckets outside the door, the chemist had a handwritten sign advertising flu jabs, and someone, no doubt one of the owners, Camilla, had chalked the day's specials on a chalkboard outside the fish and chip shop. A tabby cat sat in the window of the post office, and a shop owner was sweeping a front step. Daisy turned to go down the lane that led to the back of the bookshop. As she went past the bakery, the smell of fresh bread lingered. She inhaled and tried not to think about anything. Easier said than done.

19

Daisy woke at half past five on the morning of Maggie's procedure, though she hadn't set an alarm. Her brain had simply decided that sleep was no longer required and had nudged her awake. Her old friend anxiety enveloped her in an instant. Laying in bed staring at the ceiling for a good ten minutes, she tried to remain calm and wondered if she would be able to get back to sleep. After listening to the twins breathing in the room next door and the familiar creaks of the old building, she turned over, whipped off the duvet and gave up any pretence of rest and padded downstairs to make tea.

The kitchen felt horribly quiet without the usual morning chaos of school bags and breakfast negotiations. Miles had stayed in London with Elizabeth, who'd been having one of her nervous days about going out since the muggings, and the twins were still in the land of nod. All Daisy could think about was Maggie. Daisy had offered repeatedly to drive Maggie to the hospital, to wait with her, to bring her home afterwards, but Maggie had been absolutely adamant about going alone.

'It's routine,' Maggie had said for the hundredth time when they'd spoken the night before. 'I'll get a taxi there, they'll do their thing and Piers is coming to get me and take me to Annabelle's afterwards. No drama, no fuss, no one sitting around in hospital waiting rooms getting worked up about nothing. Don't even go there, Daise. I've worked it all out. I am fine.'

Daisy understood the logic, but didn't like it and had spent most of the previous evening resisting the urge to text Maggie every hour. The thought of Maggie sitting alone in a hospital room, minor or not, waiting to have part of her scalp removed, made Daisy feel sick with helplessness and Susannah had messaged to say that she felt the same, too.

She made herself toast she couldn't eat and tea that tasted like nothing, then sat at the little desk by the window and watched Pretty Beach wake up around her. The ferry honked in the distance as it made its first journey of the day, and she could see Nel walking briskly past the bookshop window with a coffee in one hand and her bus keys in the other. Everything looked reassuringly normal, as if the world hadn't registered that this was a day when one of the Henley sisters would be going to hospital. Maybe Daisy was dramatising everything. Possibly, but she didn't really care.

At seven o'clock, her phone buzzed with a text from Maggie.

Maggie: *Off to hospital now. All fine. Will message later. Don't worry. M x*

Daisy stared at the message for several minutes, trying to think of an appropriate response that wouldn't sound either OTT or artificially casual. In the end, she settled for

"Love you. See you later. D x" and tried not to think about what Maggie might be feeling as she sat in the back of a taxi, making her way through the traffic towards something, quite frankly, pretty daunting. At least Daisy felt as if it were daunting.

The rest of the morning passed with agonising slowness. After the joys of the school run with the twins where Daisy had little to no patience, she opened the bookshop as usual, served customers and made conversation about the weather. She talked about the latest bestsellers as if it were any other day in the shop but underneath the routine, she felt hyper aware of every passing minute. She kept calculating and recalculating how long it would be before she might expect to hear that the patch of bad skin was no more.

Xian appeared just after ten, looking more subdued than usual as she settled into her regular chair with her iPad and hip flask. Holly and Xian were now also in the know. The only other people who did. 'How are you holding up?'

'I'm fine,' Daisy replied automatically. She caught Xian's sceptical expression and sighed. 'Actually, I'm climbing the walls with worry, but there's nothing I can do about it, so I'm trying to keep busy. As she keeps saying, it's minor. I am overthinking.'

Xian tipped her hip flask and took a swig. 'Waiting is the worst part of anything medical. At least when you're the patient, you're too drugged or distracted to think about what's happening. When you're the family member, you just have to sit there and imagine all the things that could go wrong.'

'She insisted on going alone and said she didn't want anyone making a fuss.'

Xian winked. 'Sounds like Maggie and the Henleys. She's always been the independent one, hasn't she? Even when you were all little, she was the one who wouldn't let anyone help her with anything.'

'Yep, for sure she was. Right, I'll get your tea.'

The morning crawled past with excruciating slowness. Every time her phone buzzed with a notification, Daisy's heart jumped, but it was always something mundane. A delivery confirmation for new stock, a reminder about the twins' parent-teacher meetings, a message from Miles asking how she was coping. Nothing from Maggie, nothing from Annabelle, nothing to indicate whether the procedure had started, finished, or encountered any complications. All very agonising.

Just before two, her phone finally rang with Annabelle's name on the screen. Daisy answered before the first ring had finished.

'How is she?'

'She's fine. It went exactly according to plan. It was completely textbook, no complications, no surprises. She's awake, she's complaining and she's asking when she can come home.'

Daisy felt her knees go slightly wobbly with relief and had to sit down on the stool behind the counter. 'Really? She's actually okay? Thank goodness.'

'She's absolutely fine. A bit groggy, but that's normal. They are saying it went well but we won't know for sure for a while...'

'When can she come home?'

'They want to keep her for a few more hours, but assuming everything stays stable, she'll be back later. I'm going with Piers to collect her and bring her back to mine for the night, just so someone's keeping an eye on her.'

'I'll come over as soon as I close the shop.'

'See you later.'

After Annabelle rang off, Daisy found that the relief was almost as overwhelming as the worry had been. She sat behind the counter for several minutes, just breathing and letting the news settle into her bones. Maggie was okay. It had gone well. In a few hours, she'd be at Annabelle's house, probably complaining about being fussed over and insisting she was perfectly capable of looking after herself. Daisy felt sick as waves of relief washed over her. Her big sister was going to be okay.

By six o'clock, Daisy was standing outside Annabelle's front door with the tin of biscuits in one hand and a bag of books she thought Maggie might like in the other. She'd closed the shop early, collected the twins from Susannah's house, and driven over with a mixture of relief and nervous energy that made her feel slightly lightheaded.

Annabelle answered the door with a finger pressed to her lips. 'She's just dropped off on the sofa. The painkillers are making her drowsy, which is probably good.'

The twins tiptoed through the hallway with exaggerated care, clearly having been briefed about the need to be quiet around recovering patients. They settled themselves at the kitchen table with colouring books while Daisy followed Annabelle through to the sitting room where Maggie was curled up on the sofa under a cashmere throw. The bandage around her head was large and stark white against her pale skin and secured with what appeared to be enough tape to package a small parcel. She looked smaller than usual, more fragile, but she was breathing steadily and her colour was better than Daisy had expected.

'How has she been?' Daisy whispered.

'Grumpy, mostly, which is a good sign. She's annoyed that she can't wash her hair and annoyed that I won't let her answer work emails. They said there were no complications, everything exactly as they'd hoped. They've sent the tissue off for analysis, but she seemed confident that they'd got it all.'

'How long until we get the results?'

'Not sure. But she said that was really just a formality at this point. The important thing was removing it completely, which they've done.'

Maggie stirred on the sofa and opened her eyes, blinking slowly as she focused on Daisy. 'There you are. Have you been watching me sleep like some sort of creepy stalker?'

'Only for a few minutes. How are you feeling?'

'Like someone's removed part of my head, surprisingly enough.' Maggie struggled to sit up, wincing slightly as the movement made her dizzy. 'Did Bells tell you it all went according to plan? Boring, routine procedure with a boring, routine outcome.'

'She did. I'm so relieved I could cry.'

'Please don't cry. I've had enough drama for one day. Did you bring the twins? I can hear them plotting something in the kitchen.'

'They're colouring very quietly and being incredibly well-behaved. They wanted to make you a get-well card, but I told them to wait until your headache was better.'

'Headache's not too bad, actually. The painkillers are doing their job. I mainly feel woolly-headed and frustrated that I can't do anything useful.'

'You're not supposed to do anything useful. What did they say about the bandage?'

'It comes off in a few days. Then I'll have stitches for another week or so, and after that just a small scar that should fade over time. They showed me photographs of other patients and you can barely see the scars once they've healed completely.'

Daisy reached over and squeezed Maggie's hand. 'I'm so glad it's over.'

'Me too.'

The twins appeared in the doorway, clearly having reached the limit of their patience with quiet colouring. Evie was clutching a piece of paper covered in rainbow-coloured hearts, and Margot had what appeared to be a detailed drawing of a person with an enormous bandage around their head.

'We made you pictures,' Evie announced, climbing carefully onto the sofa next to Maggie. 'This one has hearts because hearts make people better.'

'And this one is you in your special head bandage,' Margot added, holding up her artwork for inspection. 'I made the bandage really big.'

Maggie examined both pictures with appropriate seriousness. 'These are exactly what I needed. Thank you very much.

Shall we put them on the mantelpiece so everyone can see them?'

As the twins arranged their artwork and settled down to tell Maggie about their day, Daisy felt the last of her worry begin to dissolve. Maggie was pale and tired, but she was unmistakably herself. It was over, the recovery had begun, and soon they would know for certain that the threat had been removed completely. It would take time for things to feel completely normal again, but sitting in Annabelle's comfortable sitting room with her sisters and daughters around her, Daisy hoped that the worst was behind them. Time would tell.

20

Daisy frowned as she looked at the screenshot on her phone. A message from Miles showed an image of a house and an email address. Right away Daisy knew the whereabouts of the house in Pretty Beach. Mile's accompanying text said it was in the Old Town and she knew precisely where it was. The house, four storey, Victorian and very beautiful was about halfway from the bookshop to Susannah's house and Daisy calculated that she would have walked past it thousands of times over the years.

Daisy: *Where did you get this from? Is it for sale?????*

Miles: *Shane Pence messaged me. He says it's not going to market officially until next week but wanted to give me a heads up.*

Daisy: *Shane Pence? How does he even know you're looking?*

Miles: *I went in there when I first mentioned it to you when the New York thing came up and then I saw him when I went for a drink with Luke last week. He said he'd keep an eye out for anything suitable in the Old Town.*

Daisy: *You registered with him?*

Miles: *Not registered exactly. Just had a chat when I bumped into him at the pub. Very casual.*

Daisy: *This is the first I'm hearing about Shane Pence and casual chats about house hunting.*

Miles: *Sorry. I thought I'd mentioned it. It was just one of those conversations that happen in Pretty Beach. You know how it is.*

Daisy: *I know how Shane is. Locals Only working.*

Miles: *He said he'd keep his ear to the ground. He'd heard about the one Julie said about but thought it might be a while. He said he would message me when one came up. Which it has.*

Daisy: *It does look nice from the outside. Very Old Town.*

Miles: *Four bedrooms, big garden, original features. Everything we talked about. There's an annexe in the old stables at the back.*

Daisy: *Sounds just right.*

Miles: *He's going away tomorrow for a few days, so wants to show it today if we're interested.*

Daisy: *Today! That's very short notice.*

Miles: *He thinks there'll be a lot of interest once it goes public. Wants to give us a first look before he goes away.*

Daisy: *I'm still processing everything we talked about. Now there's an actual house to look at today!*

Miles: *We don't have to if you're not ready. But Shane seemed to think it would go quickly.*

Daisy: *It will. What time?*

Miles: *He can do two o'clock if that works. Before the afternoon gets away from us.*

Daisy: *Two today?*

Miles: *I know it's quick, but he seemed keen to show us before anyone else gets wind of it.*

Daisy: *OK*

Miles: *No pressure. We're just looking. Getting a feel for what's available.*

Daisy: *Just looking.*

Miles: *What do you think?*

Daisy: *I think Shane Pence has very good timing. Fine. Two o'clock.*

Daisy scrolled through her contacts and found Shane's number. She'd known him since school and figured she might as well get the details straight from the horse's mouth.

'Shane Pence Properties, Shane speaking.'

'Shaney, Daise, how are you?'

'Daise! I'm well, thanks. I wondered if you might call, actually. Miles said you two were interested in having a look at the Old Town place.'

Daisy raised her eyebrows. First she'd heard of it. She was now looking at houses in the Old Town, was she? 'I have to say I'm surprised there's a house for sale down there. I walk past that road all the time and haven't noticed any for sale signs.'

'That's because there isn't one up yet and there won't be, most likely. The owners went to Canada last month and only just decided to sell. I literally got the call the other day.'

'Canada? Who was it?'

'The Harringtons. You probably don't know them. They moved to Pretty Beach about five years ago from London. Retired early and thought they'd love the seaside life.'

'And they didn't? Did Holly and Xian take a disliking? Ha.'

'They did for a while, but their daughter emigrated to Vancouver and they've got grandchildren they've never met. They decided life's too short to be on the wrong side of the Atlantic.'

Daisy could understand that. 'So they've already gone?'

'Yes. The house has been empty, which is why I thought you and Miles might want a quick look before I put it on the books properly. Once word gets out that there's a four-bedroom Victorian in the Old Town, I'll have people queuing round the block. It's got an annexe out the back there. You know that lane that goes down to the allotments, if you go that way? A lot of them are garages but this one has a flat which Miles said he was interested in for his mum.'

'It's definitely four bedrooms?'

'Four proper bedrooms, not converted attics or anything dodgy. You know what these Old Town houses are like. There will be competition for it. Miles said you're not in a chain?'

Daisy did know about the Old Town. It was the most sought-after part of Pretty Beach, with narrow cobbled streets and houses that had been part of the woodwork since Victorian times. Most of them never came on the market because they stayed in families for generations.

'What sort of price are we talking, Shane?'

Shane was elusive. 'Well, that's the thing. The Harringtons want a quick sale. They don't want the hassle of a long, drawn-out process. I think there might be room for negotiation, but don't quote me on it.'

'Room for negotiation usually means expensive to start with.'

Shane chuckled. 'It's not cheap, Daise. I won't pretend it is, but it's not silly money either. Not for what you get.'

'Which is?'

'Four beds, two baths, original fireplaces, high ceilings, big kitchen overlooking the garden and the garden's lovely. A proper walled garden with fruit trees and a little greenhouse. The sort of place you could really make a home.'

Daisy felt a flutter of excitement despite herself. 'It sounds nice.'

'It is nice. You're coming today? If it's not for you, fair enough. If it is, we can talk numbers.'

'Miles said two o'clock?'

'Correct. I'm flying off to Paris tomorrow morning for a few days, so today's the only chance I've got. After that, it'll have to wait until I'm back. Once it's all over the internet, I'll have half of London wanting to view it.'

'Two o'clock it is.'

'Brilliant. You know where it is?'

'I think so. Halfway down towards Mum's house?'

'That's the one. Number forty-two. Green front door, wisteria over the porch.'

'I know it. I've walked past it hundreds of times.'

'Well, now you can go inside it. See you at two, Daise.'

21

At two o'clock precisely, Daisy and Miles stood outside number forty-two and waited for Shane to arrive. The house looked exactly as Daisy remembered it from her countless walks over the years; a solid Victorian terrace with the green front door Shane had mentioned and a gigantic twist of wisteria that climbed over the porch. Talk about nice. A few wisteria leaves had dropped onto the path below in little scattered piles that crunched underfoot. Daisy had walked past the house thousands of times: in her youth, on her way to visit her mum, sometimes with the twins in their pushchair when they were tiny, sometimes rushing to catch the ferry on her way to school, sometimes just wandering through the Old Town because she loved the narrow streets and the way the houses leaned in towards each other like old friends.

Shane, suited and booted, pulled up in a silver estate car and bounded out of the driver's door with a lot of energy, his phone in one hand and a folder of papers in the other. 'Hello! Hi, Daise. How are you? I bumped into Bells the other day.'

'Good, thanks. Hi Shaney.'

Miles held out his hand and shook Shane's 'Hey.'

'Right then, ready for the grand tour? I've got to say, you're in for a treat with this one.'

'Hope so.' Daisy felt very odd, as if she was getting ideas above her station.

Shane unlocked the front door with a key that looked almost as old as the house itself and they stepped into a wide hallway that immediately made Daisy feel teeny-tiny. She swallowed at what looked back at her. Put it this way: she was a very long way from the new estate with the entrance hallway not much bigger than a postage stamp. Slightly worn parquet flooring appeared as if generations of feet had walked from the front door to the staircase. Daisy looked down at the intricate pattern, all little wooden blocks fitted together like a puzzle and wondered how long it would take to clean it properly. Immediately pushing that thought to the back of her mind, she stood and took everything in. The wallpaper felt as if it was dancing in front of her eyes; whoever had chosen it had perhaps been drunk or drugged or both. A mess of deep pink wallpaper roses looked like they had been there since the nineteen-eighties. A grandfather clock stood silent in the corner next to a carved wooden chair that probably weighed more than Daisy's car and looked like it belonged in a museum.

Shane gestured around the hallway, 'It's all in good condition, but as you can see, it's dated. A real lived-in feel, bags of character and all the original features you could want.' Shane pointed upwards. 'Look at that ceiling rose, you don't see craftsmanship like that in the new builds, which is why the Old Town is so tightly held.'

Character was one way of putting it, Daisy thought as she craned her neck to look at the elaborate plasterwork above their heads. It was beautiful, slightly intimidating and took her a little bit by surprise. It was almost as if, as they'd stepped in, they'd been wrapped in insulation as the old house's walls muffled everything. So quiet and solid as if the house was quite happy in its job of standing tall, solid and straight and would be for years. Daisy tried to imagine Margot and Evie charging around like a couple of fairy elephants. Sobering, quite frankly.

'Shall we start with the main reception rooms?' Shane opened a door on the left. 'This is the sitting room, the heart of the house really, if you ask me.'

The room reminded Daisy a little bit of Susannah's sitting room and the house she'd grown up in. To say it wasn't small was an understatement and the space, compared to what she had at the bookshop, seemed to stretch on forever. A bay window that looked out over a garden, a large fireplace dominated one wall, all carved wood and green tiles, with a mirror above it that reflected the room back at itself and made it seem even bigger than it already was. Built-in bookcases flanked the fireplace, and Daisy felt as if she were losing her shoes on a deep red carpet; it showed every footprint and furniture mark, as if it were keeping a record of everyone who had ever walked across it. The furniture looked like it belonged in a country house hotel rather than a family home; sofas arranged at just-so angles, side tables positioned perfectly, everything coordinated and matching in a way that suggested professional interior design rather than the gradual accumulation of things that actually happened in real life. They were far removed from Daisy's slightly boho, little bit eclectic, cobbled together style.

Miles walked to the bay window and looked out at the garden. 'Right. It's a bit bigger than I expected from what you said in your messages.'

'Yeah, these old places are massive. This is just the main sitting room. There's a dining room that seats twelve, a morning room that gets the best light, and what the Harringtons used as a study, but you could turn it into anything, really. Games room, library, home office, whatever takes your fancy. I'd snap this up if I had the finances.'

Course you would, Daisy thought as she walked to the window and stood next to Miles. A lovely but quite overgrown garden with fruit trees that looked heavy with apples and pears, and a tumbledown greenhouse looked back at her. Shane pointed to a lovely shed tucked into the far corner. 'The garden's lovely. South facing.'

'Works for me.'

'The back beds are full of herbs and there's a vegetable patch around the side. Plenty of space for children to run about.'

Daisy laughed. 'Shaney, you don't need to sell it to me.'

'Ha, sorry, Daise. Occupational hazard.'

'I went to school with you lot. I know what you're really like.' Daisy tried to imagine Margot and Evie in the house, with their school bags and art projects and the general chaos that followed them everywhere they went. It was hard to picture them in the midst of the careful ornaments, arrangements and the museum-quality furniture.

'Shall we see the dining room? It's through here, a formal dining room with original coving.'

The dining room was a long way from Daisy's current dining situation involving her table wedged into the corner of her tiny kitchen. With a table that could seat an entire cricket team, high-back chairs looked as if they'd never been sat on. A deep green on the walls made the room feel old-fashioned and formal, and there were oil paintings of stern-faced people to watch you as you ate.

'Bit grand for fish fingers and chips,' Miles said under his breath.

Daisy giggled and tried to imagine making the room family-friendly and failed completely. The whole space oozed potential; it just needed to move a tad left of field from imposing. Daisy couldn't picture the twins doing their homework at the table or herself sitting down with a cup of tea and a packet of biscuits after a long day in the bookshop. They continued to walk around. The morning room, because of course every house has one of those, was slightly less formal, with windows on two sides that filled it with light and made it feel more welcoming than the dining room. The furniture was lighter, more comfortable, though still arranged with the sort of precision that suggested the Harringtons had lived very ordered lives. A study was tucked away at the back, smaller than the other rooms but still bigger than most people's entire flats. It had built-in shelves, a desk under a large window, and French doors that opened onto a small terrace overlooking the garden. The room felt more lived-in than the others and Daisy immediately imagined lighting its tiny fire and making it cosy.

'Right then,' Shane said as they finished the tour of the ground floor, 'shall we head upstairs? The bedrooms have Victorian proportions, the likes of which I don't often see.'

The staircase was a work of art in itself, all carved wood and elegant curves, with a bannister that had clearly been polished for generations. The first bedroom had soft green walls and windows that looked out over the street. The room was enormous, with a fireplace and built-in wardrobes that could hold more clothes than Daisy had ever owned in her entire life. The size of it to Daisy was of little to no interest; the tall skirtings, clad walls, French doors and balcony were.

'It's very big.' Daisy chuckled as she realised she'd just made the understatement of the century. Everything about the house was big: the rooms, the windows, the ceilings. She felt dwarfed by the scale of it, as if she were a child playing dress-up in grown-up clothes that were several sizes too large.

On and on it went. Bathrooms were next, one with a bathtub the size of a small swimming pool and a separate shower room that the Harringtons had added during their renovations. Everything was spotless and very dated, as if no one had ever actually had a bath there or brushed their teeth at a sink. Up another set of stairs to the attic rooms, where Shane opened the door to a room completely painted in blue with cosy sloped ceilings, a skylight that filled the space with natural light, and one wall covered with framed photographs and prints. The desk was immaculately arranged; pens in a pot and a stack of notebooks next to a computer screen and shelves full of books.

They made their way back downstairs, had a look at the kitchen and then stood in the hallway again, surrounded by polished wood and the rose wallpaper. The grandfather clock seemed to be looking at Daisy, and to be fair, she was quite overwhelmed.

'What do you think?' Miles asked.

Daisy looked around at the parquet floor and the roses on the wallpaper and the grandfather clock that would probably cost more to repair than she spent on groceries in a month. It was beautiful, undeniably, but it was a world away from the cosy chaos of the flat above the bookshop. She tried to imagine the twins thundering down the elegant staircase, or herself padding to the kitchen in her slippers and dressing gown, or Miles working at his laptop on the dining room table. 'It's certainly something. I'm a bit overwhelmed.'

Shane nodded. 'These places do that to you. You know that, Daise. You've lived in one for most of your life. Your mum's house is gorgeous. Houses like this don't come up very often in the Old Town. You could do wonderful things here.'

Wonderful things, indeed, or I could stay where I am, Daisy thought.

'The garden's really lovely. Very private. No one can see in, and it gets sun all day long.'

Miles touched the bannister. 'It needs a fair bit of updating. The decor...'

'Yep, true, but structurally, nothing at all and it had a full survey done three years ago and everything's sound. New roof, rewiring, the lot. It's more a question of decoration, really. Whether you want to keep things as they are or put your own stamp on it.'

Daisy looked around at the formal furniture, the swag and tail curtains and the coordinated colour schemes and tried to imagine what it would look like with Annabelle's touch. Annabelle would be all over it like a rash, given half the chance.

Miles asked about a price and Shane named a figure that made Daisy's stomach lurch. She had to stop herself from falling flat on her back and laughing out loud. It wasn't astronomical, not for a house of its size in the Old Town, but it was more money than she'd ever imagined having anything to do with. It was the sort of money that came with mortgages that lasted decades, ginormous monthly payments and a whole lot of commitment.

Shane lowered his voice. 'That's negotiable, mind you. They want a quick sale, and they're prepared to be flexible for the right buyers. Cash buyers, especially.'

Daisy wondered what constituted the right buyers. She thought about her little bookshop with its wonky shelves and mismatched furniture, about the twins with their muddy shoes and sticky fingers, about the long line of rental properties she'd lived in since having them. She rolled her eyes at anyone being able to buy the place cash.

'I have to tell you, once it goes on the market properly, there'll be a lot of interest. The Old Town doesn't give up its secrets very often.'

Miles cut straight to the chase 'Will they take an offer for cash?'

Daisy had to stop her chin from dropping to the floor. She fell so much more in love. Not that she was impressed by money or what it could buy. Of course not.

Shane nodded. 'I could try.'

'When do you need to know?' Miles asked.

'Well, I'm back from my break at the beginning of next week, so that gives you the weekend to think it over.'

'Yep.'

Daisy couldn't wrap her head around anything. Mile's voice told her that he was prepared to move quickly and go ahead with her or without. They hadn't even discussed it.

Shane lowered his voice. 'Look, between you and me, I'll just keep this quiet and let you think about it. A few days won't make a whole lot of difference. Once this place hits Rightmove, I'll be fighting off the enquiries. I'll tell the Harringtons the listing was delayed for a bit. If we're talking about the possibility of a cash buyer not in a chain, it will be a deal breaker.'

Miles nodded as if it were nothing to him. As if he were doing a deal like the ones Daisy often heard him discuss on video calls all day long. Almost like he was negotiating the price of his lunch. Daisy walked out of the front door in a daze. Who would have thought? Her world, which was already spinning, went a little bit faster as someone up above tapped it on the top and gave it a good old further spin.

22

The things going on in Daisy's head had reached dizzying amounts. It was funny really, she'd gone from the road in front of her being quite boring apart from it being fraught with financial worries to a road which was throwing left forks and right turns her way willy-nilly. Despite the lurching this way and that, she knew which road she preferred, although she definitely did not like the bump in the road that had come with what was going on with Maggie.

It was strange to have something not right with Maggie. As far as Daisy was concerned, Maggie had just always been there; solid, reliable, determined, straight to the point and had always, always, always had Daisy's back. It had been that way for the whole of Daisy's life and that had now changed. Every single little thing that had gone on in Daisy's life, including the bungee jump, going to uni, the bookshop, having the twins, through all of it, Maggie had been there, standing in the wings, backing Daisy up, and now it seemed that Maggie and her wings were wobbling. Something had knocked one of the Henley girls for six, upended their secure unit and didn't Daisy know about it. Just the thought of it made a horrible, panicky feeling swirl in

Daisy's stomach, and all sorts ran through her head, none of which she wanted to contemplate.

As she climbed the stairs to the flat above the bookshop, in contrast to her brain, the building was quiet. The old walls almost sighed out as if they had settled into the final part of their day. The twins had been asleep for over an hour and the only sounds were a few creaks and knocks here and there of the old timber as it tucked itself up for the night. Daisy paused on the small landing and looked through the gap in the bedroom door. For a second or two, she just stared and smiled; both girls were fast asleep, Margot with her arm flung over her pillow and Evie curled up like a cat with her duvet pulled right up to her chin. Clean school uniforms were folded neatly on the chair, ready for the morning rush and their little mushroom night light glowed from the corner. Safe, tight, sweet, loved. It flashed through Daisy's mind that it must have been what she, Annabelle and Maggie had looked like when they were the same age as Margot and Evie. Then they were safe. Now, not so much. Life had changed that in more ways than one.

Tiptoeing past their room, she headed to the bathroom, having earmarked a very long, very quiet, very self-indulgent bath with nothing except decompressing in mind and perhaps a read of her book. Turning on the taps, she poured in a long stream of fancy bath oil donated to her by Annabelle and undressed as she watched water cascade into the old enamel tub, the sound echoing off the tiles. Steam began to rise and fog the glass and as the bath filled, Daisy sat on the edge of the tub in the dim light and tried to think rationally about Maggie. The procedure was over and it had gone well and that was the end of it, hopefully. As she hopped in the bath, she crossed her fingers that it would work some or any magic. Getting into a deep, hot bath had delivered in the past many a time; upset, have a bath, celebrating, have a bath, tired, have a bath, panicking, have a bath and repeat ad infinitum.

Settling in, Daisy sighed as her brain fizzed. Once upon a time, nearly the only thing in her head had been getting through the night with twins; after that, it was swiftly replaced by worry about finance. Now there was so much more and many things vying for her attention: the nomination, Maggie, New York, the Old Town house, the filming request and everything else that seemed to be spinning faster than she could keep up with.

About ten minutes into her bath, her phone, which was on silent, lit up beside her. She frowned to see Maggie's name going across her screen.

'Yeah, they didn't get everything.'

'Sorry, what do you mean?'

'It's a bit deeper than they thought. They said that might be the case all along.'

'What do you mean they didn't *get* everything?' Daisy's voice sounded tiny and she gripped the edge of the bath as if somehow that might help her. It so did not help.

'They found more when they were in there. It's spread a bit further. Nothing dramatic, but they need to go back in and get the rest of it out.'

Daisy closed her eyes and tried to keep her voice steady. 'When?'

'They want to do it as soon as possible. Get it all sorted properly this time.'

'Right.' Daisy swallowed hard and forced herself to sound calm and practical rather than terrified. 'That's good then. Better to be thorough.'

'That's what I said. No point messing about with it.'

There was a pause and Daisy could hear Maggie's television in the background, some cooking programme. Jamie Oliver. The normality of it made everything feel more surreal. 'Are you okay?'

'I'm fine. It's all very routine. Just a case of finishing the job properly.'

'I thought she said they'd got it all. How long?'

'It's still completely routine. Depends how it goes.'

Daisy felt tears prick at her eyes and was grateful that Maggie couldn't see her face. Maggie'd been the strong one for so long, the one who sorted things out and didn't panic, now the tables had turned and Daisy was struggling. The news felt bigger than anything she knew how to handle. Also, she didn't *want* to handle it. Selfish old Daisy? Perhaps, perhaps, perhaps.

'Daise? Are you still there?'

'Yes, sorry. I'm here.'

'Look, I've spoken to Mum and Bells. We're all going round to Annabelle's tomorrow evening for supper. We can then talk it all through properly. Are you free?'

Daisy wanted to scream. 'Of course I'm free.'

'Good. I want to get everything straight before I go in. Make sure everyone knows what's what and that there isn't any drama.'

'There won't be any drama.'

'There will if Mum starts carrying on. You know what she's like when she gets worried.'

Daisy did know. Susannah's way of dealing with worry was to spring into action, usually involving elaborate meal planning and a need to reorganise everyone's lives. It came from a good place, but it could be overwhelming when what you really wanted was to be left alone to process things. 'We'll keep her calm.' Daisy did not feel calm. She didn't want to be calm. She hated having to be calm. Being calm felt all sorts of wrong.

'Will we, though?' Maggie laughed. 'She'll have me eating seventeen different types of soup and taking enough vitamins to stock a chemist.'

Despite everything, Daisy smiled. 'The soup will be good, though.'

'The soup will be revolting. That green one with all the bits in it nearly finished me off before.'

'I'll talk to her and make sure she doesn't go overboard.'

'Thanks. And Daise?'

'Yes?'

'Don't you start going all weird on me either. I need you to be normal, not all worried and treating me like I'm made of glass.'

'I won't.'

'Promise?'

'I promise.' But even as she said it, Daisy knew it was a lie. How could she be normal when her big sister, the one who'd always been the strongest of all of them, was facing something that might change everything? How could she pretend not to be scared when the thought of losing Maggie made her feel like the ground was shifting under her feet? She would have to suck it up, though. A big, old, deep, fat line in the sand had just been drawn and Daisy Henley was adamant that even if it killed her, she would step up to it.

'Right then. I'll see you tomorrow at Annabelle's, about seven, she said.'

'See you then.'

'We'll get it all out in the open rather than having separate conversations with everyone. The twins will keep everyone distracted if things get too heavy.'

After Maggie hung up, Daisy sat in the cooling bath water and let the tears come. Oh, how those tears poured, my friends. Blub, blub, blub and blubbing some more. There may have been an amateur dramatics switch flicked on. One of the Henley girls booed indeed. She cried for her sister, for the unfairness of it all, for the way life seemed determined to throw complications just when things had started to feel settled. She cried for her mum, having to go through it. She pretty much bawled until she felt empty and exhausted.

Then, feeling as if there was not a single tear, sob or strange wail left, Daisy got out of the bath and wrapped herself in an old baby towel that was soft from years of washing. Gritting her teeth, she nodded as she thought about the line she'd be stepping up to. Daisy decided to be strong and not to be defeated. She would have to be brave and normal and everything Maggie needed her to be. Right there, though, sitting in a towel with cute pink bunnies on it, she allowed herself to be scared. Very, very scared, indeed.

23

As soon as Daisy walked into Annabelle's kitchen, she could feel the tension in the air. Annabelle looked at her and made a secret slitting motion with her finger across her throat, took a glass down from a floating shelf and poured Daisy some wine. Daisy had just come down from upstairs, putting the twins to bed. Piers was sitting on the sofa near the fireplace with a concerned look, Susannah's face looked like thunder and Maggie was perched at the kitchen island with a glass of wine in her hand and was shaking her head.

Maggie's voice was oddly hesitant. 'Mum, you see this is what I don't want. Do. Not. Fuss. It's nothing and I am fine. I've told you this over and over.'

Annabelle interrupted. 'Mags, sorry, but you are *not* fine. You're about to have your scalp operated on. Again!'

Maggie narrowed her eyes and bit back. 'Don't call me Mags.'

Daisy sighed heavily. She felt as if the conversation alone was causing her pain. It was clearly the same for Susannah and Annabelle. Maggie continued on. 'It's not that major.'

'For God's sake, Maggie! It's horrendous. I'm not going to sit here and continue playing this charade with you! Honestly!' Susannah raised her voice and all three of her daughters stopped. Susannah rarely got cross, but when she did, people stood to attention.

The kitchen went silent except for the hum of the Aga and Piers shifting on the sofa. Daisy took a large gulp of wine and wondered how they'd got to this point so quickly. Ten minutes before, she'd been upstairs reading the twins a bedtime story about a mouse who lived in a teapot and now she was standing in the middle of what felt like a family crisis. If there was one thing about the other Henley women, it was that they were strong alpha characters. All of them stubborn, all of them dynamic, all of them wanting so very much to get their own way. All of them emotional and scared.

Susannah stood by the window with her arms folded and her jaw set. Daisy kept her mouth shut. When Susannah did a funny pursed lip thing at the same time as she shook her head, it meant that she was way past the point of diplomatic conversation. She'd clearly been holding back her feelings about Maggie's situation and had reached the end of her patience with pretending everything was normal. Her hair was messed up where she'd been running her hands through it, and there were spots of colour on her cheeks that appeared when she was upset or angry.

Maggie had taken note and sounded less defiant, but not much. 'I know you're worried, but getting worked up about it isn't going to help anyone and I don't want this.'

Susannah snapped and did not look impressed. 'I'm not getting worked up! I'm being realistic about what's happening to my daughter. There's a huge difference. You are being unreasonable, expecting us to go along with this parody that you're fine!'

Annabelle moved around the kitchen island and stood next to Daisy and attempted to look calm. She picked up the wine bottle and topped up everyone's glasses as if they were going to need fortification for whatever was coming next. Annabelle put on her tactful voice. 'Perhaps we should all sit down and talk about this.'

Maggie raised her voice. 'No, Bells! Not that voice. God help us all if you're going to start doing that. Mum's having a panic attack and I'm trying to talk her down from it.'

'I am not having a panic attack!' Susannah's voice pitched higher. 'I'm having a perfectly reasonable reaction to being told that my daughter needs brain surgery!'

Maggie slammed her wine glass down on the marble worktop. 'Now you're being dramatic! It's scalp surgery. There's a huge difference. Where did you get brain surgery from?'

Susannah didn't look best pleased. 'You see, that's precisely what I mean. From where I'm sitting, it all sounds bone-chilling. If there is one thing this family has always had, it's our health, and now look. To be honest, girls, I don't know what to do or think, which is also throwing me. I just don't want this to be happening.'

Daisy felt caught between wanting to support her mum and wanting to respect Maggie's obvious desire not to be treated like an invalid. She'd been in the position before with her family, trying to mediate between different approaches to handling crisis, and it never ended well for anyone involved. Piers, clearly having similar thoughts, got up and put his arm around Susannah's shoulders.

'Maybe we should listen to what Maggie actually wants to tell us,' Daisy suggested carefully.

Maggie closed her eyes, tutted and shook her head. 'Thank you. That's exactly what I've been trying to say.'

Susannah fixed Daisy with a look that could have stripped paint. 'And what exactly does Maggie want to tell us? That we should all pretend this isn't happening? That we should act like it's perfectly normal for one of my children to need surgery on her head? Nope, I am not doing that.'

'I want to tell you that I'm handling it. That I've got good doctors, that the prognosis is excellent and that I don't need everyone falling apart around me. I am allowed to handle this exactly as I want to.' Maggie stated.

'Who's falling apart?' Susannah demanded. 'I'm not falling apart. I'm being a mother.'

'You're being a mother who's making this harder than it needs to be.'

Piers patted Susannah's back and cleared his throat as if he was considering saying something diplomatic, then clearly thought better of it and reached for his beer instead.

Annabelle walked to the other side of the kitchen and took a dish of halloumi out of the Aga and slid it into the middle of the island. She then opened a jar of fig compote, decanted it into a dish and popped it next to the haloumi. 'Right, everyone take a breath. We're all on the same side here.'

Maggie reached for a piece of halloumi. 'I can manage my own medical treatment.'

Susannah nodded 'You're trying to be brave about something terrifying, and I'm not going to apologise for being frightened,' Susannah's voice cracked slightly on the last word and Daisy felt her heart contract. 'Let me tell you girls: I'm worried.'

Maggie softened. 'I'm not frightened and this isn't helping. The surgeon is going to cut it out of my scalp and it will be gone. The end. Honestly, she said it was as simple as that. It's just that the first effort missed a bit.'

Susannah took a fork from the top of a napkin, speared it into a piece of halloumi, changed her mind and put it down again. 'I can't eat. Tell me what would help and I'll do it.'

Maggie rolled her eyes and started laughing. 'Stop looking at me like I'm dying would be a start.'

'I'm not...'

'You've been looking at me weirdly ever since I told you about the first procedure and it's making me feel as if this is much worse than it is.'

Susannah's face crumpled. 'I'm sorry. I just don't like this.'

'Every time you ask me how I'm feeling or whether I need anything, you get this look on your face like you're already grieving for me.'

'I just want to help. It's always been the same where you three are involved. I want you to be okay. I wish it were me who had this, not you. I'd rather just go through it myself.'

'I know. But the best way to help me right now is to treat me like I'm still the same person I was before we found this thing. Not like I'm made of ice or something.'

Daisy sipped her wine, wished that Miles wasn't in London and tried to process what was happening. She'd been so focused on her own worry about Maggie that she hadn't considered how exhausting it must be for Maggie to manage everyone else's reactions on top of her own fear. It was the same dynamic she'd fallen into when the twins were born and everyone had wanted to help, but their help had often felt more like additional responsibility. Sometimes in the early days, she would have preferred to have been left alone and to get on with things on her own.

Annabelle bustled around the kitchen. 'What do you need from us? Practically, I mean. What would actually be useful?'

Maggie considered the question for a moment. 'I need you to stop acting like this is the end of the world. I need you to still get annoyed with me when I'm being difficult instead of treating every conversation like, well, you know. It's not helping. At all.'

Daisy wasn't entirely sure how she was going to stop the worry from showing on her face. 'We can do that.'

Maggie made a face. 'Yesterday I got a box with seventeen

different types of herbal tea and a selection of organic soups that probably cost more than most people spend on food in a month.'

'Who from?'

Susannah looked slightly sheepish. 'I thought you might need organic nutrition.'

'I need normal.' Maggie was adamant.

'Point taken,' Annabelle said. 'No more care packages. No more special treatment. No more walking on eggshells. We'll go back to being horrible to you. I much prefer it that way, anyway.'

Daisy chuckled. 'Me too.'

'I know you've been talking about this among yourselves because you all get this look when I walk into a room, like you've just stopped discussing something important.'

Daisy felt heat creep up her neck because that was exactly what had been happening. She'd spent hours on the phone with Annabelle and her mum discussing Maggie's situation, trying to work out how best to support her, without actually asking Maggie what kind of support she wanted. 'We were trying to work out how to help.'

'I know. But it makes me feel like I'm a problem to be solved rather than a person who's dealing with something difficult.'

'It's fair enough.' Piers said from the sofa. 'It makes sense that you don't want to be treated differently. We'll all go back to taking the Michael out of you.'

'At least someone gets it.'

Susannah shook her head and her voice faltered. 'I just love you so much and the thought of anything happening to you makes me feel completely helpless. I literally feel as if someone has pulled the rug out from under me and I'm flat on my back wondering what the hell is happening.'

'Nothing's going to happen to me. The surgery is routine, the recovery is straightforward, and in six months this will all be a story we tell about how we overreacted to a minor medical procedure.'

'Is it really that minor?'

'It's really that minor. The surgeon does three or four of these procedures every week. For her, it's like changing a tyre. For me, it's slightly more significant than that, but it's still not exactly life-threatening.'

'But they have to take some of your scalp,' Annabelle said, and Daisy could hear the same fear in her voice that had been in Susannah's.

'They do and then they close it up again and I go home with some painkillers and instructions to take it easy for a few weeks. It's not pleasant, but it's not dangerous either. Let me tell you now. If I mention needing a bit of help and you immediately start planning military-style logistics, I will kill you. I don't need a rota or anything like that. I might need one of you to pop round to make sure I haven't run out of milk.'

'No rota. This is just something that needs doing, so we're going to do it and then move on.'

The conversation continued for another hour as they worked through the practical details of Maggie's surgery and recovery. Who would drive her to the hospital, who would pick her up, what each of them would and wouldn't do. By the time they'd finished talking, the tension in the room had dissipated considerably. Susannah had stopped looking like she was attending a wake, Annabelle had put away her tendency to organise everyone's life, and Daisy felt a smidgeon less stressed. Not that she was happy about it because she most definitely wasn't, but she felt slightly better.

Maggie topped up her wine. 'Now that we've got that sorted, can we please talk about something else? I'm sick of it, to be frank.'

'What do you want to talk about?' Annabelle asked.

'Daisy's house viewing would be good. I want to hear all about this Victorian mansion Miles is trying to talk you into buying. I mean, because yeah, we all assumed that was going to happen in Daisy's life. In fact, not that long ago, we were sitting around this very table before that wedding and you were not in a good place, Daise.'

Daisy felt all eyes turn to her and realised she'd been so focused on Maggie's situation that she'd completely forgotten about the house viewing. It felt like it had happened weeks before and she wasn't sure she had the energy to process another major life decision. 'It was interesting.'

'Interesting good or interesting bad?' Susannah asked.

'Interesting complicated. It's a beautiful house, but it's also, I don't know, overwhelming.'

'Did you like it?' Maggie asked.

'I did, but it represents a big change for Miles and me...'

'That's not necessarily a bad thing,' Annabelle said. 'Sometimes a change of surroundings can be exactly what you need.'

'Maybe. But it might also be exactly what I *don't* need. I love the flat above the bookshop. It feels like home in a way nowhere else ever has.'

'You could make the house feel like home, too,' Piers said. 'It just takes time.'

'What does Miles think?'

'He's keen. Shane reckons it will get snapped up if Miles, I mean, we, I think, don't go for it.'

Piers nodded. 'In a heartbeat. That won't be on the internet more than a day.'

'Do the twins know?'

'God no! I haven't even decided!'

'They'll have opinions.'

'They definitely will.'

Daisy sighed. She was no closer to knowing what the right choice was than she had been when Shane had first sent Miles the listing.

'So, if you decide to move in with him and you want to buy it, how will that work?'

Daisy raised her eyebrows. 'I think he's decided to buy it with or without me.'

'Oh.'

'Wow.'

'I know.'

'How long do you have to decide?' Susannah asked.

'Shaney wants an answer sooner rather than later. He's going away and thinks there'll be a lot of interest once it goes on the market properly.'

'That's not very long.'

'No. It feels like the sort of decision that should take months to make, but we, or rather Miles, hasn't got long.'

'Sometimes the best decisions are the ones you make quickly, before you have time to talk yourself out of them.'

'And sometimes the worst decisions are the ones you make quickly because you felt pressured.'

Maggie sipped her drink. 'True. But you'll never know which type this is until you make it.'

'Very helpful, thanks.'

'I try to be useful.' Maggie deadpanned.

Despite the stress of the evening, Daisy giggled. The banter was what she'd missed during all the worry about Maggie. Whatever else was happening, they still had each other, thankfully.

'Right, I think we've covered enough major life decisions for one evening. We need to eat.'

Maggie laughed. 'We've established that I'm not dying, Mum's not allowed to send any more care packages, and Daisy's having an existential crisis about whether a millionaire buying her a house will change her fundamental identity.'

As Daisy watched Annabelle tip a packet of designer microgreens onto a huge platter, the house decision loomed large in her mind. Deep down, she already knew what she was going to do. Problem was she hadn't yet told Miles.

24

The next morning, Daisy met Susannah at the top of the cliff path that led down to the beach. A pale grey sky promised rain at some point, but it had held off and the sea stretched out in strips of calm and silver towards the horizon. Susannah, wrapped in an old waxed jacket and walking boots good for tramping across beaches and clifftops, was already there when Daisy arrived.

Susannah kissed Daisy's cheek. 'Morning. I thought we could walk down to the point and back. Get some sea air in our lungs and clear our heads after last night. Did you hear from Bells about the girls?'

'Yes, they're fine.'

'I need a good dose of Pretty Beach air in my lungs.'

'You and me both.' Daisy nodded, though she suspected the walk had been arranged for reasons beyond fresh air and exercise. Susannah had suggested it in a text at seven that morning and Daisy was fairly sure that Susannah wanted to debrief on how Maggie was. As they made their way down a narrow path that zigzagged between gorse bushes and patches of seagrass,

Daisy smiled as they stood to the side to let a couple with a dog pass.

The path was well-worn from generations of Pretty Beach residents who'd used it to reach the beach and Daisy could navigate it with her eyes shut. She'd followed it since she'd been small enough to need her hand held, first with her mum and sisters, then later as a teenager when she'd wanted somewhere to think, and more recently with the twins when they needed to burn off energy and she needed the therapeutic sound of waves on shingle. The beach itself was empty except for a man walking a dog near the water's edge and an elderly couple sitting on the sea wall with a thermos of tea between them. The tide was out and a wide expanse of sand and pebbles crunched underfoot as they made their way towards the far end where the beach curved around the headland.

'How are you feeling about everything?' Susannah asked as they settled into the rhythm of walking together. 'Last night was quite intense.'

Daisy chose her words carefully. 'I think we all needed to hear what Maggie actually wanted from us instead of guessing and getting it wrong.'

'Probably. Though I'm not sure I'm going to find it easy to stop worrying just because she's asked me to.' Susannah rubbed her forehead. 'Between you and me, this is my worst nightmare.'

Daisy saw lines of concern around Susannah's eyes and she was more than aware that Susannah was trying to put on a brave face. The worry about Maggie was written all over her features despite her best efforts to hide it. 'You won't stop worrying. I know I won't, not until the surgery is done and the threat is gone.'

'Correct, it's harder to put into practice not worrying than anyone might think. In fact, Daise, I hate it when people say "try not to worry". What a stupid thing to say to someone when it's clear that they're worrying.'

'It's the not knowing I don't like.'

'I keep thinking about when you girls were little; when you had problems I could actually fix. A scraped knee, a nightmare, someone being mean at school. I could put a plaster on it or make you a hot chocolate or march into school and sort it out. This is so different. I feel as if someone has dropped a bomb on me and flattened my world. Trust me, I have prayed that this will just go away, when in fact, the opposite has happened. I have begged for it to be happening to me instead, then I wake up and it's still the same.'

'Their problems get bigger and your ability to fix them gets smaller. I can see it in my future. It's happening already.' Daisy understood Susannah's feelings. She'd been having the same realisation about the twins, watching them grow more independent and knowing that soon enough their problems would be beyond her ability to solve with cuddles and biscuits.

As they navigated around a patch of seaweed that had been left by the tide, the smell of salt and vegetation from dark green tangles hit Daisy's nose. She stood on a piece of seaweed until it popped.

Susannah shook her head. 'I'm worried she's not telling us how serious this really is. You know what Maggie's like. She's always been the one who doesn't want to worry anyone else. She truly hates not being top dog. What if this is worse than she's letting on and she's trying to protect us from the truth?'

'What makes you think that?'

'Just a feeling. The way she was so quick to dismiss our concerns, the way she kept saying it was routine and minor. It felt like she was trying *too* hard to convince us it wasn't a big deal.'

Daisy considered this as they walked alongside a rock pool. They stopped for a minute and peered down as it reflected the grey sky. She'd had the same thought herself, having her own little nagging worry party that Maggie was downplaying the seriousness of her situation to spare the rest of them. She'd even considered phoning the surgeon. However, she'd also seen how exhausted Maggie had become from managing everyone else's emotions on top of her own, and she wondered whether her mum's instinct was right or whether it was just the natural anxiety of someone who was used to being able to fix things. 'Did you ask her directly about whether she was telling us everything?'

'Not really. I do wonder if it's just my need to feel in control of a situation I can't actually control?'

Daisy didn't have an easy answer or any answer. They'd reached a point where the beach curved around a rocky outcrop and gave way to a smaller, more sheltered cove. The rocks were covered in mussels and barnacles, and pools of seawater caught between them reflected the sky here and there. Climbing over slippery stones, they found a flat rock to sit on that was just out of reach of the waves and for quite a while neither of them said anything at all.

'What did Piers say about it all after I went home?' Daisy asked. 'He's normally full of wisdom, but he was very quiet last night.'

'He didn't say much after you'd gone. No one did.'

'He must be worried as well.'

'I guess all we can do is wait and see how it goes. Blimey, I've certainly spent so long thinking about it, which is pointless.' Susannah sighed and picked up a piece of driftwood and turned it over in her hands and traced the grain with her finger. Daisy could see her trying not to cry. She patted her mum's leg.

'I do think she'll be fine. I've googled it, Mum. Plus, Maggie's too stubborn to let anything get the better of her.'

Despite clearly being very worried and on the point of tears, Susannah smiled. 'She is stubborn, isn't she? She always has been, even as a really tiny child. Once she'd made up her mind about something, there was no changing it. Actually, all three of you are the same. It must be a Henley thing.'

'Exactly, it runs in the family. That's where Margot gets it from. If Maggie has made up her mind that this surgery is going to be routine and straightforward, that's probably exactly what it's going to be.'

They sat watching the waves roll in and retreat, leaving foam and seaweed scattered across the sand.

Susannah changed the subject. 'Anyway, how are you coping? The award, the bookshop getting nominated, and this house business with Miles. It's for sure all come at once. You've got a lot on, Daise.'

Daisy dismissed everything on her plate. 'Ahh, I'm fine. I don't have bad problems these days, apart from Maggie's prognosis. I've got the Independent Retail Alliance coming to do that filming, so that will be interesting.'

'Gosh, I'd forgotten about that, what with everything with Maggie. It's a lot. You're so busy.'

'It's good busy though. I do keep feeling like I've got too many plates spinning that if I take my attention off any one of them for too long, everything's going to come crashing down, but yeah, I'm fine with that.'

'That's exactly how I felt when you girls were small.' Susannah nodded. 'It was like I was constantly juggling competing demands and never quite managing to get everything right. You just get on with it and struggle through.'

Daisy was surprised to hear her mum had felt the same way. 'It never felt like that to me. Did it get easier?'

'In some ways. The daily logistics got easier as you all became more independent. But the emotional side got harder. When your children are small, you can protect them from most things. When they're adults, you have to watch them face difficulties and know that your ability to help is limited.' Susannah sighed. 'Trust me, Daise, you never stop being a parent.'

'I'm starting to understand that with the twins. You just have to let them get on without you from what I've seen so far.'

'They have to learn to navigate the world on their own eventually.'

'It's tricky not to want to wrap them in cotton wool.'

'What are you going to do about the house?' Susannah asked, changing the subject to something marginally less emotionally fraught.

Daisy fibbed. She *did* know, but she hadn't yet told anyone. 'I honestly don't know. I like being the sort of person who lives above a bookshop and it just really, really suits me there, Mum. Gosh, I wouldn't say no to that house, but I'm settled where I am now. Do you know what I mean?'

'Houses are just buildings, Daise. You make them into homes by living in them the way that feels right to you. What does your gut tell you?'

Daisy's gut was currently a mess of conflicting instincts and competing desires, but underneath, she knew and she decided to tell her mum. 'My gut says maybe to stay put.'

'What does Miles think?'

'He's all in for buying it.'

'The Old Town is nice…'

'It seems like a very expensive way to find out whether we're compatible.'

The tide had turned while they'd been sitting on the rock. Small waves were now reaching closer to their feet. They stood up and began making their way back across the rocks towards the main beach, stepping to avoid the patches of seaweed that had become slippery with the rising water.

'I'd best get back.' Daisy inclined her chin in the direction of the town.

'Thanks for listening to me worry about Maggie. I know she asked us not to fuss. I can't help myself, Daise.'

'I know. I'm the same.'

'Whatever you decide about the house, make sure it's what *you* want, not what you think you *should* want. You've built something wonderful with the bookshop and the life you've created for yourself and the twins. Don't let anyone convince you to change it unless you're genuinely excited about what might replace it.'

As they walked back along the beach together, their footprints joined the pattern of marks left by early morning dog walkers and joggers. The wind had picked up and Daisy did her jacket up. Going back towards Pretty Beach, the sea air had done Daisy the power of good. She was now clearer about several things.

25

Despite everything that Daisy had going on, she'd had to park it all and get on with running her business. It was directly before the Independent Retail Alliance were due to arrive to do the filming. Daisy stood on the library ladder in a very pretty, floral high-neck dress that Annabelle had insisted she borrow for the occasion. The bookshop had been cleaned from its absolute top to very bottom and didn't Daisy know about it. Every surface had been sprayed and wiped, the books were in perfectly curated-not-curated jumbles of piles and stacked everywhere on shelves and Daisy had upped the lamp and fairy light quota exponentially. She stretched up to thread new blue and white Pretty Beach bunting, delivered the day before by local seamstress Clemmie, across the top of the fiction section. The little triangles of blue and white did a very good job of pulling the colours of Pretty Beach into the bookshop, but nothing for Daisy's nerves.

The bookshop looked better than it ever had. Daisy had tidied and thought through every little corner and arranged just about everything that didn't move to showcase the cosy charm that had won the bookshop the nomination in the first place.

The library trolley she'd rescued from Facebook Marketplace sat in its usual spot and the seasonal reads arranged on it looked as if they'd been placed by a professional stylist rather than a mum of twins who, before starting the bookshop, had never really styled much of anything in her life.

The fairy lights that had multiplied over the months twinkled from every available surface, almost smug in the spot they'd ended up in in life. New additions to the fairy light party had been wound around picture frames and draped over the corners of shelves in a way that looked oh-so casual but had actually taken Daisy the better part of an hour to achieve. The wingback chairs had been hoovered, plumped and positioned just so and the little side tables here and there were placed in the right spots for little lanterns and tealights and absolutely ready for cups of tea.

Fresh flowers from Susannah's garden filled three huge mismatched white jug vases placed at strategic points around the shop. The whole place smelled of a three-wick lavender and vanilla candle burning on the counter, old books and a faint trace of beeswax polish Daisy had used on the front of Uncle Dennis's old desk. As she adjusted the bunting to hang in perfect swags between the shelves, Daisy's mind wandered to the house in the Old Town and the decision that loomed over her and Miles. To be fair, it was mostly Daisy with the decision overwhelm; Miles had been sold by both the gloriousness of the house and Shane's sort of casual sales technique whereby he was more than certain that the place would be snapped up as soon as it hit the World Wide Web. They'd walked past it twice since the viewing with Shane, once on their way to collect the twins from school and once on a deliberate detour where Daisy had stood looking up at the front of the house, wondering if she had inhabited someone else's body or perhaps was living in a twenty-four-seven dream.

Both times the house had looked exactly the same and just as gorgeous; solid, imposing, the delightful twist of wisteria over the heavy green front door, elegant proportions and very special Victorian brickwork underneath. Both times Daisy had found herself with an image in her head of her walking up the path with shopping bags and children's school bags, unlocking the door and stepping into the hallway with its perfect parquet flooring and beautiful old staircase. That was where it had ended, though, and yet again she'd thought about how much she loved living by the bookshop.

Wondering about it all and how her life was almost unrecognisable from when she'd been in the tiny new build house on the estate fifteen minutes from Pretty Beach, she climbed down from the ladder and moved it along to the next section of shelving, her dress catching slightly on the metal rungs as she repositioned herself. The dress felt floaty and lovely and a little bit strange after months of her normal floral cheesecloth shirts, tucked into wide leg jeans and topped with soft slouchy cardigans. However, Annabelle had been spot on that it was the right vibe and simply popping it over her head had made her look put-together and feel good.

Climbing back up, to the elevated position perched at the top of the ladder, Daisy could see the whole shop spread out below her, every carefully arranged corner and lovingly tended display sitting there doing its thing. The poetry section with its hand-lettered shelf markers, the new arrivals table positioned to catch customers as they walked through the door, the children's corner with its pastel cushions and low shelves painted in the palest shell blue. Daisy swallowed and shook her head as she remembered the first day she'd stood outside what had been Uncle Dennis's mess of a place. With her hands cupped over her eyes, she'd peered in through the glass and hadn't quite known what to think. Now, something very nice looked up at her. The precious place she'd poured her heart, savings and every spare moment into creating showcased her hard work. Every book had been chosen by her, every lamp positioned to create exactly the right atmosphere, every detail considered and reconsidered until it felt on the nose right. As the sun went in and out and clouds moved across outside, a few different shadows fell on the floor. Daisy smiled to herself as the old building creaked gently; the familiar sounds of timber settling and expanding had become as much a part of the bookshop's character as the wonky shelves and the temperamental coffee machine tucked behind the counter. She loved it all more and more.

Stepping down from the ladder, she looked up at the bunting and nodded, quite pleased with herself, and quietly, though she'd never admit it, she was flooded with self-satisfaction. The blue and white triangles worked well and added just that little bit of a Pretty Beach coastal touch to the old books and lovely things. As she rolled the library ladder and moved it back to its usual position, her thoughts turned to Maggie and the surgery. Despite all Maggie's reassurances and the family's promise to treat the whole thing as routine, Daisy was far from rational about it all. Inside her head and heart, the old anxiety that was way too much of a friend kept popping up its head. When she'd spoken to Maggie the night before to check how she was feeling, Maggie had been trying to sound so very normal and matter-of-fact that it hadn't felt real. They'd talked about work and the weather and the latest Pretty Beach gossip as if nothing significant was happening, which was exactly what Maggie had asked for but somehow made Daisy feel more worried rather than less.

For Daisy, the magnitude of the surgery and the casual way everyone was discussing it made her *very* uncomfortable. Surgery, even routine surgery with excellent outcomes, as far as she was concerned, wasn't what she wanted anyone in the Henley family to be going through. At the end of the day, it was still someone cutting into her sister's head with sharp instruments. The fact that it happened to other people every day of the week, according to Maggie, didn't make it feel any less significant for Daisy.

Walking to the front window, she looked out at the laneway to check for any sign of the Alliance people who were due to arrive within the hour. The narrow street looked exactly as it always did, cobblestones gleamed after an early morning drizzle of rain, the table outside the florist over the road was loaded down with zinc buckets full of flowers and a cat was picking its way carefully between the puddles. As Daisy pulled back the old cage security door, the irony wasn't lost on her that she would be spending the morning being interviewed about her successful business, whilst in real life, the bookshop at the moment was the last thing on her mind. She was more worried about the house thing and whether Maggie would be alright than the award nomination. Bottom line: she could have done without the filming. Success, it turned out, didn't solve your problems.

Checking the time on her phone, her stomach fluttered with nerves at the thought of being interviewed and having to articulate what made the bookshop special when she wasn't entirely sure she understood it herself. She'd muddled along right from the outset. All she could really put her finger on was that it felt right, safe, comfy and happy all at the same time. How did you put that into words? She was well aware that somehow she'd created something that customers seemed to love when they walked through the door, that people kept coming back for reasons that went beyond just buying books and that the only way was up.

The bunting fluttered slightly in the draught from the old windows and Daisy just stood and stared for a moment. Whatever happened with the house decision, whatever the outcome of Maggie's surgery, whatever changes lay ahead for all of them, at least she was now mostly in charge of her own destiny. That alone was priceless.

26

The crew arrived just after ten, and Daisy was relieved to see they were nothing like the daunting professionals she'd been imagining in her head. One of them, Alicia, turned out to be a woman about her own age in smart casual clothes, a large printed scarf, tennis shoes and a bubble of dark curls, accompanied by Tom, who carried what looked like a glorified iPhone setup rather than the massive cameras Daisy had been dreading. As she watched them come in the door, Daisy felt her whole body sigh in relief as she took them in and wondered why she'd worked herself up so much. Rather than arriving with all sorts of technical filming paraphernalia, they each had regular-looking black backpacks and Tom was pulling a silver case behind him. Not that intimidating at all.

After shaking hands and introducing themselves, Alicia looked around, raised her eyebrows and shook her head. 'Well, this is going to be easy enough. Not our hardest job of the week, eh Tom?'

Tom chuckled. 'Had worse.'

'This is perfect. It's exactly the sort of authentic independent bookshop atmosphere we want to capture. Very Instagram-worthy but in a genuine way, if you know what I mean.'

Daisy smiled. 'Thanks, I do my best. Tea? I'll pop the kettle on.'

Tom nodded as he started to unpack his equipment. 'We had a coffee on the train, but it wasn't up to much. How good is that fast train? Mind you, good job we weren't paying for it, otherwise we would have needed to take out a mortgage.'

Daisy busied herself with the kettle, grateful for something to do with her hands while Tom set up a light and tested various angles with his iPhone mounted on what looked like a very expensive tripod. The whole operation was much more casual than she'd expected, rather than the professional production she'd been nervous about.

'Right, if it's okay with you, we will start with some general shots of the space. Then, again, if you're up for it, Tom will film you doing normal bookshop things, just moving around naturally, arranging books, that sort of thing. Try to forget we're here.'

'Easier said than done.' Daisy chuckled, very glad that she'd taken Annabelle's advice and worn the dress.

'You'll be fine.' Alicia looked around. 'With what we've got to work with here, this is going to be a no-brainer from our side of the fence.'

After an hour or so and what felt to Daisy like a lot of still pictures, Tom started filming from lots of different angles. Then it was her turn and she began her usual routine of straightening shelves and repositioning displays. She showed them the library trolley and explained how she'd found it on Facebook Marketplace, demonstrated the way the fairy lights created different moods throughout the day, and talked about the regular customers who'd made the wingback chairs their own personal reading spots. Tom filmed with both an iPhone and a vlogging camera and occasionally asked her to repeat something or move to catch better light, but mostly he followed her around as she went about the business of being a bookshop owner. It wasn't that hard at all.

Alicia watched one of the videos back. 'This is brilliant. You're a natural at this. Very relaxed and genuine.'

Daisy hooted. 'I don't feel relaxed! I suppose talking about books is easier than talking about a lot of things, though.'

'That's exactly why this works so well. You're not trying to sell anything or prove anything, you're just sharing something you love with people who might love it too. That really does come over well.'

They'd been filming for about forty minutes and were just starting to wrap up when there was a sound from somewhere behind the bookshop that made Daisy frown, make a funny face and wonder what it was. It was a sort of gurgling, gushing noise that seemed to be coming from the direction of the hallway that led to the stairs up to the flat.

Tom lowered his camera. 'What was that?'

Before Daisy could answer, the noise got louder and was joined by what sounded suspiciously like water. Daisy's stomach dropped as she realised what was happening. She rushed towards the back of the shop. 'Oh, no! That's not good. That's really not good.'

She pushed through the door that led to the hallway and was greeted by the sight of dripping water from the ceiling and drops on the walls. Water was already beginning to pool on the wooden floor of the hallway.

'Where's your stopcock?' Alicia called from behind her, apparently unfazed by the domestic emergency unfolding around them.

'I have absolutely no idea!' Daisy called back over the sound of dripping water. 'I should know that, shouldn't I? I should definitely know where the stopcock is in my own building.'

'Most people don't,' Tom said helpfully as he filmed the

chaos. 'This is actually quite good footage. Very authentic small business challenges.'

'Ahh! Don't put this in the promotional video. The Independent Retail Alliance probably doesn't want to showcase businesses that flood during interviews.'

'On the contrary. This is exactly the sort of real-life content that people connect with. There is nothing staged about this. You can't make this up if you tried!'

The water was coming from what looked like a pipe that ran along the ceiling towards the flat upstairs, though it was hard to tell exactly where the breach was. Daisy stood in the middle of the rapidly expanding puddle and tried to remember anything useful about plumbing while Alicia searched for something that might be a water shut-off valve.

'Found it. I think this is it anyway. Cross your fingers.'

Alicia turned off the water, and mercifully, the gurgling pipe sound diminished, though water continued to drip from the ceiling and plop into a couple of puddles that had formed across the hallway floor.

Daisy surveyed the damage, 'Okay, so that's not how I imagined this morning going.'

Tom was still filming everything. 'At least it waited until we'd finished most of the interview.'

'Most of it?'

'We've got everything we need about the shop and the award,' Alicia assured her. 'This just adds a bit of extra character to the story for the socials. Of course, we'll send everything to you for approval. It might look rubbish when it's been edited, but it might be great. You never know.'

Daisy looked around at the water dripping from the ceiling and pooling on the floor and laughed. 'True, actually. I've learnt that you can never tell what people will like, either. Character is one way of putting it. I'm not sure soggy and incompetent is the image the Independent Retail Alliance wants to project, but what do I know?'

'Are you kidding? This is perfect. It shows that running an independent business isn't all fairy lights and award ceremonies. Sometimes pipes burst and you have to deal with it while you're wearing your best dress and trying to look professional for the cameras.'

'I suppose when you put it like that, it does sound quite authentic.'

'Exactly. Real life happening to real people running real businesses. Much better than some polished corporate presentation.'

Tom continued filming as Daisy mopped up the worst of the water. The whole situation was so absurd that Daisy had stopped caring.

As they finished mopping and surveyed their handiwork, Alicia clapped her hands lightly together 'Right, I think we've got some brilliant footage here. The contrast between the beautiful bookshop and the domestic chaos is exactly what people want to see.'

'Really?'

'Really. It shows that you're human, that running a small business comes with unexpected challenges, and that you handle those challenges with humour. That's much more compelling than someone who pretends everything is always perfect.'

'I certainly can't pretend that. Not after this morning. What a disaster. I'm so sorry.'

'Don't be silly, we love pipes exploding.'

Tom packed up his equipment while Daisy tried to assess the damage to the hallway and sent a message to Suntanned Pete. The water had mostly been contained, though there were definitely stains on the walls and she hoped that the floorboards would dry out. Still, it could have been much worse, and at least it had happened while people were there to help rather than when she was upstairs asleep.

'This is going to make a much better behind-the-scenes video than anything we could have planned. People will remember the bookshop owner who handled a burst pipe with dignity while wearing a floral dress.'

'I'm not sure dignity is how I'd describe it.'

'Trust me, you were very dignified. Competent too. Most people would have panicked.'

'I think I did panic, just quietly.'

'Well, it didn't show. You'll see when we send you the final edit.'

After they left, Daisy stood in her damp hallway wearing her borrowed dress and surveyed the aftermath of the morning's events. The bookshop itself was unscathed, the bunting still hanging perfectly and the fairy lights twinkling away as if nothing had happened. Only the hallway showed evidence of the domestic emergency that had turned her professional promotional opportunity into that good old small business owner's reality: problems and real life.

She thought about calling Miles, then decided it could wait until she'd changed out of Annabelle's dress. The bookshop felt peaceful after the morning's excitement, the carefully arranged displays exactly as she'd left them before the world had briefly turned chaotic. Whatever the final video looked like, at least it would be honest about what running a small business actually involved. It wasn't all bunting, nominations, fairy lights and recognition that she knew without a doubt. In actual fact, right from the word go, the bookshop had been about a wing, a prayer and bootlegging from the inside out. It included burst pipes and emergency repairs and the sort of challenges that nobody mentioned in business plans as far as Daisy could work out. Which didn't really matter anyway; business plans were for other people. All she wanted to do was pay her bills and be happy in Pretty Beach.

27

It was the morning of Maggie's surgery. Not only did Daisy feel as if it wasn't a good day, it was grey and still, with a sky that made everything look washed out and slightly unreal, which was appropriate, really. Daisy had been awake since five, she'd made tea and warmed a cinnamon bun, checked her phone seventeen times and tried to pretend that it was just another ordinary old run-of-the-mill morning in Pretty Beach. Inside, Daisy felt far from normal. The thought of Maggie having her scalp sliced open had been making her feel sick for days.

The twins had stayed with Susannah and Maggie had asked Daisy to drop her at the hospital at eight fifteen, which had meant leaving Pretty Beach at half past seven to allow for traffic and the inevitable confusion of finding the right car park at the hospital. Daisy had offered to stay the night at Maggie's to make the morning easier, but Maggie had declined.

As Daisy drove through the narrow streets of the Old Town towards Maggie's place, Pretty Beach looked exactly as it always did in the early morning. The fresh fish kiosk was open and doing its thing, a jogger in bright yellow trainers pounded along the seafront, and the ferry was chugging towards the harbour with its usual cargo of commuters and early tourists. Everything was standard, as if Pretty Beach hadn't registered that this was a day when one of its residents would be going through something significant.

Maggie was waiting outside when Daisy pulled up. She got into the passenger seat without ceremony, buckled her seatbelt, and settled back without saying much. Daisy could tell Maggie was purposely making herself look and sound calm. She wasn't fooling anyone.

'Thanks for doing this. I know it's early.'

'Don't be silly. I have had earlier mornings than this with the twins. This is practically supper time. Of course I was going to drive you. How are you feeling?'

'Fine. A bit tired. I didn't sleep brilliantly, but that's probably normal in a situation like this.'

Daisy wanted to fire off a million more questions. She had to fight the urge to pummel Maggie with words and ask if she was nervous or scared or having second thoughts. However, if there was one thing Daisy knew, it was how to read her sister and Maggie was clearly only up for small talk, if that. They'd had enough conversations about feelings and fears over the previous few weeks. Reading the room from Daisy's point of view showed that Maggie needed someone else to handle the logistics while she focused on getting through the day.

They drove through the centre of Pretty Beach and as they reached the edge of town and joined the main road that led inland towards the hospital, the landscape began to change. The small winding roads of Pretty Beach gave way to a dual carriageway, they passed the modern housing estate Daisy had lived on before the bookshop and the feeling in the car, though it was unspoken, began to get more and more tense.

'Do you remember when you had the twins?'

Daisy chuckled. 'How could I forget?'

'I don't think any of us will forget that in a hurry.'

'Nope.'

'This feels different, doesn't it?'

Daisy felt as if she was treading on eggshells. She wasn't sure what Maggie wanted her to say. The dynamic of their relationship had always been Maggie playing the confident big sister role. This suddenly felt distinctly different. 'This is routine surgery with a good outcome. Not the same thing at all.'

'I know. I was just thinking about how strange it is to be driving to hospital as the patient rather than the visitor.'

'Yeah.'

'When you're visiting someone else, you spend the whole journey worrying about what you're going to find when you get there. When you're the one going in, you already know what's going to happen, so at least that bit is certain, I suppose.'

Maggie's voice was calm and matter-of-fact, but Daisy caught something underneath it that was so very far from normal, it made Daisy grab the steering wheel very tightly. Knowing that Maggie wouldn't like it, she had to stop herself from reaching over and squeezing her hand.

The traffic was lighter than Daisy had expected, and they made good time through the outskirts of the town and onto the ring road that would take them to the hospital. Daisy wondered what it would be like after the surgery. Indicating left to pull out, she checked her blind spot, pulled into the fast lane to overtake a lorry loaded with building supplies. 'Well, the traffic's a dream this morning.'

'Thank goodness. What's happened about the house in the Old Town? You've been very quiet about the whole thing since you went to see it.'

Daisy was surprised that Maggie was thinking about her domestic arrangements when she was on her way to have surgery. She was glad to talk about something, if truth be told. 'I'm still thinking about it, but the owners have delayed putting it to market for a bit, their end, so that's good. We'll have to decide one way or another, though. At least, Miles will.'

'You don't sound convinced. What's holding you back?'

'Okay, I am going to sound very selfish, but whatever. I like my life the way it is. I like living above the bookshop and being able to walk to school and having everything I need within a few streets of each other.'

'You could still have all that from the Old Town. It's not exactly the other side of the world.'

'I suppose. I don't know. I just like my little life, but I know Miles can't live in that tiny flat forever.'

The landscape around them got more urban, more functional. Retail parks and roundabouts, car dealerships and fast food restaurants, the sort of anonymous commercial sprawl that could have been anywhere in the country. It was the opposite of Pretty Beach, and as always, when Daisy was away from home, she couldn't really wait to get back.

'What does Miles think?'

'He's very keen. The thing is, it's alright for him in a way. He can just snap his fingers and buy it. Do you know what I mean? We regular mortals down here on earth can't do that. It's the one thing where we are *very* different.'

'Right, you don't like that?"

'Don't get me wrong. He doesn't show off or anything. I think he genuinely wants to buy a good house, especially with Elizabeth getting older and needing somewhere permanent to settle. Then there was all that mugging stuff. I mean, you can see his point about why he wants to get her out of there.'

'She sounds quite isolated from what you've told me.'

'She is.'

The hospital signs started appearing along the roadside, directing them through a series of roundabouts and traffic lights towards the main entrance. Daisy felt her stomach tighten for many reasons as they got closer. Once they reached the hospital, Maggie would disappear into the medical system and Daisy, Susannah and Annabelle would have to wait, trying not to imagine all the things that could go wrong.

'Are you nervous?'

'A bit. More about the recovery than the actual surgery. I hate being laid up and dependent on other people.'

'You won't be dependent. You'll just be temporarily requiring a bit of extra help.'

'Same thing, really.'

'No, it's not. Dependent suggests you can't manage at all. You'll just need someone to do the shopping and check you're not overdoing things. There's a difference.'

'If you say so.'

The hospital appeared ahead of them, an ugly, not very efficient-looking sprawling complex of brick and glass buildings connected by covered walkways and surrounded by car parks that seemed to stretch for miles in every direction. Signs directed them towards different departments and visitor areas, and Daisy tried to navigate the right way while avoiding ambulances and delivery vehicles that seemed to approach from every angle.

She found a parking space and turned off the engine. 'This is it then.'

'This is it.'

'Ready?'

'As ready as anyone can be for having their scalp removed and opened up by strangers.'

'Don't say it like that.'

Daisy could tell Maggie was nervous. She'd been fiddling with the little designer logo on her handbag the whole way and her leg hadn't stopped jigging. For all Maggie's calm practicality and insistence that everyone treat the surgery as no big deal, she was clearly way out of her comfort zone. And rightly so as far as Daisy was concerned; she was facing something involving anaesthetics and scalpels and a recovery period more than taking the rest of the day off work. Daisy pushed the button on her seatbelt. 'You don't have to be brave for my benefit.'

'I'm not being brave. I'm just trying to get through it without falling apart.'

'You could fall apart a little bit if you wanted to. I wouldn't mind.'

'I mind.'

Daisy understood completely. 'Right, well come on then.'

'Yep, let's get this over with.'

28

Daisy couldn't take her eyes off Maggie, who, in striped pyjamas, was wedged into the corner of the sofa in the room off Annabelle's kitchen. A large white, almost turban-like bandage that was wrapped around her head was so dramatic and big that it was comical and had already elicited more than a few laughs. Not that essentially any of it was funny, but everyone involved had seen the comical side and had a little chuckle. With one hand wrapped around a cup of tea and the other resting on a cushion, Maggie, for sure, looked delicate; her skin was pale, going to the loo tired her out and she'd had trouble eating. None of it made Daisy happy, but overall, as far as any of them knew, the surgery had gone well. Maggie had come home from hospital and had surprised everyone by accepting Annabelle's offer to stay at her house. Maggie's acceptance of help had been the only sign needed for the Henley women that things weren't at all usual. They had rallied around and then some.

Daisy smiled. 'I still can't believe you agreed to let Bells look after you. You've spent the last few months insisting you didn't need any help from anyone.'

Maggie sighed. 'It turns out having surgery makes you realise that independence is overrated when you can't reach the loo without feeling a bit woozy.'

Annabelle shimmied around the kitchen island with a small wooden board covered in baking paper and three just-out-of-the-oven caramel and sea salt cookies. 'She's been a model patient, actually. Very well-behaved for someone who usually refuses to let anyone do anything for her.'

Daisy rolled her eyes. 'Oh my goodness. Have you made the sea salt cookies? Things must be bad.'

Maggie hooted. 'She's been fussing over me like a hen. She tried to cut up my toast into eight triangles for me. Luckily, I can still do that, and yes, this is the second batch of home baking we've seen already.'

Annabelle tutted. 'You were having trouble with the knife because of the painkillers making you dizzy.'

Daisy smiled as she participated in and watched the familiar dynamic play out between the three of them. At the same time, she tried to gauge how Maggie was *really* coping beneath the usual Henley girls' banter. For sure, with her headgear, Maggie didn't look great. Because of the laughing and banter, to anyone looking on, they'd probably assume that Maggie was okay and on the mend. Daisy knew better. The bandage made Maggie look smaller somehow, more vulnerable than any of them were used to seeing her and bottom line, she just no longer looked like Daisy's very capable, very much more grown-up older sister. Someone had rearranged the steps the three girls usually sat on and Daisy was not very comfortable on her perch.

Susannah came in from the garden with a mug of tea, displaying the same look she'd had on her face since she'd learnt of Maggie's diagnosis; a look that appeared as if she was jovial and fine. Anyone who really knew her knew that she was far from it. Susannah had been trying to follow Maggie's instructions about not making a fuss, but it was clearly a struggle and

Daisy, for one, didn't blame her. Maggie looked in a bad way and it was obvious she didn't feel great either. Despite all her bravery, she'd caved and had for once listened to advice.

'How's the pain?' Susannah asked as she sat down on the sofa next to Daisy.

Maggie replied in a tone that meant she didn't want to discuss it. 'Manageable. The doctor said it would be worse for the first few days and then gradually improve. So, I'm more or less right on schedule.'

Annabelle gestured with the plate of cookies. 'The stitches come out soon, assuming everything's healing properly, correct?'

'Yep. She said the procedure went exactly as planned. No complications, clean margins, everything looking good. Just as I told you all.' Maggie pointed to the coffee table. 'It's all there in the notes.'

Daisy noticed that Maggie's hand trembled slightly as she lifted her mug, though whether from the medication or just the general exhaustion that came with recovering from surgery, it was impossible to tell. Daisy didn't like any of it. Sadly, she had little choice. It didn't really matter whether she liked it or not. It was happening right in front of her eyes. 'Have you heard anything about the test results?' Daisy asked carefully. 'From what they removed?'

'They said it would take some time for the full report. She was confident they got everything. As I said, the margins looked clean and there was no sign it had spread anywhere else.' Maggie brushed it off. 'Routine procedure, routine outcome, routine recovery period. Nothing dramatic or surprising about any of it. The worst thing is this bandage. I did tell you all this ages ago.'

There was something in the way Maggie spoke that made Daisy wonder if Maggie was trying to convince herself as much as the rest of them. For all her insistence that the surgery was minor and straightforward, the reality of having part of your scalp removed was bound to be more unsettling than anyone wanted to admit.

'What about work?' Daisy asked.

'I've postponed anything that requires serious strategic thinking until my brain isn't full of cotton wool.'

'That must be difficult for someone who usually has her fingers in every pie.'

'It's an education in delegation. Turns out the world doesn't actually end if I'm not available to micromanage every detail of every project.'

'A revolutionary discovery,' Annabelle said dryly. 'Guess what? We're coping without you, Mags. Maybe you should have surgery more often if it teaches you to let other people do their jobs.'

Susannah held her hand up. 'Don't even joke about that. I don't want any of you to have any sort of surgery for the foreseeable future.' Susannah was sharp and loaded with emotion.

Maggie reached for a cookie and clearly wanted to change the subject away from her medical situation. 'Enough about me and my various inconveniences. What's happening with everyone else's lives? Daise, have you and Miles made a decision about that house yet?'

Daisy felt all eyes turn to her and realised she'd been so focused on Maggie's recovery that she'd barely thought about the house decision. 'The owners put it on hold for a bit.'

'So, it's not gone to the open market?' Annabelle asked.

'It will do soon. Miles keeps saying we should trust our instincts, but our instincts seem to be pointing in several different directions at once.'

'Yes, I had similar feelings after surgery. I trusted my gut to accept help.'

'Very self-reflective of you, Mags.'

'I'll probably go back to being my usual pragmatic self once the drugs wear off.'

'Promise?' Annabelle asked.

'It's quite humbling actually, realising how much you depend on other people when you can't manage everything yourself.'

'Welcome to the human race,' Susannah said with a smile. 'The rest of us figured that out years ago.'

'Better late than never.' Maggie nodded.

29

Daisy tucked her legs underneath her on the sofa and balanced her laptop on her knees, as she cradled a mug of chamomile tea in both hands. It had been a long day and with the twins finally settled upstairs after the usual round of negotiations about extra stories and drinks of water, Daisy had retreated to the sitting room and didn't want to come up for air. Miles was in the shower after a long day that had involved three client calls to New York and a trip to check on Elizabeth at her flat. The sitting room was quiet except for the sound of water running through the pipes, thankfully not gushing out and the distant hum of traffic from the main road that led out of Pretty Beach.

Daisy navigated to the email about the awards ceremony and started to read through. She'd been putting off researching the gala venue for weeks, partly because she'd been too busy with the bookshop and everything else going on in her life and partly because thinking too hard about the whole thing made her a total and utter bag of nerves. She'd put the whole thing to bed and treated it as if it were a distant obligation that would sort itself out without requiring too much attention from her.

However, the date had slowly crept around and whether she liked it or not, Daisy had to be organised and find out what she was letting herself in for.

Clicking through the various things in the email and then the website, she scrolled through. The Independent Retail Alliance website was sleek and professional and in fleece pyjamas curled up on the sofa, the whole thing felt quite bizarre. The home page featured photographs of award winners from previous years, all of them looking confident and successful in the sort of clothes that suggested they knew exactly what they were doing and had never experienced a moment of impostor syndrome in their lives.

Daisy felt her stomach drop as she looked through the information about the year's awards ceremony, as she took in the details she'd skimmed over when the invitation had first arrived. The venue was in Bath, in a Georgian hotel masterpiece that had apparently hosted everyone from Jane Austen to Charles Dickens and was available for hire by organisations with enough budget to afford chandeliers and marble columns.

'Oh,' Daisy said aloud to the empty room. 'Oh dear.'

The photographs of the venue showed grandeur, grandeur, and more grandeur. Daisy had been trying not to think about it for a reason and now she knew why; ballrooms with gilded ceilings and crystal chandeliers, elegant staircases that swept down from galleries lined with classical statuary, dining rooms where the tables alone were ginormous, all made her feel out of place. For sure, though, everything was beautiful; there was no doubt about that.

Scrolling through more photographs, she read the venue's history, learning that it had been the social centre of fashionable Bath society for over two centuries and had hosted balls forever. The building had been restored to its original Georgian splendour, which meant it looked exactly as impressive as it would have done when Jane Austen was writing about the social hierarchies that played out in its elegant rooms.

Clicking through to the programme for the evening, Daisy gulped. 'I'm really going to have to stand up in front of all these people and make a speech if I win or get runner-up.'

The agenda was more elaborate than she'd expected, starting with a reception where winners and guests would mingle over champagne and canapés, followed by dinner in a spectacular ballroom and then the awards ceremony itself. There would be speeches from the chairman of the Independent Retail Alliance, the mayor of Bath, and several of the nominees. At least she hadn't been asked to give a speech. The whole evening was scheduled to last until nearly midnight, which meant she'd be playing the game for over six hours.

On finding the list of other award winners, Daisy felt another flutter of anxiety as she read through their credentials. There was a woman who'd started a chain of zero-waste grocery stores that now had branches across three counties, a man who'd built a vintage clothing empire from a single shop in Brighton, and a couple who'd turned their farm shop into a destination that attracted visitors from across Europe. All of them sounded like they'd been running businesses since before Daisy had even thought about opening a bookshop, and all of them probably knew exactly what to say when handed a microphone and asked to inspire other independent retailers. She still felt as if she was wading around in the dark without a clue.

She clicked through to the dress code information and winced at the words 'black tie' in bold letters, followed by several serious paragraphs explaining what this meant for both men and women attending the event. Evening gowns were strongly encouraged, cocktail dresses were acceptable if they were sufficiently formal, and there were detailed guidelines about appropriate colours, hemlines, and accessories that made

Daisy realise she'd never attended anything that required the same level of sartorial planning.

The water stopped running upstairs and Daisy could hear Miles moving around in the bathroom. When he came down, he would probably wonder why she was sitting in the dark with only the glow of her laptop screen for company. With a sense of doom, she stayed curled up on the sofa and continued scrolling through photographs of previous awards ceremonies, trying to understand what she'd got herself into. The images showed exactly the sort of elegant evening she'd been avoiding thinking about. Men in fitted dinner jackets and women in gowns that looked like they'd been chosen by personal stylists, all of them holding champagne flutes and engaging in animated conversation that suggested they were eating up their surroundings. Everyone looked like they belonged, like attending black tie events in Georgian ballrooms was a regular part of their social calendar rather than a terrifying one-off experience.

After finding a video from the previous year's ceremony and watching the award winners give their speeches, noting how confident they all seemed as they stood behind the lectern and delivered what sounded like carefully prepared remarks about innovation and community spirit and the challenges facing independent retail, Daisy hoped she wouldn't win. None of them appeared to be reading from notes or struggling to remember what they'd planned to say, and all of them managed to sound both humble and authoritative in exactly the way Daisy was certain she'd never manage.

'Right. This is definitely a bigger deal than I thought.'

Miles appeared in the doorway wearing his dressing gown and with his hair still damp from the shower. 'Talking to yourself? What's a bigger deal than you thought?'

'This awards thing. I've just been looking at the venue online and it's all chandeliers and marble. I'm going to need to curtsy at someone when I walk through the door. I've been putting it off because of Maggie, but it's looming and fast.'

'Sounds impressive.'

'Sounds terrifying. Everyone else who has won awards looks like they were born to attend black tie dinners in Georgian ballrooms. I look like someone who runs a small bookshop in a seaside town and has never owned a dress that cost more than fifty pounds.'

Miles sat down beside her and picked up the laptop and scrolled through the same photographs. 'It's very grand, but that's appropriate, isn't it? You've won a significant award for your business. It deserves to be celebrated somewhere impressive.'

'It's just a little bookshop. We're not exactly changing the world here.'

Miles joked. 'You're preserving something very important.'

Daisy giggled. 'When you put it like that, it sounds almost noble.'

'It is noble and most people are very impressed even if you aren't.'

Daisy leaned against his shoulder. 'This is all very surreal. We're going to have to get on with it and have fun.'

'I like that plan of attack.'

'I think I'll be fine once I'm there. You're looking at a woman who gave birth to twins on her own and let me tell you that was no easy feat. I am sure I can manage a few canapes and a smile.'

'Standing up and saying thank you for an award hasn't got anything on that and you're good at challenges even when you don't think you are.'

'If I do win, which I don't think I will and I mess up the speech, it'll only be in front of hundreds of people and probably recorded for posterity.'

'If you win, you'll be fine and I'll get to sit in the audience and see how lucky I am.'

Daisy considered all of it and decided it was about time she started to back herself and acknowledge that her little bookshop was actually a success rather than just a lucky accident. Beefing herself up felt a little bit alien, but she was going to give it a jolly good go. 'I should probably think about what I say about being nominated if anyone asks, or maybe I just wing it and hope for the best.'

'I reckon just be honest. I guarantee half the people there will be feeling exactly the same way. The difference is that you actually deserve to be there, which puts you ahead of at least some of them.'

'How do you know I deserve to be there?'

'Because I've seen what you've built, and I know how hard you've worked for it. Because customers travel for miles to visit your shop, and because you've created something that matters to people beyond just buying and selling books.'

'You're biased.'

'I'm informed. There's a difference.'

Miles closed the laptop and shifted so he could put his arm around her properly. 'You'll be more than fine.'

'Of course, I'll just be mingling with hundreds of strangers in formal wear while standing in a room that once hosted Jane Austen. So my cup of tea.'

Daisy stood up and stretched and nodded. The venue might be grander than anything she'd experienced before, but the reason she'd be there remained the same. She'd built something worth celebrating, even if she was only just beginning to believe it herself. She was going to own it and enjoy the ride.

30

Daisy had not long been back from a very long walk to the lighthouse with the twins, after which she'd arrived at Annabelle's house tired and happy. The purpose of the lighthouse walk was to let the girls run off some steam and get some fresh air and it had been successful. They were now sitting in the small, snug room next to Annabelle's kitchen, watching a movie and eating popcorn.

Maggie's head was still bandaged but not quite as heavily and she had some colour back in her cheeks. The careful application of a wide soft headband hid what was going on underneath and mostly though still delicate, she was looking more herself again. She had a bit of her old self back and was no longer moving around quite as cautiously. With a glass of spritzer in her left hand, she was staring at an iPad and cross-checking a delivery email with packages Annabelle was holding up from the other side of the kitchen.

'Four dresses, two cocktail, one full length, one taffeta bow.'

Annabelle tapped on each packet. 'Check, yep.'

Daisy laughed. 'Thank you for doing this for me.'

Annabelle shook her head. 'You left it so late, Daise! How can you be like that?'

Daisy shrugged. 'I'll be fine. I'm not really bothered by what I wear.'

Maggie tutted. 'There was no way you were going to this without looking the part. You will be representing the Henley family, say no more.'

Annabelle rolled her eyes. 'What on earth were you thinking, not having sorted this out?'

Daisy chuckled. 'I was happy to go in that sparkly number in your dressing room.'

'Technically, that's a cocktail dress.' Annabelle lowered her voice. 'Anyway, this has given me an excuse to shop and get a new dress. Piers never needs to know.'

Maggie chortled. 'Do you really think he doesn't know about your shopping habits?'

'He doesn't know the specifics,' Annabelle chuckled as she started cutting through the plastic wrapping on the first package. 'What he doesn't know won't hurt him has been my motto from day one. I started as I meant to go on and yes, I am available for marriage guidance sessions.'

'He knows you well enough to know that helping Daisy shop for a dress would involve you buying yourself something,' Maggie bantered. 'He's not stupid.'

Annabelle pulled the first dress from its packaging. 'He knows better than to say anything. Right then, let's see what we've got here. Err, hmm, right.'

The first dress, navy blue with sequins scattered across the bodice, was not great. The cut was all wrong, hitting at an awkward length neither cocktail nor evening wear, and the neckline gaped.

Maggie swore and wrinkled her nose. 'Oh dear. That's not right at all. I hope things improve.'

'It looked much better online.' Annabelle held the dress up

against herself and frowned. 'The description said midnight navy, but this looks more like what happens when you put a white wash in with dark colours.'

Daisy reached out to feel the fabric. 'Hmm. It's quite scratchy too. I'd probably rub myself raw before I even got to the venue.'

Maggie shook her head. 'Cheap sequins. You'd leave a trail of sparkles everywhere like some sort of discount fairy godmother. Nope, not digging that. We'll mark that one as a fail. It needs to be returned right away. I don't think there's any point in you even trying it on, Daise.'

Daisy took the dress from Annabelle to get a better look. 'Plus, the shape is all wrong. Look at where the waist is supposed to sit. That would hit me somewhere around my ribcage.'

'Right, dress number one is definitely out. Cheap and nasty though it is most definitely not cheap.' Annabelle looked on in disgust. 'Let's try the second one and hope it's an improvement.'

The second dress was deep, almost black green with what appeared to be enough fabric to upholster a small sofa. The shoulders had padding suited to a rugby player and the waist was gathered with an oversized flower that looked like it belonged on a Christmas present rather than a dress. The colour was lovely, but everything else about it screamed nineteen-eighties office party gone wrong.

Daisy side-eyed. 'Bells! That's hideous! I'm not going as a green tent.'

'The shoulders alone would need their own postcode,' Maggie observed. 'You'd have to turn sideways to get through doorways.'

Annabelle giggled. 'Shoulder pads are having a moment. Honestly, that looked nice on the website. That is *absolutely* awful. Well, you're not trying that on either.'

Maggie laughed. 'Those shoulders have more structure than most people's conservatories.'

'The green is pretty, though,' Daisy offered. 'Very, umm, rich.'

'A good colour won't help if you look like you're wearing a small marquee.' Maggie winced. 'Maybe try it on, but I think right out of the bag it's a no from me.'

Daisy stroked an enormous satin flower-type construction around the waist. 'And what's with this? It's the size of a small child. People would think I'd wrapped myself up as a present.'

Daisy whipped her clothes off and pulled on the green dress and all three of them fell about laughing.

'A very large, green present with delusions of grandeur. Or, in fact, an actual pheasant.'

Annabelle laughed. 'Sarah Ferguson vibes. Say no more. Dress number two is also rejected. I was trying to go for the wow factor.'

'What's the third one?' Daisy asked, eyeing the remaining packages with growing scepticism.

'This one's the full-length backless black number.'

The third dress looked promising when it first emerged. It was indeed black, appeared to have reasonable proportions, and the length looked appropriate for an evening event. There were no obvious sequin disasters or shoulder pad catastrophes to worry about. As Annabelle held the dress up properly, the neckline looked dubious; it plunged so dramatically and the back dropped so deeply that it would have required scaffolding for Daisy to actually wear it.

Daisy took in the full scope of it. 'Yeah, I don't think I can go in that. I'd need boob tape and, well, I don't know, just about every tape known to man.'

'It's quite something. You'd get an award for most creative use of body tape.'

'I'd spend the entire evening worried about falling out of it. That's not the sort of confidence boost I need when I'm already nervous.'

'Plus, you'd freeze to death,' Maggie added practically. 'It's

Bath, not July in Ibiza. You need more coverage than a few strategically placed strips of fabric. Nope.'

Annabelle sighed. 'What a nightmare! It is rather more revealing than the website suggested. The model must have been wearing some sort of industrial-strength undergarments. Online shopping for evening wear is always a gamble. This, Daise, is why I told you not to leave it so late.'

Daisy shrugged and waved her hand in front of her. 'It's fine. I'll just wear the sparkly one of yours. We'll send this lot back pronto.'

Annabelle gathered the black dress up and laid it out beside the others. 'That leaves us with the taffeta one-shoulder bow number. Please let this one be wearable because I'm running out of options.'

'What exactly is a taffeta bow dress?' Daisy asked nervously. 'That sounds like it could go very wrong very quickly.'

Annabelle unwrapped the final package and started to peel off reams of tissue paper. When it finally appeared, she held it up and all three of them fell silent. Floor length, fitted, deep black and very plain except for a large fabric bow over one shoulder.

Daisy nodded and sounded hopeful. 'Oh, that's completely different from the others.'

Maggie sighed. 'It's beautiful. Let's hope it fits.'

Annabelle touched the bow. 'The bow detail gives it something special without being over the top.'

'It looks really, really expensive.'

Annabelle coughed. 'It's an investment piece. An investment for other occasions, not just this one.'

'What other occasions am I likely to have for wearing something like this?' Daisy asked with a laugh. 'This awards thing is probably the fanciest event I'll ever attend.'

'I meant for all of us.'

Maggie chuckled. 'If you say it's an investment, that means it is extraordinarily expensive.'

Daisy joked. 'We'll need to timeshare it.'

'It's a dress one wears to win an award.' Annabelle added.

'Assuming I actually win this award. Don't forget I am just a nominee.' Daisy pointed out. 'I might just be the token small-town nominee who makes up the numbers.'

'Don't be ridiculous. Those women from the alliance were practically writing poetry about your bookshop. If they're not pushing for you to win, I'll eat my shoes.' Annabelle noted.

Maggie laughed. 'That would be quite a sacrifice.'

'Right, get this dress on. I want to see if it fits as well as it looks.'

Daisy pulled the dress on, wriggled the bow over her shoulder and raised her eyebrows. It fit beautifully and as she smoothed down the skirt, Annabelle squealed.

'Oh my God. Daise, you look absolutely incredible!'

Daisy fiddled with the bow. 'The bow's a bit wonky.'

'Turn around slowly so we can see the whole effect.' Maggie commanded. 'That is something else. Thank goodness!'

Daisy did as instructed and looked down as she turned. Truth be told, simply stepping into the dress had made her feel fabulous. She walked over to the mirror above the fireplace, stood on her tiptoes and studied her reflection. She had to admit the dress was stunning and fit her like it had been made specifically for her body. 'I do quite like it.'

Annabelle looked exponentially pleased with herself. She gloated. 'Quite like it? It's stunning! You look like a successful and confident person without being over the top, which is exactly what you are.'

'The bow really isn't too much?' Daisy asked, pointing to the dramatic shoulder detail.

Maggie nodded. 'The bow is perfect because the rest of the dress is so plain.'

'I suppose this is really happening. I'm actually going to an awards ceremony in an amazing dress.'

'You're going because you've achieved something worth celebrating,' Maggie corrected. 'The dress is just the wrapping paper.'

'Very expensive wrapping paper,' Daisy said with a nervous laugh.

'Worth every penny if it helps you feel confident,' Annabelle said. 'And you do look confident. Confident and successful and like you absolutely belong at a fancy awards do.'

'You're both very sure I'm going to win,' Daisy observed. 'I probably won't win…'

'You'll look fabulous while not winning. There's something to be said for losing in style.'

'Very reassuring, thanks.'

Maggie nodded, pursed her lips and clapped her hands together. 'Miles is going to be knocked sideways.'

31

Daisy pushed open the back gate to Annabelle's house and walked through the garden with a bottle of wine in one hand and a bag of cinnamon buns in the other. Annabelle's garden looked lovely; little plops of sun bounced off the greenhouse, an old lichen-covered bench under an apple tree showcased lovely striped cushions and a rambling rose going over the shed made Daisy smile. She could hear voices coming from the kitchen and the sound of Piers laughing at something. The twins had gone ahead and were already somewhere inside and Miles followed in behind her with a pack of beers and a bunch of flowers.

As they walked in, Daisy felt her shoulders relax. The kitchen was full of her family and the Henley noise she knew and loved well. Something delicious smelling was coming from the Aga, and Annabelle, in a striped shirt with her sleeves rolled up, was standing on the far side of the island stirring something in a large white bowl. Maggie sat on one of the high stools with a glass of wine, her bandage barely visible under a silk head scarf tied over her head and to the side. Susannah stood by the window with her hands wrapped around a mug of tea, talking to Piers, who was leaning against the worktop with a beer in his hand.

'There she is.' Maggie spotted Daisy and smiled 'How did the afternoon go?'

'Fine, nothing dramatic to report. Evie lost her reading book, but we found it under the car seat. Margot decided she wanted to walk the long way home so we could see if the ducks had any babies.'

'Any luck with the ducks?'

'Not yet, but she lives in hope.'

Daisy put the wine and cinnamon buns on the worktop and kissed Annabelle on the cheek. Suntanned Pete was sitting at the small table near the window with a beer. He raised his glass when he saw her. 'Daise, how are we?'

'Good, thanks.'

'Where are the girls?' Daisy asked.

'They went up to build something with Lego. They said it was going to be a castle.'

'They'll be there for hours then. Excellent.'

Piers kissed her hello and passed her a glass of wine that Annabelle had already poured. 'How was your day?'

'Good. Busy. I had three people ask about when the next book club meeting was and someone wanted to know if I could order in a specific biography that's apparently only available from a publisher in Edinburgh.'

'Can you?'

'I can try. It's about a Victorian explorer nobody's ever heard of, but the customer seemed very keen.'

'That's the beauty of independent bookshops.' Pete fiddled with the mirrored sunglasses on his head. 'You can actually get things done for people instead of telling them to check online.'

Susannah turned away from the window and Daisy could see right away that something was different about her mum's face. She looked lighter somehow. Susannah had been trying to hide how worried she'd been about Maggie, but the strain had been showing around her eyes and in the way she held her shoulders.

Daisy kissed her. 'Mum, you look better.'

'I *feel* better. Much better, actually.' Susannah smiled in Maggie's direction. 'We have news.'

Maggie swivelled around. 'I finally got the rest of my test results back this morning.'

'Everything's fine. Better than fine, actually. The surgeon got all of it, clean margins, no sign of any spread, no need for any further treatment. I'm officially in the clear.'

Daisy felt her knees go a bit wobbly and she sat down heavily on the nearest stool. 'Really?'

'Really, really. The report came back completely clear. She said the surgery was textbook perfect. They got it all.' Maggie touched the scarf in the place where the initial problem had been.

Susannah made a noise that was somewhere between a sob and a laugh and put her mug down on the windowsill. 'I don't think I could have coped with much more uncertainty.'

Miles raised his beer. 'That's brilliant news. What a relief.'

Pete shook his head. 'Thank the good lord.'

Daisy stood up and hugged Maggie. 'I'm so relieved I could cry.'

'Nope, no crying. I've had enough emotional scenes to last me a lifetime.'

'I thought you said you weren't scared.'

'I wasn't scared exactly, but I wasn't exactly looking forward to the possibility of having to go through all this again either.'

Annabelle joined the hug and Susannah wrapped her arms around all three of her daughters. 'I don't care if you're sentimental or not. I've been worried sick. I am so, so relieved.'

Miles took a picture with his phone. 'One for the family album.'

Evie appeared in the doorway. 'What's happened? Is Aunty Maggie not poorly anymore?'

'That's right, sweetheart. Maggie's going to be absolutely fine.'

Margot launched herself at Maggie. 'Does that mean you don't have to wear the bandage anymore?'

'I have to wear it until everything is better, but after that, no more bandages.'

Daisy sat back down and gulped her wine. The relief was *so* intense, it felt almost physical, as if she'd been holding her breath for a long time and could finally exhale properly. She looked around the kitchen at everyone talking and laughing and felt overwhelming gratitude that Maggie was okay. 'What did the surgeon actually say?'

'She said it was straightforward. The margins were clear, which means they got all the abnormal tissue, and there was no sign that anything had spread. She's confident that's the end of it.'

'What about follow-up appointments?'

'I'll need to go back for check-ups, and then again in six months and a year. After that, it'll just be annual skin checks and that sort of thing.'

'That's it?'

'Just regular monitoring to make sure nothing new develops.'

Susannah wiped her eyes with the back of her hand. 'I feel like I've been waiting in limbo for a long time. I kept thinking there would be complications or more surgery needed.'

'I did tell you all that I would be fine.'

Annabelle took a large wooden paddle from underneath the island, unwrapped wax paper from cheese and spooned onion, garlic and balsamic jam into two small dishes. Daisy watched everyone settling into the news and felt as if she could jump up and down in excitement that things had returned to normal. Nothing special or fancy, just the three sisters and Susannah in the kitchen doing their thing. It had all been hanging on a knife's edge and now it was better. Maggie was going to be fine and everyone she cared about was in the same room, making noise and fussing over each other. It struck her that this was exactly what happiness looked like, not some grand dramatic moment but just ordinary people in a kitchen being relieved together.

'How are you actually feeling? Not the official medical report, but how do you *feel*?'

'Tired, mostly and relieved, obviously, but also a bit strange. I didn't want to tell anyone, but I mean, I spent weeks preparing myself for the possibility that this might be more serious than we thought. I had plans for what I'd do if I needed more treatment, how I'd handle time off work, all sorts of contingencies. Now I don't need any of those plans and I feel a bit lost.'

Daisy understood completely. She'd totally kept her thoughts to herself, been doing the same thing, mentally preparing for worst-case scenarios and researching treatment options she hoped they would never need. 'I think that's normal. It's like when you're rushing to catch a train and then you find out it's been delayed. You don't know what to do with all that adrenaline.'

'Exactly.'

Miles came over and refilled their wine glasses. 'What are you two whispering about?'

'Just processing the good news,' Maggie said. 'It's harder than you'd think.'

'I can imagine. You've been living with uncertainty and now suddenly there isn't any uncertainty anymore.'

'Right. I don't know what to worry about now.'

Piers started to open a bottle of champagne. He held it up. 'French, it's been waiting patiently for the right moment and this is it. One of my sisters-in-law getting the all-clear from surgery.'

'Here's to getting the all clear.' Pete raised his beer.

'To surgeons who know what they're doing and thank goodness for the amazing staff and nurses.' Susannah added.

'And to sisters who worry about each other even when they're told not to,' Maggie looked at Daisy and Annabelle with raised eyebrows.

Daisy was more than thankful for the kitchen full of the sounds of normal family life again - Annabelle clattering around with pots and pans, the twins giggling upstairs, conversation flowing without the undercurrent of worry that had been there for ages.

'What's the plan for work?' Miles asked. 'Are you going back full-time right away?'

'Next week, probably. I've been working from home.'

'What about the headscarf situation?'

'I'll probably keep covering the area for a bit longer just because it's still quite red and obvious. Vanity, really.'

Pete chuckled. 'I was just thinking that you look quite elegant in a headscarf. Very nineteen-fifties film star.'

'I feel more like a nineteen-fifties housewife.'

The conversation drifted here and there as Daisy sipped her wine and observed. Pete chatted about one of the latest holiday cottage disasters, Miles talked about his work situation with the New York clients and Daisy listened with half her attention while the other half just soaked up the normalcy of it all. It had been missing from the Henley family gatherings since Maggie's news. The shadow of Maggie's diagnosis hanging over everything had now, thank goodness, gone and good riddance, too.

Daisy scooped up a piece of cheese, popped it on a cracker and added a blob of onion jam. 'Yum, Bells, you've outdone yourself with this, as usual.'

Maggie nodded. 'Delicious. Anyway, are you ready for the big awards ceremony? Shame they're not live streaming it.'

Miles laughed. 'I'm glad they're not.'

Pete helped himself to some cheese. 'This is a big deal, Daise. You're representing Pretty Beach at a national awards ceremony.'

'No pressure then.'

'None at all,' Miles laughed. 'Just the entire town's reputation resting on your shoulders.'

Daisy winced. 'That's exactly what I need to hear right now.'

Pete raised his eyebrows. 'What are you going to say if you win?'

'I probably won't win.'

'But what if you do?'

'I haven't thought about it. I suppose I'll say thank you and try not to trip over my dress.'

Susannah smiled. 'You should prepare something, just in case. A few words about what the bookshop means to you and to Pretty Beach.'

'Like what?'

'Like how it's given you a purpose and a place in the community. It's brought people together. It's proof that small independent businesses can thrive if they offer something genuine.'

'That sounds very grand when you put it like that. I just wanted somewhere to live and a way to make money. Everything else was accidental. Nah, I'm not planning a speech. I'll wing it if it happens.'

A couple of hours later, the twins were in bed in Annabelle's spare room, Pete had taken Susannah home and Daisy was sitting rugged up underneath a blanket on a bench in the garden looking up at the stars. The relief about Maggie settled in as if in little layers.

Miles patted her leg. 'All good?'

'Better than good. I'm just happy to be here and have us back to normal and all of us being here together. Everyone is healthy and happy. No crises to manage or problems to solve.'

'Yep.'

'So different from a year or so ago. I was still living in that tiny house on the estate, working different jobs to make ends meet, worried about everything all the time. Now I have a business that's doing well, a nomination for a national award, a relationship that makes me happy, and my sister just got the all-clear from surgery. It's a lot of good news all at once.'

'I like good news.' Miles noted.

'Me too. I'm still processing the evening.'

'Good processing or complicated processing?'

'Good processing. Definitely good processing.'

'It was nice to see Maggie looking like herself again.'

'I didn't realise how much the worry was showing until I saw her without it.'

'Same with your mum. She was trying to hide how scared she was, but it was written all over her face.'

'We all were. Even when we were trying to be normal and supportive, we were all terrified.'

'And now you're not.'

'Now we're not.'

They sat sipping their drinks and listening to the sounds of Pretty Beach settling down for the night.

'Are you ready for this awards thing?'

'As ready as I *can* be. I'll try not to embarrass myself when I have to make conversation with proper business people.'

'You run a successful independent bookshop that's been nominated for a national award.'

'Whatever happens, it'll be something to celebrate.'

'Like today was.'

'Exactly like today was.'

32

Daisy cracked an egg into a frying pan and watched it sizzle alongside two others in a little pool of lovely hot oil. The kitchen at the bookshop smelled fantastic; all Sunday morning bacon fat and toast. The kind of weekend breakfast smell that made everything feel slow, comfy and indulgent. With the twins at Susannah's, it had to be said that the morning had been a whole lot less frantic than Daisy's regular weekday mornings. With a nice easy lie-in and a late opening of the bookshop, she'd fried bacon until it was crisp around the edges, added thick sliced black pudding and sausages, grilled tomatoes until they were soft and slightly charred, and warmed baked beans in a small saucepan and had two pieces of bread from the bakery waiting to be fried. Life behind the bookshop was good.

Miles sat at the little wooden table by the window with a mug of coffee in both hands, still in his pyjamas. His hair stuck up at odd angles, he had a slightly rumpled look, appeared as if he had slept well, and had an air about him that he was in deep relax mode. Daisy liked that Miles very much. They chatted away as Daisy took a pan from the copper rail underneath the shelves Pete had put up, added some duck fat and dropped in some sliced mushrooms.

'How many eggs do you want?' Daisy asked, though she'd already cracked three into the pan, she knew Miles's appetite for a good old-fashioned fry-up.

'Two, thanks. Though those look perfect, so I might manage three.' Miles winked.

'I know what you're like with a full English.'

'You know me too well.'

Pretty Beach Radio played from a little speaker on the worktop and Suntanned Pete's voice filled the kitchen. Daisy chuckled as Pete bantered in the middle of reading out the weather forecast. He'd noted that the weather promised a mild day with the possibility of showers and that it was perfect weather for walking up to the lighthouse, going out on a boat and or staying indoors and doing nothing much at all. Pete's voice continued. 'I've got a message here from Jean at the post office who wants everyone to know that new stamps featuring British butterflies are now available. She says they're perfect for anyone who collects stamps or just wants to send a nice letter. Jean also wants to remind everyone that the post box outside the chemist is still being emptied twice a day, despite what some people might have heard to the contrary.'

Daisy smiled as she turned the eggs carefully with a spatula. Pete's radio show always made her laugh because he took his job very seriously. He read out birth announcements and death notices, advertised lost cats and found bicycles, and generally kept everyone informed about the small details of life in their corner of the world.

Miles joked. 'I must go and buy some stamps.'

Pete's voice continued from the speaker. 'Here's something for anyone who's interested in local history. Margaret from Pretty Beach Historical Society has found some old photographs of the harbour from the 1920s. She's going to display them in the library next month and she'd love to hear from anyone who might be able to identify some of the people in the pictures. Margaret says there are some wonderful shots of the fishing fleet and the old ferry, back when it was still powered by steam.'

Miles reached across to turn the radio up slightly. 'I love these local history stories. It's amazing what people find tucked away in attics and cupboards. Pete is so serious. Honestly, he cracks me up.'

Daisy nodded. 'Mum's got boxes of old photographs she keeps meaning to sort through. She says some of them go back to when her grandparents lived here. Goodness knows what else is upstairs here. Uncle Dennis liked to hoard a thing or two.'

Daisy moved the eggs over, poured the oil from the black pudding pan into the frying pan and pushed four triangles of bread down into it and tried not to think about either the calories or her cholesterol levels.

Pete continued as the pan sizzled. 'A quick reminder about parking in the town centre. Roy from the council wants everyone to know that the restrictions around the church are still in place despite the road works being finished. He says people are still parking there who shouldn't be and tickets will be issued if it continues, as noted on the community Facebook page. Charlie from the council also wants to thank whoever's been putting the wheelie bins back in the right places after collection day. He says it makes his job much easier and he appreciates the help.'

As the bread finished frying, Daisy divided the breakfast between two warmed plates; eggs in the centre, surrounded by bacon, sausages, grilled tomatoes and black pudding tucked alongside. The beans went in a small pool beside everything else and the fried bread, looking golden, was tucked around the top of the plate. Artery-friendly it was not.

Miles raised his eyebrows and rubbed his hands together. 'Do I or do I not love a fry-up?'

'I've learned that you do. I won't be able to get that dress on at this rate. There are about two weeks' worth of calories on this plate. Oh well...'

As they tucked in, a song finished and Pete's voice drifted from the radio again, this time with a request for information about a missing cat called Tiddles who'd disappeared from the Old Town area. He described Tiddles as a large ginger tom with white patches and a tendency to turn up in unexpected places. The owner was offering a reward and asking anyone who might have seen him to put a post on Facebook or call in at the bakery.

'There's nothing worse than losing a pet.' Daisy noted. 'Actually, a lost child is much worse, not that, thankfully, I know about one of those.'

Miles's phone rang just as he was tucking into his second piece of fried bread. He glanced at the screen and frowned slightly before answering. 'Shane? Hey.'

Daisy could hear the estate agent, Shane's, voice coming through the phone, though she couldn't make out the actual words. Whatever Shane was saying made Miles sit up straighter and put down his bread.

'Right, I see. When did this happen?'

More talking from Shane's end, urgent and animated by the sound of it. Miles looked across at Daisy with an expression she couldn't read.

'How serious are they? Do you think they'll actually make an offer?'

Daisy put her knife and fork down and topped up her tea from the teapot.

'No, no, I understand completely. It's fine to phone me on a Sunday. You're just keeping me informed.'

Shane's voice continued through the phone and Miles nodded even though Shane couldn't see him.

'What sort of timescale are we talking about?'

The answer to this question made Miles's eyebrows go up significantly. He caught Daisy's eye and made a face that suggested the news wasn't ideal.

'Right. Well, I appreciate you letting me know. Can you give me until later today to think about it?'

More conversation, brief this time, and then Miles hung up and put his phone back on the table.

'What was that?'

'The house. I told you that Shane texted me to tell me that the owners decided they wanted to get going quickly after the initial delay. He said that as soon as it hit the internet, it went nuts. He's had loads of enquiries. Someone else has seen it now and they're very interested.'

'Did he say who they were?'

'A couple from London. They've apparently been searching for eleven months and haven't found anything they like until now. He said they spent over an hour there yesterday and asked very detailed questions about everything.'

Daisy pushed beans around her plate with her fork and tried to process the information. She'd been putting off thinking about the house thing, telling herself it would just fade away. Apparently, time had just run out and push had come to shove. 'What did Shane say about their situation? Are they serious buyers?'

'Very serious, according to him. They're cash buyers, no chain, ready to move quickly. Exactly the sort of people sellers want to deal with.'

'Like you, then, if that's still what you want to do.'

'I guess so. Meaning it comes down to who makes the better offer and who can move fastest.'

'Or who Shaney prefers. The Pretty Beach way will come into play here.'

Miles wrinkled his nose. 'What? What's Shane got to do with it?'

'If we want it, I mean *you* want it. You'll get it over them. Hands down without a doubt about that.'

'How does that work if they offer more money?'

'Trust me on this. Pretty Beach beats to its own drum where things like this are concerned. There's no way they will get it unless, of course, you offer something silly. If you're in the game, you'll win.'

Pete's voice came through the radio again, cheerfully announcing that the Pretty Beach Gardening Club would be holding their annual plant sale in the community centre car park. He read out a list of the sorts of plants that would be available, from bedding plants to established shrubs, and reminded everyone that proceeds would go towards maintaining the public gardens near the seafront. Pete's announcements felt strange against the backdrop of the suddenly urgent house situation. Here was Pretty Beach going about its regular business while Daisy and Miles faced a decision that upped the relationship stakes.

'What do you want to do?' Daisy asked.

'I want to buy the house. I've wanted to buy it since the moment we walked through the front door. This just forces my decision. I don't know why I stalled when Shane said they were ready to go.'

'Even with competition?'

'*Especially* with competition. I don't want to lose it to someone else when we've already decided it's perfect.'

'Have you decided that?'

Miles put down his fork. 'I thought *we* had. Haven't we?'

Daisy considered. Had they decided? They'd talked about the house extensively, visited it twice, and discussed the practicalities, but she wasn't sure they'd ever actually made a firm decision to proceed. She had certainly not said yes to moving in and she'd told him she was happy in the bookshop.

'We've talked about moving in together, about making things more permanent between us. This house would be perfect for that when that time comes. I know you need time.'

The radio moved on to music, something gentle and folky. Daisy thought about the house as she'd last seen it, with its elegant proportions and period features and garden that would be lovely in summer. It was undeniably beautiful and it would suit their needs perfectly, but the urgency of Shane's call had unsettled her. 'Do *you* actually want to live there?'

'Yup. I am sick of the flat. It's tiny. I want to wake up in that bedroom with the view over the garden and the lighthouse in the distance. I want a proper base when I go to and from New York. I want to have breakfast in that kitchen and watch the golf in that sitting room. I want your mum to come for lunch and sit in the conservatory. I want the girls to have friends over and use that garden for football and trampolines and whatever else they're into. I need to put down roots, Daise.'

Daisy put her head to the side. 'That sounds lovely when you put it like that.'

'It sounds lovely because it *would* be lovely. We could be really happy there, Daise.'

'We're really happy here just as we are.'

'We are, but we could be really happy there too and there would be more space for everyone, including my mum when she comes to visit or live, hopefully.'

Daisy looked around the little kitchen where they were sitting. It was small, slightly cramped when more than two people tried to use it at the same time, but it was also cosy and familiar, completely hers and she loved it. Not only that, she really didn't like the idea of leaving it. 'How long did Shane say?'

'He wants to know as soon as, if we're, I, am going to make an offer. The other couple are coming back to measure rooms and look at it again, and he thinks they'll put in an offer straight after that.'

'It's such a big decision.'

'It's not long at all. But we've been thinking about this for ages already. It's not like we're starting from scratch. This is the first house that has come up in the Old Town since I've been looking. It's literally the *only* one.'

'I suppose so, yes.'

They finished their breakfast while the radio continued and then Miles stacked their plates in the dishwasher and wiped down the worktops. As Daisy cleared the table, the house went through her mind. 'Shane's putting quite a bit of pressure on us, isn't he?'

'He's doing his job. If there are two serious buyers interested in the same property, he needs to manage the situation.'

'Or he's trying to create urgency so we'll make a decision quickly.'

Miles mused. 'Possible, but you are the one telling me it's one in one out in the Old Town.'

'True. If they're cash buyers with no chain, they probably are quite serious. Properties like that don't come up very often. Which is another thing that makes me nervous.'

'Why does that make you nervous? You are not filling me with optimism that you want this.'

'I'm sorry. I know I should be jumping for joy and I know how unsettled you've been. I don't know. I just like what we've got now.'

'Daise, I think I'm going to just buy it and go with the flow.'

'As you do. Oh yeah, just buy a house just like that!'

'I didn't mean it to come out with that. Look, it solves many problems. The annexe thing would be brilliant for Mum. I would be here without any dramas. Let's leave the moving in together thing and play it by ear.'

Daisy nodded. 'Yes, let's.'

33

Daisy turned the key in the ignition and pulled away from Annabelle's house with Maggie in the passenger seat beside her. As they drove through the narrow streets of Pretty Beach towards the Old Town, Daisy rattled on about the house. Maggie had insisted on having a look at the house and after a quick call to Shane, it had been sorted and they were meeting him there.

Maggie adjusted the silk scarf on her head and settled back into the passenger seat. 'So, Miles is going to buy it, but you're not moving in? Have I got that straight?'

'That's about the size of it, yes. He wants to get out of that tiny flat and settle somewhere permanently in Pretty Beach. The house solves all his problems with space and gives his mum somewhere to live if and when she moves down.'

'But it doesn't solve *your* problems?'

'I don't really have problems that need solving. I like where I am.'

They drove past the harbour where fishing boats bobbed at their moorings, seagulls wheeled overhead and the water sparkled as one of the Pretty Beach ferries chugged out to sea.

Pretty Beach looked peaceful, unhurried and completely happy with itself.

Maggie frowned. 'So, you're staying put above the bookshop. Is that what you're telling me? Doesn't make sense, Daise, but whatever works for you.'

'For now. I'm not ready to give up my independence. The bookshop is the first place that's ever felt completely mine, and I'm not in any hurry to change that.'

'And he's fine with that arrangement?'

Daisy shrugged. 'He says he is. He wants to be settled somewhere permanently, with the New York thing coming up and he wants his mum to have options about where to live. The house gives him both of those things, whether I'm there or not. You know how rarely they come up in the Old Town and money is not an issue. It makes sense.'

They turned left at the post office and drove up the hill towards the Old Town, past a little row of cottages that lined a narrow street. The houses were old with slate roofs and small front gardens filled with flowering shrubs and all painted in the soft colours that Pretty Beach was known for, pale blues, pinks, yellows and greens that caught the light and made the whole street look like something from a postcard.

'What about the relationship side of things?' Maggie asked. 'Doesn't living separately defeat the point of being together?'

Daisy shook her head. 'Why would you say that? It's been working fine. This just means we each keep our own space as well.'

'Very modern of you.' Maggie winked.

'Very *practical* of me. I've got the twins to think about and they're settled where they are. Moving them into a big house feels like a lot of upheaval. Mags, you know how many times they've moved. I'm not ready to do it and I don't think they are.'

Maggie pressed her window down slightly and let the sea breeze blow through the car. Salty, Pretty Beach coastal air filled their noses. 'What does Miles think about you staying where you are?'

'He understands, or at least he says he does. I don't know, he's gone from being quite angst-y about it all to being laid back and completely the opposite. He knows how important stability is for the girls and me, after all the moving around we did when they were smaller. He can see that they love living above the bookshop. Yeah, I don't know. I think we both now get it.'

'And what about when his mum moves down? Won't that change the dynamic quite a bit?'

'I don't know. I guess we cross that bridge when we come to it. It's another reason why I'm staying put.'

They reached the crest of the hill and the view opened up before them, showing the whole sweep of Pretty Beach laid out below. The harbour looked tiny and the ferry was just a speck on the horizon. The lighthouse stood white and stark against a blue sky, and beyond it, the sea stretched away to meet the clouds in a line that seemed to go on forever.

'It's beautiful up here. I forget sometimes how lovely it is to live somewhere like this.' Maggie noted.

'Every time I come up this way, I remember how lucky we are to call this place home.'

They drove through the most exclusive part of Pretty Beach, where houses changed hands rarely and usually stayed within the same families for generations.

'So, what's the deal with Miles and his New York work?' Maggie asked as they navigated around a tight corner, faced an oncoming car and had to reverse to give way. 'Wasn't that what he was getting his knickers in a twist about? How's that going to work if he's living here permanently?'

'It's no different to what he's doing now. He's worked it out so he only has to go over there once or twice a month, sometimes less. Most of the work can be done remotely these days, and the meetings he does need to attend in person are usually just sign-off sessions for deals he's been working on.'

'How the world has changed, eh? That sounds manageable.'

'He was worried at first that it might mean too much travelling, but it's turned out to be much more flexible than he expected. The time difference actually works in his favour because he can have calls with New York clients in the afternoon here.'

'And you're not worried about him jetting off to America all the time?'

'Not really. It's just work travel and it's not like he's disappearing for weeks at a time. It's the fast train that makes it doable; otherwise, it wouldn't work.'

Turning onto the road the house was on, Maggie shifted in her seat and squinted out the windscreen. 'Which one is it?' Maggie craned her neck to look at the houses they passed.

'The one with the green door and the wisteria over the porch.'

'Oh, that one. I remember walking past it when we were little. Didn't someone famous live there once? Like years and years ago?'

'I don't know. We'll have to ask Mum.' Daisy pulled up outside the house and turned off the engine. The building looked even more impressive than she remembered from her visits with Miles and Shane.

'I can see why Miles wants it. It's gorgeous!' Maggie enthused.

'It really is.'

'You're *mad* not to move in, Daise. Fruit loop.'

'I'm quite content in my little flat above the bookshop.'

Maggie got out and stood on the pavement as they waited for Shane to arrive. 'It looks enormous and wow, it's so nice. Bells will be beside herself.'

'It's beautiful, no question about that.'

'And you're definitely not tempted to move in right away?'

Daisy considered. Was she tempted, really? The house was undeniably lovely, and the idea of waking up every morning to views of the garden and the sea beyond was not a horrible one. But something was telling her not to jump in with sixteen feet. 'I'm tempted by the idea of it, but I'm not ready for the reality of it. Does that make sense?'

'No, it does *not* make sense in any shape or form. Who even are you? You're nuts and bonkers. It's spectacular and the twins would love this garden.'

'I've spent so many years not knowing where I was going to be living from one month to the next that having my own space feels precious. I'm not chucking that out the window.'

'You have a point.' Maggie gestured in the direction of the back garden. 'So that's the annexe back there. It would work for Elizabeth, would it? Has she agreed to move down then?'

'Not totally, but Miles is worried about her being on her own. This gives her a way out without feeling like she's imposing on anyone. She's still going on about not being a burden.'

'So, yeah, it ticks a lot of boxes. It really is a beautiful house.'

'It is, Mags, I just need to do things at my own pace, though. For now, this arrangement works for both of us. He gets to settle down properly in Pretty Beach, and I get to keep my independence. Who would have thought it all started with the twins chucking ice cream at him?'

'I hope another set of twins are in the air.'

'No chance!'

'What if he starts pressuring you to move in?'

'No idea. Right now, I still need my own space.'

'You know what I think? You're a bit bonkers, but I think you're being very sensible. You've got a good thing going with the bookshop and you're not ready to change and the best relationships are the ones where both people can be themselves without having to compromise everything they've built.'

Daisy nodded. She could see both sides of it, but after years on her own with only worry as her companion, she was both cautious and content; content with the life she'd built for herself and the twins and cautious about what she did with it. She wasn't sure what was on the cards, but whatever it was, she was absolutely one hundred per cent certain of one thing and that was that she would do things on her terms, selfish or not.

Not only that, she would not act in haste and would move when *she* was ready to and not before. For someone who had spent years feeling like life was something that happened to her rather than something she controlled, there was no way she was *ever* going back to how she'd felt before. If there was one thing she learnt from being on her own, it was that she had to look after number one. Selfish or not, she was going to roll with that.

34

Daisy pushed open the blue gate to Susannah's house and walked up the path between the lavender bushes that lined either side. The evening air carried the smell of something delicious cooking and Daisy could hear voices and laughter coming from inside the house and the sound of cutlery being arranged on plates. The twins had run ahead and were already through the front door, calling out greetings to Susannah.

Daisy sighed as she slipped off her shoes. The house looked exactly as it always did; welcoming, gorgeous and slightly chaotic; plant pots clustered around the front door, a collection of wellington boots was lined up against the wall, a huge, very symmetrical pile of firewood was stacked in the porch and the little bench seat on the right was topped with striped cushions. Daisy had grown up in the house, had brought the twins there when they were babies, and loved how, as soon as she walked up the path, she felt a comfort from being somewhere that had remained constant through all the changes in her life.

When she went inside, Susannah was standing at the Aga stirring something in a large pot, her hair had escaped from its usual neat arrangement and her apron was slightly flour-dusted. Annabelle sat at the scrubbed pine table with a glass of wine, and Maggie, with her feet tucked up under her, was in the chair by the window. The twins had already disappeared somewhere into the depths of the house and Radio 4 was playing from the windowsill.

Susannah smiled as Daisy walked into the kitchen. 'There she is. My award-nominated daughter. How are you feeling about tomorrow night?'

'Terrified,' Daisy admitted, accepting a glass of wine that Annabelle passed to her. 'Miles is looking forward to it, so there is that.'

'You're going to have a whale of a time. Those people know what they're doing by the looks of it.'

Daisy sat down at the table, sipped her wine and looked around at her family. The kitchen had seen all sorts over the years; countless family discussions, happiness, celebrations, teenage shenanigans, sadness, homework problems, relationship dramas and major life decisions. She loved the nostalgia of it all and let it wrap itself around her and take her under its wing.

'Have you decided what you're going to say if you win?' Annabelle asked as she topped up her glass of wine.

'I've written something down, but it sounds terrible when I read it out loud. Either too formal and businesslike, or too emotional and rambling. I won't win anyway, but when I thought about winging it, I didn't think it would be a good idea.'

'What are you going to say?'

'Just thank you, really. Thank you to the people who nominated me, thank you to Pretty Beach for supporting the bookshop, thank you to all of you for helping me get to this point.' Daisy felt a prick at the corner of her eyes as emotion welled up.

Susannah turned away from the stove and wiped her hands

on her apron. 'That sounds perfect. Simple and heartfelt, which is always the way to go.

'It doesn't sound perfect when I try to say it out loud. I either gabble through it so fast that nobody can understand me, or I slow down so much that I sound like I'm reading the shipping forecast.'

The twins thundered back into the kitchen wearing what appeared to be every piece of fancy dress clothing Susannah owned. Margot had on a purple velvet dress that trailed on the floor behind her, topped with a feathered hat that kept slipping over her eyes. Evie sported a combination of sequinned top, tutu and fairy wings, several strings of beads around her neck that clinked when she moved and she clip-clopped in a pair of Susannah's heels.

'We're dressed up like Mummy for her important dinner,' Margot announced, adjusting her hat with seriousness.

Daisy managed not to laugh at the sight of them. 'Much more elegant than I'm going to look tomorrow night. You look lovely, girls.'

'Can we practice what you had on those cards? We can be your audience and clap when you finish.' Margot asked.

'That's actually not a bad idea,' Annabelle said. 'You need to practice saying it in front of people anyway.'

'I don't think you and the twins count as representative of tomorrow night's audience,' Daisy protested.

'Practice is practice,' Maggie pointed out. 'Besides, if you can say it coherently in front of us lot, you can say it coherently in front of anyone.'

Susannah took a navy blue Le Creuset pot out of the Aga, took off the lid and slid a loaf of bread from it onto the table. Cutting it into thick slices, she then dished out six bowls and put a casserole dish and a ladle onto a wicker table runner. The smell of rosemary and garlic filled the kitchen and Daisy felt her stomach rumble as she realised she'd been too nervous to eat much during the day.

Susannah nodded. 'Right, after dinner, we'll go into the sitting room and you can practice your speech while we pretend to be distinguished award ceremony guests.'

'This is already embarrassing and I haven't even started yet.'

'It's not embarrassing, it's preparation,' Annabelle corrected. 'You'll thank us tomorrow when you're standing up there feeling confident when you've won.'

Daisy offered a piece of bread to the twins and inhaled the delicious smells. The casserole was exactly the sort of comforting food Susannah specialised in, rich and warming and slowly cooked all day long. As the conversation moved this way and that and everyone tucked in, Daisy relaxed. The mixture of chat, banter, teasing and unwavering support was exactly what she'd needed.

'What time do you need to leave tomorrow?' Susannah asked.

'Around lunchtime. The ceremony doesn't start until around seven, but Miles wants to drive slowly and maybe stop somewhere on the way, so I'm not rushing around at the last minute.'

'Very sensible. You don't want to arrive feeling frazzled.'

'I'm going to arrive feeling frazzled, whatever happens. I just hope I can hide it well enough that nobody notices.'

After dinner, they moved into the sitting room with coffee and the last of the wine and Daisy settled onto the sofa. Everything was cosy and just so; little wicker lamps on top of the fireplace, family photographs covering every surface and books stacked on the shelves that lined the walls. The twins had rearranged themselves into even more elaborate outfits and were positioned on the sofa, a very demanding expectant audience.

Maggie settled herself into an armchair by the fireplace. 'We are now distinguished members of the Independent Retail

Alliance, gathered in Bath to celebrate excellence in independent business. Daisy Henley, please take the stage.'

Daisy giggled and felt ridiculous. 'It's too weird practising in front of you lot.'

'Pretend we're strangers and very serious business people who've never met you before.'

'I know you too well to pretend you're strangers and I'd rather not think about it.'

'Stop procrastinating and give us your speech.'

Daisy pulled out her phone and tapped. 'When I first opened The Bookshop Pretty Beach,' she stopped and looked around at her family. Margot and Evie both had very wide eyes. 'This is hopeless. I can't concentrate when you're all staring at me.'

Susannah waved her hands in little encouraging movements. 'We're not staring, we're listening attentively. Carry on.'

'When I first opened The Bookshop Pretty Beach, I never imagined it would become more than just a way to make ends meet.' Daisy paused and glanced at her notes, then looked up again. 'I was a single mother with twins, living in rented accommodation, working different jobs to pay the bills. The idea of owning my own business seemed impossible and implausible for someone like me.'

'Good start,' Annabelle muttered. 'Personal but not too personal.'

'But sometimes impossible things become possible when you have the support of an extraordinary community. Pretty Beach didn't just accept my little bookshop, it embraced it. Customers became friends, people found us online and came to visit, and what started as an attempt to create something nice became quite meaningful.'

The twins had stopped fidgeting as much and were listening intently. Margot's feathered hat had slipped sideways and Evie's fairy wings rustled every time she moved.

'The bookshop became a place where people pottered with

books, reconnected with old favourites and found exactly the book they didn't know they were looking for. But more than that, it became a place where community happened. Mums with young children could sit and chat and elderly customers could spend a bit of time browsing and chatting without feeling rushed or unwelcome.'

'You're getting into your stride now.'

Daisy found that once she'd started, the words came more easily than she'd expected. 'This nomination means more to me than I can adequately express, not just because it recognises what I've built at the bookshop, but because it celebrates the values that independent businesses bring to their communities. We're not just shops, we're gathering places. We're not just selling products, we're creating connections. We're proof that our beautiful country needs good old-fashioned shops back.'

'Brilliant! That's exactly right.'

'I am accepting this award for every small business owner who's ever worried about competing with larger companies, anyone like me who's bootstrapped something from nothing, and every community that's chosen to support local businesses over corporate alternatives. Thank you to the Independent Retail Alliance for this recognition, thank you to my customers for their loyalty, and thank you to Pretty Beach for being the sort of place where dreams can come true. Most of all, thank you to my sisters and my mum.'

The sitting room was quiet for a moment after she finished, and Daisy felt her cheeks flush with embarrassment. 'That was terrible, wasn't it? Too long, too sentimental, too much about me and not enough about business?'

'Perfect.'

'Really?'

'Really.'

Margot started clapping enthusiastically, her oversized dress rustling with each movement. 'That was much better than the lady who did the prizes at school. She just said thank you and sat down.'

Daisy put her phone back in her pocket. 'I probably won't win, but at least if I do, I know I can get through it without completely embarrassing myself.'

'You're going to be wonderful.' Susannah got up and hugged Daisy. 'I'm so proud of what you've achieved and tomorrow night, everyone else will see what we've always known about you, whether you win or not. We are Henley women and we are capable of extraordinary things when we put our minds to it. I am so proud, Daise! So proud.'

'Thank you. You've all helped me so much.'

'Rubbish.'

Daisy felt a strange mix of being way too emotional and very content, both at the same time. Truth be told, she wasn't that bothered about the actual event itself or indeed whether or not she won the award. She was bothered about being in Pretty Beach and being surrounded by people who knew her completely and loved her anyway. At the event, she would be in a room full of strangers, wearing an expensive dress and trying to sound like she belonged among successful business people. That held not a lot of clout for her because she was exactly where she'd always belonged, in her mum's house with her sisters and daughters, being *herself*. For sure, new challenges and new experiences were good, but whatever happened, she had people around her who loved her rain or shine. She was exactly where she belonged, in the place she'd created for herself and her daughters. Bottom line of it all was that really, when push came to shove, she didn't care about a lot else.

She nodded as she watched Evie and Margot quickly move on and start talking to Maggie about the scar under her scarf. The speech was ready, the dress was hanging in her wardrobe, Miles would be by her side, and her family believed in her totally, utterly and completely. That felt just so blooming good.

For the first time since receiving the nomination, Daisy felt a little bit excited about the evening. Whatever happened at the ceremony, she would represent Pretty Beach and independent bookshops. She would hold her head high. She'd rock the one-shouldered dress. She'd be, act, see and do like a Henley girl through and through. She wasn't going to argue with that.

35

Daisy adjusted her seatbelt for the third time and glanced down at her jeans and floral shirt as Miles navigated the car through the narrow streets leading out of Pretty Beach. Her dress was hanging carefully in the back of the car, protected by layers of tissue paper and a garment bag that Annabelle had insisted was absolutely essential for transporting couture. Not that the dress was couture, or that Daisy even really knew what that was, but it felt like it to her. The plan was to have a nice bath at the hotel once they reached Bath; a bath in Bath had to be done. Meaning that they could travel comfortably, maybe stop for a cup of tea and arrive in good time without any stress.

'You're very quiet,' Miles observed as they joined the main road to take them up and away from Pretty Beach, inland towards Bath. 'Second thoughts about the whole thing?'

'Not second thoughts exactly, ha, more like forty-seventh thoughts. You know these things aren't my cup of tea. I'm trying to remain open-minded and calm.'

Miles patted Daisy's leg. 'Fake it til you make it.'

'Trust me, that will be happening.'

The countryside rolled past the windows as the Pretty Beach

Hills loomed in the far distance. As Miles continued driving, fields dotted with sheep gradually gave way to small villages and market towns, lovely old church spires poked up into the sky and gorgeous patchworks of English fields lined with hedgerows accompanied their journey. Daisy, not having been out of Pretty Beach that many times in her existence, watched life pass the window and there wasn't much chatting going on in the car at all. As her brain decompressed, she couldn't quite believe she was on her way to an awards ceremony for running a successful business. Everything felt slightly surreal. Here she was with a little bookshop people loved, sitting beside a man she very much loved. Oh, how much her life had changed.

Daisy frowned. 'What did the schedule say on the invitation?'

'Reception starts at six-thirty with drinks and mingling. Dinner at seven-thirty. Awards ceremony, then dancing and more drinks until whenever people decide to give up the ghost.'

'Dancing? In that dress. I can hardly move in it.'

'I'll pick you up and twirl you around.'

Daisy giggled. 'I'll probably want to go straight back to the hotel room and put my pyjamas on. Hair up, bra off and relax.'

'Yeah.'

Daisy made a face. 'What exactly do you think mingling entails?'

'Schmoozing with people you don't know. Don't worry, I'm an expert.'

Miles reached across and squeezed her hand and then looked back at the road. 'You'll be fine once you're there. These events are always tiring, though. Having to small talk with people you don't know and smile all the time.'

'Are you speaking from experience?'

'A bit. I've been to a few corporate events over the years. The format's usually the same, whoever's organising. Drinks, dinner, speeches, more drinks. Most people are just pleased to have an excuse to dress up and eat good food. If the drinks are flowing, some people get absolutely plastered, which is either very funny or very not.'

'I guess some people must love it.'

'Tonight, I'm not in the driving seat though, I'm the plus one. I get to sit back, have a few bevvies and observe while you do all the work.'

Daisy joked. 'What? I'm relying on you to charm your way around the room and make contacts for my business. I want you to find me a silent investor, or what is it? Seed investor or something...'

'Hmm, I didn't know I was now an employee of The Bookshop Pretty Beach.'

'I'll get you a contract of employment issued pronto.'

'Anyway, I have a bit of news.'

'Right, good news, I hope.'

'Shane messaged me this morning regarding the house. It's all systems go. Solicitors, paperwork and the like...'

'Wow, it's going quickly since the offer was accepted.'

'It is. Look, Daise, you just do whatever you want to do. We don't have to change anything.'

'Okay.'

'I need to settle.'

'Yes.'

'We'll play it by ear.'

'Yep.'

They stopped for tea at a pub about halfway to Bath, and Daisy kept checking her watch every few minutes to make sure they weren't running late. She felt all sorts of out of kilter, as if the day was passing both too quickly and too slowly at the same time. As if something very big and even more significant was just ahead of her in her future and she wasn't quite sure what it was or whether she wanted it in the first place. Safe to say she wasn't feeling herself at all.

An hour or so later, Bath appeared gradually as they crested a hill, spread out ahead of them like something from a period drama. Daisy leaned forward, taking in the honey-coloured stone of Georgian structures and elegance that seemed to ooze from the buildings. Her stomach fluttered with nervous excitement as they joined a line of traffic and the car crept along. Daisy couldn't take in Bath fast enough and it unravelled like a painting, all soft golds, pretty beiges and greys, domes and spires, chimneys and crescents. As if the whole place had been quietly stitched together by someone with a grand, old, beautiful English city in mind. The planner had done well adding history in layers, terraces upon terraces, golden honey stone, columns and windows that watched the world. Daisy, it was safe to say, right from the word go, was smitten.

As Miles drove, Daisy gaped at sweeps of majestic buildings, ornate wrought iron balconies, stone steps to painted front doors, rings of townhouses in grand continuous loops. All of the beautiful English city things. The detailing was exquisite; columns with carved capitals, cornices jutted just so, circular windows set high under the eaves, old gas lamps, pavements wide and neat. Fabulous.

As they drove further in, the buildings shifted with tiny shops tucked into Georgian shells, cafes with awnings and boutiques slotted behind railings. High, arched windows displayed books, baskets of soap, and racks of scarves in jewel tones. A chemist with its name carved in stone above the door. A tiny tea shop with twisted glass and a wooden sign swinging in the breeze. All of it gorgeous with lovely, quiet old buildings standing as if looking down on everything going on below them, strong, elegant, quietly asserting themselves as though they'd been there long before and would be there long after.

Everywhere she looked, there were little details Daisy just couldn't get enough of. Fanlights above heavy front doors, delicate egg-and-dart cornicing, window boxes bursting with trailing ivy and the most beautiful fretwork ever. All surrounded by the softest, muted, loveliest sounds and colours; hues of stone gold, muffled tyres on damp cobbles, rumbling buses winding their way through the streets, soft pops of bronze, footsteps, distant voices, a bit of laughter spilling out from somewhere behind a steamed-up café window.

Daisy gushed. 'It's beautiful. So impressive. Maybe I should actually get out of Pretty Beach a bit more often. This is breathtaking.'

'It really is. I thought you would like it. It's a perfect setting for your big night. You're going to remember this forever.'

After parking the car, with Miles in charge of the garment bags, Daisy dragged her suitcase behind her around onto a crescent with a cobbled pavement, looked at the hotel and raised her eyebrows at what presented itself. Wide steps up to an ornate door flanked by sculptured bay trees, a huge old coach light dangling overhead, iron railings, a doorman in tails, classical music. *Hello, Daisy, you have arrived.*

Daisy stood back and gaped after they'd been helped inside and Miles went to the desk. All around, softly painted panel walls enveloped her, beautifully upholstered sofas sat next to each other, a huge old fireplace winked from a far wall and coffee tables were perfectly stacked with posh books and candles. Swag and tail curtains, a glorious decorative ceiling, chandeliers by the dozen, a cluster of white orchids arranged just so. Daisy gripped the handle of her bag as if it were a life raft and gulped. She was a very, very, very long way from the bookshop at Pretty Beach. As she watched Miles at the counter, her mind zoomed to the desk in her little shop, to the thrifted library trolley, to being perched precariously on one of the book ladders, to practising her speech in front of her sisters, mum and girls. Chuckling to herself, she shook her head. Oh, how ridiculous and funny. Suddenly, she went cold as a penny dropped as clear as day; she'd been nominated as the blow-in from a little coastal town just to tick a box for some posh, fancy corporate person behind a desk somewhere who had to put the "independent" bit in the Independent Retail Alliance. By the looks of the hotel, the event was a much bigger deal than she could have imagined, and there was no way in the world that she had even a smidgeon of a teeny tiny chance of winning. At least she wouldn't have to give an acceptance speech, there was that.

The room, once they'd arrived upstairs, was more of the same; all upholstered sofas, plump cushions, peplum curtains, oversized bed, lush carpet and a bath bigger than Daisy's bedroom. So overawed by it all, Daisy hadn't said much at all. As she parked her suitcase by the end of the bed, Miles smiled.

'Right, now, what's the plan? You're going to have a bath in Bath, is that right?'

Daisy peered in at the enormous clawfoot bathtub in the centre of a marble-floored bathroom. 'Yes. That was the plan. Goodness, you might have to send out a search party after I get in that bath.'

'Rightio. How about I leave you to yourself, then?' Miles checked his watch. 'We've got a while. I might stroll down to the corner there and pop into that pub we saw as we came in. Work for you?'

Daisy could barely speak; she was that overwhelmed. Miles hadn't clocked what was going on in her head at all. Clearly, he was much more used to gallivanting around in posh hotels than she was. Truth be told, she was happy to be left on her own to get herself together a bit. Her old anxious friend had arrived with a bang deep in her veins. She needed to take action, calm down and recalibrate. A bath in Bath would facilitate that. 'Yep, that would be great.'

'Then we'll get ready and go down for a pre-event drink in the bar, if you like or whatever suits you. I'm easy. This is all about you.' Miles kissed her on the cheek, 'See you in, what, an hour or so?'

Daisy nodded and hung her dress carrier on the outside of the wardrobe and started to take the dress bag off. 'Yes, great, see you later.'

Walking to the window, Daisy looked out and closed her eyes for a second. She couldn't quite believe where she was, what she was doing or really how in the name of goodness she had arrived there. One minute she'd been standing in a hallway in a tiny new build on an estate a fifteen-minute ride from Pretty Beach, wondering how she was going to keep things together, now she was in a very fancy hotel room as a small business owner who'd been nominated for a national award. Her world had for sure taken a turn and moved in mysterious ways. A teeny tiny little part of her wished it would slow down a bit and remain the same. Fat chance of that; it was flying around doing its own thing.

36

The dress was in its place, Daisy's skin sheened with iridescent-hued body lotion courtesy of Annabelle, her clutch bag was tucked under her arm, her hair loosely piled into an updo and Miles wasn't looking too shabby in a dinner suit by her side. Daisy stood with a flute of champagne in her right hand, feeling as if she had a small child or a large bird perched on her shoulder when in fact it was a gigantic taffeta bow. Everything around her sparkled, twinkled and glowed; the people, the outfits, the room and the drinks. She tried to let it rub off on her so that she, also, radiated sparkliness. As she looked around, a glorious, elaborate plasterwork ceiling soared high above, the walls were lined with beautiful pictures and mirrors and all around everything felt, looked, smelled and showcased grandeur.

Miles was a pro at working the room and talking the talk. Daisy, in fact, was pretty much gobsmacked by him and very nicely pleased. He'd obviously picked up on her feelings and run with them by taking charge. Daisy liked that very much. She stood listening to a woman from Oxford who ran a chain of independent shops that sold antiques at the same time as wondering how she was going to get to the ballroom elegantly without tripping over her dress.

Miles squeezed her hand and whispered in her ear. 'You look stunning.'

Daisy whispered back. 'Right back at you. I feel like I'm playing dress-up.'

'You don't look like you're playing dress-up. You look like you were born to wear that dress. Ask me how I know.'

Daisy giggled. 'I don't feel like that.'

'Jane Austen used to attend balls here. We are following in distinguished footsteps.'

'Ha, I am used to seeing her in Uncle Dennis's attic.' Daisy gestured around. 'There are a lot of people here.'

'All here to celebrate independent businesses like yours. You should feel proud of being part of this, Daise. It's a big deal.'

A tall woman with silver hair approached them with a genuine smile of recognition. 'You must be Daisy Henley. I've seen photos. I'm Sarah Evans-Jones, I'm presenting the award in your category tonight, which is why I recognised you. I wanted to introduce myself and say how delighted we are that you're here.'

Daisy was a bit taken aback to be recognised. 'Thank you so much. It's wonderful to be here, though I have to admit I'm rather nervous about the whole thing.'

Sarah nodded and blinked rapidly. 'Perfectly natural. I was rather intimidated when I attended my first awards ceremony twenty years ago. I was, still am, actually, an independent retailer, so I know what it feels like to be in your shoes. The secret is to remember that everyone here is just pleased to meet you and hear your story.'

Daisy nodded. 'I feel like I'm making it up as I go along half the time. I've only just started learning what I'm doing and I find myself here doing this. Crazy really.'

'That never changes! I've been in retail for years and I still feel like I'm making it up as I go along half the time. You've found your niche and you're good at it and that's what this evening is about, celebrating people who've built something special.'

'Thank you, Sarah, that's so nice.'

37

Daisy could still feel the enormous bow on her shoulder as if it itself were a guest at the awards event. To her left, a portly man dressed in a tuxedo which didn't fit and a floppy bow tie had kept her entertained for most of the meal with long tales of stories about all sorts and how he had started his independent retail journey selling fruit and veg from the back of a Ford Transit van. Another nominee, a woman to his left, had started at a market stall selling boho-style dresses she had made herself and, although still independent, had gone on to have stores all around the world. Chatting away to them was quite an eye-opener for Daisy and her nerves had been completely obliterated as she sipped on her champagne. She was being thoroughly entertained by entrepreneurs whose tales were leaps and bounds ahead of her, but full of so much inspiration.

Rather than sitting there feeling like a duck out of water, in actual fact, she was loving soaking up the atmosphere, listening to the chat and watching as Miles did the same with the people on his right. All in all, she was having a very good night. After finishing a spectacularly soft and crunchy pavlova drizzled with a raspberry coulis that she could have eaten about ten of, Daisy settled back in her chair and listened to Mike, the portly man, tell her how one of the hardest things to negotiate in the retail business was taking on new premises and paying rent. It went through Daisy's mind that currently, that was not a problem of hers. It has been solved for her by her mum without either of them really appreciating it. Yet again, Daisy realised how lucky she was to have the support of the Henley family.

As a beautiful long, narrow platter of cheese, quince paste and artisan biscuits was placed in the centre of the table, the actual awards ceremony itself began. The lights were lowered, a hush descended and the MC began to talk about how the awards had come to be. She then moved on to divulge background information on the alliance itself and proceeded to give a long spiel about the history of the Independent Retail Alliance and how its work and fundraising had become an important part of the industry. Daisy sat back, sipped on her drink, observed and listened. All of her former nerves and worries were no longer; listening to other people's stories, hearing about journeys and learning from other business owners' ups and downs had made her see that her worries had been unfounded. Susannah had said to her just before she'd left that if she learnt one thing from the event, it would have been worth going to. For sure, Daisy had learnt a lot more than one thing. Oh yes, she'd hoovered up all sorts of things and made a few new acquaintances to boot.

Having Miles by her side had been the icing on the cake and the whole episode had turned, very surprisingly, into a lovely evening. On top of that, the hotel itself and the fact that she was looking forward to spending the day in Bath the next day meant that, all in all, she was having a lovely time.

Watching intently, Daisy looked behind the podium on the stage where a large screen displayed the list of categories for the various awards. She listened as each category was called out and watched the accompanying promotional videos on the screen.

The MC then proceeded to introduce each nominee and their business, announce a winner and a runner up and the same scenario was repeated for another category until it came to the category for the bookshop. Daisy gulped as she realised her name and business would be showcased and watched the first couple of videos, and then, all of a sudden, it was the bookshops' turn.

'Our final nominee in this category is Daisy Henley, The Bookshop Pretty Beach.'

On the screen, there was a short video of the place she had created, showing to the whole room. Daisy watched in complete amazement as her little bookshop filled the enormous screen in front of her. There were the fairy lights she'd strung up months before, twinkling away like tiny stars against the dark wooden shelves. The library trolley she'd rescued from Facebook Marketplace sat in its usual spot, loaded with books and topped with a vintage jug full of flowers from her mum's garden. The wingback chairs looked impossibly inviting, positioned just so near the windows where the afternoon light streamed in and made everything look golden and warm.

The camera panned across the children's section with its low shelves painted in soft shell blue, then moved to show the poetry corner with its hand-lettered shelf markers that she'd spent hours perfecting. Every detail felt magnified on the big screen, from the mismatched vintage mugs lined up behind the counter to the bunting she'd hung between the biography shelves. It was her world, her creation, displayed for hundreds of people in evening dress to see and judge.

She could hear her own voice coming through the speakers, talking about how the bookshop had become more than just a business, how it had given her a purpose and a place in the community. The words sounded strange and formal when played back in the grand dining room, so different from the casual conversation she'd had with Tom and Alicia that morning when the pipe had burst and they'd all ended up mopping water from the hallway floor.

Miles reached for her hand under the table and squeezed it gently. Around them, people were muttering appreciatively at the images on screen, and she caught fragments of conversation about how charming it looked, how authentic, how different from the sterile chain stores that dominated most high streets. The man beside her, who'd been telling stories about his fruit and vegetable stall all evening, leaned over and whispered that it looked exactly like the sort of place he'd love to browse for hours.

The video showed customers in the shop, people she recognised from Pretty Beach, going about their usual routines of browsing and chatting and settling into the comfortable chairs with cups of tea. There was Xian in her usual spot by the window, iPad in hand and silver hip flask discreetly topped up. Daisy felt a strange disconnection between the elegant woman in the black dress sitting at this formal dinner table and the person on screen in the floral dress, moving around the bookshop. The contrast was so stark it felt almost surreal, as if she was watching someone else's life being celebrated while she sat in borrowed bling pretending to belong among all the successful business people.

But as the video continued, she began to recognise the significance of what she'd created. It wasn't just about selling books or making money, though both of those things mattered. It was about creating a space where people felt welcome, where community happened naturally, where the simple act of browsing for something to read became an opportunity for connection and conversation.

The dining room around her felt impossibly grand in comparison to the cosy intimacy of the bookshop on screen. Crystal chandeliers hung overhead, dropping light on tables laden with more silverware than most people could dream about. The walls were lined with oil paintings in gilded frames, and the ceiling soared high above them with elaborate plasterwork that spoke of centuries of wealth and privilege. It was beautiful, undeniably, but it was also formal and slightly intimidating in a way that made her appreciate the unpretentious comfort of her own little shop.

As the video drew to a close with a shot of the bookshop's hand-painted sign and the blue and white bunting fluttering in the Pretty Beach breeze, Daisy felt a surge of pride that surprised her with its intensity. She had built something worth celebrating, something that mattered to people beyond herself. The bookshop might be small and the profits low, but it had become exactly what she'd hoped for: a place where books and people and community came together in ways that felt natural and necessary.

The screen went dark and the lights came up slightly as the presenter prepared to announce the winner in her category. Daisy's heart hammered against her ribs as she realised that in just a few moments, she would either be celebrating the achievement of being nominated or walking up to accept an award she still couldn't quite believe she deserved. Either way, she knew that watching her bookshop on the enormous screen, seeing it through the eyes of people who understood what independent businesses meant to their communities, had already given her something more valuable than any award could represent.

The winner turned out to be a woman called Caroline and her farm shops and Daisy couldn't believe it as her name was called as runner-up. She watched as the elegant woman Caroline, who Daisy had previously chatted to, made her way gracefully to the stage. Caroline looked completely at ease in the spotlight, accepting her award with a confident smile and looking right at home in the fancy room. Her speech was polished and articulate, thanking the judges and talking about the importance of supporting local food producers and sustainable farming practices.

Daisy applauded enthusiastically, genuinely pleased for Caroline even as her own emotions swirled between pride at being runner-up and a tiny stab of disappointment that she hadn't won outright. The rational part of her mind knew that being runner-up in a national competition was an extraordinary achievement for someone who'd started her business on a whim, but the part of her that had been secretly hoping for outright victory deflated a tiny bit. Who ever likes coming in second?

'Now the runner-up, again, as announced, is Daisy Henley of The Bookshop Pretty Beach,' Sarah smiled from the podium, suddenly the spotlight was on their table and everyone was looking at her expectantly.

Miles squeezed her hand once more and whispered, 'Go on then, you brilliant woman.'

Daisy stood up carefully, mindful of her dress and the unfamiliar height of her heels, and made her way towards the stage. The walk felt endless, with hundreds of pairs of eyes following her progress across the dining room. The enormous bow on her shoulder seemed to have developed a life of its own, shifting slightly with each step and making her hyper-aware of how formal and unfamiliar her outfit felt. The stage lights were brighter than she'd expected, and for a moment, she felt blinded as she climbed the steps to accept her award from Sarah. The crystal trophy was heavier than it looked, beautifully engraved with the Independent Retail Alliance logo and her name in elegant script. Holding it made everything feel suddenly real in a way that the nomination letter and the evening's formality hadn't quite managed.

'Congratulations, Daisy,' Sarah said warmly, positioning her for a photographer who appeared at the edge of the stage. 'Would you like to say a few words?'

The microphone was thrust towards Daisy before she had time to panic properly about speaking to the room full of people. She looked out at the sea of faces in evening dress, all of them turned expectantly towards her, and felt her carefully prepared speech evaporate from her memory completely. 'I honestly didn't expect this. When I opened the bookshop, I was just trying to create some stability for myself and my daughters. I never imagined it would lead to standing here in a room like this.'

Her voice steadied as she found her rhythm. 'This recognition means more to me than I can express, not just because it validates what I've built at the bookshop, but because it celebrates the values that independent businesses bring to their communities. We're not just shops selling products, we're gathering places where people can connect with each other and with stories that matter to them.'

The room was completely quiet, and she could see people nodding in recognition of what she was saying. Miles beamed.

'The bookshop exists because of the extraordinary support of the Pretty Beach community, and because of my family who believed in the idea even when I wasn't sure I believed in it myself.'

After a round of applause, Miles stood up to hug her as she reached their table. He whispered in her ear. 'That was perfect.'

Daisy put the trophy carefully on the table in front of her. Runner-up in a national competition for independent retailers. Not bad for someone who'd started out with no idea what she'd been doing, who'd listened to an orange man in wraparound mirrored sunglasses, decided that he might have been onto something and jumped in at the deep end. Not bad for a Henley girl, at all.

38

Daisy was a bit floaty and a lot lovely as she got out of the shower in the hotel room upstairs from where the gala had taken place. She was so on a high from being announced as a runner-up that she felt as if she was sitting on a puffy cloud, having a little ride around seeing what the world looked like for successful people. Once back in the room, she'd taken off the bow dress, frankly pleased to get it off, had a quick shower, scrubbed off her makeup and taken all the pins out of her hair. Miles had done the same, minus the makeup and pins, and both of them were decked out in the fancy velour hotel robes provided by the hotel, sitting on the balcony overlooking a sea of twinkling lights as Bath below them showed off. Daisy had thoroughly enjoyed herself, felt oddly special, a tad glowing and strangely honoured.

Tapping her phone, she smiled as she looked through social media posts and stories from the Independent Alliance and caught a glimpse of herself standing on the podium as a runner-up. The position had also come with a monetary business grant, which was going to go down well. All of it swam around her eyes and her head in a lovely, delicious, happy swirl. Daisy Henley was on fire and didn't it feel nice.

Miles had made them a cup of peppermint tea, it sat in front of them, its steam rising up into the air. She snuggled into her dressing gown and smiled. 'Wasn't that all so well done? I really enjoyed myself.'

'It was really good.'

A text came in from Annabelle.

Annabelle: *Did you have a lovely evening, Daise? WhatsApp us!*

Daisy picked up her phone and scrolled through until she found the family group chat. She pressed the video call button and Annabelle's face appeared on the screen, followed quickly by Susannah and then Maggie, squeezing into view. They were all in Susannah's kitchen, the Aga and scrubbed pine table visible behind them.

'There she is! Look at you in that fancy hotel robe. How did it go? We've been dying to hear everything.'

'It was absolutely brilliant! I can't quite believe it all happened, to be honest. I came runner-up in the Independent Retail Alliance Awards.'

Susannah clapped her hands together, Annabelle squealed with delight, and Maggie raised a mug of tea. 'Runner-up! Oh, darling, that's absolutely wonderful. Tell us everything. What was the ceremony like? We've been dying to hear!'

'Once I got there and started talking to people, it was actually really lovely. Everyone was so nice, and the other nominees had such interesting stories about their businesses. Yep, I was fine. Dare I say it, I thrived hearing other people telling me their stuff.'

'That's great. What about the venue? How was that?' Annabelle leaned closer to the screen.

'It's amazing here. Wait, let me show you the lights of Bath around us.' Daisy turned her phone around so the camera faced outwards. She panned slowly across the view from the balcony, taking in the honey-coloured Georgian buildings of Bath spread out below them. Street lamps dotted the curved terraces and crescents and everything sparkled on the calm, clear evening. 'This is the view from our hotel room. It's absolutely gorgeous.'

'It looks like something from a period drama. How beautiful.'

Daisy turned the phone back to face her. 'The awards ceremony was in a hall where Jane Austen used to go to balls. Can you imagine? I kept thinking about that while I was standing on the stage in that dress. Thanks again for helping me with that. I most certainly looked the part.'

'Did you give a speech as runner-up?'

'I did, and it wasn't nearly as awful as I thought it would be. The whole thing was surreal, really. There I was in this incredibly grand ballroom, surrounded by people in evening dress, and they showed a video of the bookshop on this enormous screen. It looked so lovely, all the fairy lights twinkling and customers browsing and the wingback chairs. I almost didn't recognise it as the same place where I spend my days.'

'What was the dress like? Did the bow stay in place?'

'It felt enormous at first, but by the end of the evening, I'd forgotten it was there. The dress was absolutely perfect, Bells. Thank you for choosing it. I felt like I belonged there, which was half the battle.'

Miles moved so that his face popped into the edge of the phone screen. He leant down to kiss the top of Daisy's head. 'She was magnificent. I was so proud I could barely sit still.'

Daisy heard herself gushing. 'And the runner-up prize comes with a business development grant, which will help with any improvements or expansions I might want to make.'

'That's fantastic,' Susannah beamed. 'Well done, you.'

'Congratulations!'

Maggie beamed. 'So proud of you, Daise.'

Susannah nodded. 'Right, well, we'd better let you get some rest now that you're a global superstar.'

Daisy chuckled. 'Ha.'

Annabelle smiled. 'The girls are tucked up in bed. They're going to be so happy.'

'They will.'

'You've had a big day, and you'll want to enjoy Bath tomorrow.'

'We want to have a wander around the city and maybe visit some of the bookshops. There's supposed to be a lovely independent one near the cathedral that I'd like to see.'

Maggie raised her eyebrows. 'Take lots of photos. I want to see everything. The hotel, the city, the bookshops, all of it.'

'I will and thank you all for being so supportive about tonight. I know I was nervous about the whole thing...'

'Don't be silly. Right, we're going to let you enjoy that balcony.' Annabelle made shooing motions with her hands.

'And well done again, darling,' Susannah added. 'We're all so very proud of you.'

After they'd said their goodbyes and the call had ended, Daisy put her phone down on the small table between the balcony chairs and leaned back. The air was cool against her face, and she could hear the distant sounds of Bath settling down for the night. A few cars moved through the streets, an odd voice or two drifted up from the pub on the corner as the night drew to a close and there was the occasional laugh or snatch of conversation from a few hotel guests coming from the direction of a large conservatory to their left.

Miles gestured to Daisy's phone. 'That was nice. You can see how proud they are of you.'

Daisy nodded. Talk about happy. For so long, she'd seen herself as someone who was just getting by, making the best of difficult circumstances and hoping nothing would go wrong. Now she felt different. The evening had shown her another version of herself, one that she wanted to make further acquaintance with. 'I keep thinking about standing on that stage and looking out at all those people in their evening dress, holding that trophy, talking about the bookshop as if it were something really significant. It felt like I was describing someone else's life.'

'You're the one who opens the shop every morning, who knows exactly which books to recommend to which customers, who created that atmosphere that makes people want to linger for hours. You're the one who turned Uncle Dennis's dusty old building into a place where community happens. It's your life.'

'Weird really.' Daisy nodded as she watched the lights of Bath twinkle below them and let the satisfaction of the evening wash over her as she listened to the distant sounds of the city. 'The most surreal part was seeing the video of the shop on that *enormous* screen. All those fairy lights and wonky shelves and mismatched furniture, blown up huge for hundreds of people to see. I kept thinking they'd realise it was all held together with optimism and second-hand finds from Facebook Marketplace. Thank goodness the burst pipe wasn't in there.'

Miles laughed. 'Everything looked genuine and lived-in, not like some corporate idea of what an independent bookshop should look like.'

'I want to remember this feeling. Not just the award, but the confidence. The knowledge that what I've built is valuable, even if it doesn't look like traditional business success. Do you see what I mean?'

'Yeah, let's have another drink before we put this night to bed. Get the most out of it and this amazing view.'

Miles got up and called through from the fridge and the mini bar. 'This is well-stocked. Can I tempt you with vodka, whiskey, gin, a mini bottle of champagne? Pimms? A strange concoction in a can involving rum and I think chia seed?'

Daisy called back, 'Actually, I don't think I fancy any of that. Is there hot chocolate?'

Miles held up a packet of chocolate powder and wiggled it. 'There's a bottle of milk in here, too.' He flicked the kettle on as he nodded, then held up a packet of mini marshmallows. 'This is my kind of hotel. I can do you a nice hot chocolate with marshmallows on top.'

'Works for me,' Daisy smiled back. Five minutes later, they were sitting in the same position, looking out over Bath, decompressing and chatting about the phone call with Daisy's sisters.

'They seemed really pleased for you, didn't they?'

'Yes, they did. I feel great, calm and like something good is going to happen with my business and everything.'

'It's a shame you didn't win, really, isn't it?'

Daisy shook her head. 'Oh, I won, Miles. I won absolutely.'

'What?'

Daisy nodded as lots of things dawned on her. It was as if her head were one of those old-fashioned penny machines where you drop in the coins and wait to see if they will ever fall off the edge. She smiled as all the pennies dropped over the edge all at once in a dirty great fall. 'I've won at being Daisy. Finally, finally, finally. My business is going well, my girls are safe, I've got you, my family are okay, and I have a home. I still live in Pretty Beach, the only place I want to be. Really, what else is there to win?'

'When you put it like that. So, I take it you're happy, Daise?'

'Just a little bit.'

'Well, we'll have a nice day tomorrow just to top it all off, and then I don't know about you but I'll be ready to get back to Pretty Beach. Same for you?'

'Always.'

Buy my new book Love From Pretty Beach at Amazon

LOVE FROM PRETTY BEACH

Love from Pretty Beach

Gorgeous, small-town women's fiction and swoon-worthy escapist romance set in a beautiful British seaside town. If you're looking for a happy ever after with divine characters, settle in and say hello to Pretty Beach.

When five-year Pretty Beach resident Darby decides her life is at a complete and utter dead-end, she decides on a whim to start something she's been wanting to do for years. She flips up the lid of her laptop and hits go. That's when life gets really interesting and the little town by the sea she's settled into starts to wrap her in its charm. We watch from the sidelines as a whole new journey unravels...

Full of Polly's unique trademarks; a gorgeous setting, lose yourself escapism, tumbledown old house, the dreamiest romance ever, ever, ever. If you are a Babbette and part of the Pollyverse you will need supplies.

POLLY BOOKS

(Reading Order available at authorpollybabbington.com)

Love from Pretty Beach

The Bookshop Pretty Beach
    Whispers at The Bookshop Pretty Beach
    Always at The Bookshop Pretty Beach

A Cottage in Lovely Bay
    Sunshine in Lovely Bay
    Forever in Lovely Bay

One Nice Day in Lovely Bay
    One Sweet Day in Lovely Bay
    One Perfect Day in Lovely Bay

The Summer Hotel Lovely Bay
    Wildflowers at The Summer Hotel Lovely Bay
    Seashells at The Summer Hotel Lovely Bay

POLLY BOOKS

The Old Ticket Office Darling Island
    Secrets at The Old Ticket Office Darling Island
    Surprises at The Old Ticket Office Darling Island

Spring in the Pretty Beach Hills
    Summer in the Pretty Beach Hills

The Pretty Beach Thing
    The Pretty Beach Way
    The Pretty Beach Life

Something About Darling Island
    Just About Darling Island
    All About Christmas on Darling Island

The Coastguard's House Darling Island
    Summer on Darling Island
    Bliss on Darling Island

The Boat House Pretty Beach
    Summer Weddings at Pretty Beach
    Winter at Pretty Beach

A Pretty Beach Christmas
    A Pretty Beach Dream
    A Pretty Beach Wish

Secret Evenings in Pretty Beach
    Secret Places in Pretty Beach
    Secret Days in Pretty Beach

Lovely Little Things in Pretty Beach
    Beautiful Little Things in Pretty Beach
    Darling Little Things

The Old Sugar Wharf Pretty Beach
    Love at the Old Sugar Wharf Pretty Beach
    Snow Days at the Old Sugar Wharf Pretty Beach

Pretty Beach Posies
    Pretty Beach Blooms
    Pretty Beach Petals

Printed in Dunstable, United Kingdom